# PRAISE FOR *THE CHOICES SHE MADE*

We all have to make difficult choices in life, and in Felicia Ferguson's debut novel *The Choices She Made,* Madeline Williams goes from an innocent teenager to a ruined girl who's afraid of the powerful family of the boy who attacked her. But her widowed father stands by her, no matter what she decides, and this unconditional love helps her to make the hardest decision ever.

After giving up the boy she loved and the life she'd planned, Madeline, now a single mom, has a teenaged daughter who wants answers. When they return to Blue Springs, Texas, for the summer, the past comes back to haunt Madeline. The very boy who assaulted her, now a divorced man, has to answer to charges brought by several other women. Madeline tells her daughter the truth, and again has to make a difficult decision. Will she step forward and share her secret with the world, or will she keep quiet to protect the child she loves?

A touching story that mirrors today's headlines and focuses on the agony of women having to deal with horrible memories and tough decisions. It moved me more than I can ever say. A story that will touch your heart and strengthen your faith.

—LENORA WORTH, author of *Seeking Refuge*

There is something to be said for the tenacity of an up and coming author. Felicia Ferguson has that tenacity in her book, *The Choices She Made.* As we follow Madeline through her story we find well-written plots, beautiful description, and yummy adventure. Ferguson takes the reader on a well-penned story and when it ends, you wish it hadn't. I completely loved it. Satisfying. Enjoyable. A must read.

—CINDY SPROLES, Best-Selling, Award winning author of *What Momma Left Behind*

# THE
# CHOICES
# SHE
# MADE

FELICIA FERGUSON

The Choices She Made

End Game Press books may be purchased in bulk at special discounts for sales promotion, corporate gifts, ministry, fund-raising, or educational purposes. Special editions can also be created to specifications. For details, contact Special Sales Dept., End Game Press, P.O. Box 206, Nesbit, MS 38651 or info@endgamepress.com.

Visit our website at www.endgamepress.com.

Library of Congress Control Number: 2022932713

ISBN: 978-1-63797-045-4

eBook ISBN: 978-1-63797-044-7

Cover by Greg Jackson, Thinkpen Design

Interior by Typewriter Creative Co.

Printed in the United States of America

10 9 8 7 6 5 4 3 2 1

# TABLE OF CONTENTS

# CHAPTER ONE

*Blue Springs, Texas*
*March, 1997*

M ADELINE WILLIAMS'S HEAD LOLLED AGAINST hard, wooden planks as she blinked awake.

*Bang.*

*Bang.*

*Bang.*

Blurred browns, yellows, and grays gelled into familiar shapes. Stall door. Clean straw. Water trough. She took a quick breath of the dry, musty air that surrounded her, trying to will her mind to connect all the pieces. Make sense of the chaotic sounds and images pinging at her. A cow's loud call rang out from the adjacent stall, drawing her back to the here and now. Startled, Madeline clenched her rough denim shorts, the hems frayed by the slice of scissors.

Through a mental fog, her mind blanked. Then remembered ... His voice low, heavy. His breath sickly sweet from the plug of Skoal. His hands insistent and unyielding.

Shaking, she pulled her cut-offs into place as she surveyed the dusty stall. He was gone.

Relief choked her as she drew her knees to her chest, rocking. Part tremble, part a silenced reach for solace. She curled tight into a ball until slowly, gently, a cocooning blankness descended, boxing the stark terror away and leaving an odd clarity of thought in its absence.

A long, plaintive *moo* split the air, followed by an answering call echoing some distance away.

*Must've separated mama and baby for sale.*

With a curious detachment, Madeline turned in to the boards as they vibrated under the cow's hooves accompanied by another long, mournful moo and reply.

*Poor things. I hope they at least go to the same buyer.*

"Donnie!" a loud, unfamiliar drawl commanded. "Get that cow under control before she tears the place down."

Madeline jerked. She was in the stall next to that cow, wasn't she? Scrambling to her feet, she slipped unnoticed out of the pen and into the bright hallway where a harried cowgirl tugged a bouncing four-year-old toward the women's bathroom. Madeline ducked her head and brushed by them, heading for the cattle auction's main building.

*How long was I gone? Where is John David?*

"Lot twenty-eight." The cry burst clear and raucous through the arena entry up ahead, bouncing off the walls. A cowboy glanced left, right, then locating the men's room, tipped his hat to her and hurried on his way.

Madeline sagged against the cold cinderblocks, dodging the man's gaze. She'd left for popcorn at lot thirteen. She had to get back before the gavel fell on this one. Dad would be worried. She took in a deep breath, desperate to steady the tremors, but a whimper escaped her lips.

John David knew everyone in there in some way or

another. What if he was already bragging about his conquest? Skin crawling, she buried her face in her hands. There was no choice but to go in.

Madeline tried another deep breath and this time shoved the fear and humiliation to the back of her mind. When she reached the door of the arena, she paused and squared her shoulders. She'd survived Mom's death ten years ago. She could survive this.

Madeline pushed open the door and stepped through. "Sold to bidder twenty-five," the auctioneer cried. The crowd turned to discover the winner's identity, affording her the briefest moment of incognito as she fled to the comfort of Dad's presence.

The creepy feeling along her skin told her John David was near the cattle entrance, but her eyes darted around the arena anyway, finding him standing just outside the gates. His hand rested on one of the bars, poised to jump the fence to help the wranglers.

She could feel his eyes track her to the seat next to Dad. Hunching her shoulders, she curled inward hoping somehow to hide from his penetrating gaze.

Dad looked up from his sales notes as she settled beside him. "The steers'll be up soon." Brow wrinkled, his navy eyes studied her.

Madeline's chest tightened. *Can he tell?*

"Where's your popcorn?"

She stifled a ragged sigh and lied. "They ran out."

He nodded. A few minutes later, their lot number was called, and the cowhands herded their steers into the arena. "There was a cow-calf lot with the cow confirmed pregnant that came through. Highest seller so far, but still a ways off last year's prices. Doesn't look too good for us, Pumpkin."

Madeline tried to mumble some sort of response, but thankfully the gate opened and their lot pushed into the arena.

A man with a clipboard leaned over to the auctioneer. "Whatcha got for us now, son?" the auctioneer asked.

"Ten yearling Angus cross steers. Local rancher been fattening 'em up all winter, and they're looking good."

"Yessir, what say y'all? How 'bout we start out this lot at one thousand?" The auctioneer started his chant, pointing out the ages and weights of Dad's steers. Spotters yipped and hawed as bidders tipped hats, rubbed noses, and raised hands. Bidding hopped between three men, but Madeline only watched one.

John David's consistent nods finally tired the others, and he won the lot with a record price for yearling steers— or so the auctioneer crowed. "Sold to John David Billings, son of the fine owner of this auction house, Tommy Billings. Building your own herd to finance your run for governor, are ya' John David?"

Madeline sank in the seat as the auctioneer continued to josh the heir to the Billings' family fortune. Only the next lot pushing through the gate diverted his attention.

"'The last shall be first,' huh, Pumpkin?" Dad asked with a wide grin, his jubilation evident to all. "Bet your grandpa is looking down from heaven green with envy at the price we got today." He rose and headed to collect the check, stopping between the benches to grasp hands and trade smiles with congratulatory ranchers and cowboys. Then he slung an arm around Madeline's shoulder and steered her down the hall, planning out the future for their unexpected income. Something about paying down bills. Eating dinner out to celebrate. And maybe repainting the tractor.

Madeline forced a smile and what she hoped would be received as a supportive nod.

Within minutes they reached the office, joining the line of cowboys collecting their winnings and making payments. They were two men away from the registration table when a loud guffaw pounded through the room.

*Tommy Billings.* Madeline cringed. She prayed the wealthy blowhard wouldn't see them, but there was no avoiding the man.

"Well, there he is. Biggest sale of the day. Congratulations, Jim." Tommy hustled around the table with a huge grin and shook Dad's hand. "Jim, I swear this girl of yours gets prettier every day. Good thing she takes after her mama instead of you." His smile sobered with believable sympathy. After a sorrowful glance her way, Tommy mumbled, "God rest her soul."

Madeline prayed for the floor to open up beneath her. A moment later, Tommy flashed a jovial smirk. "You know, Madeline, I took a shine to your mama back in the day. By then I'd inherited five thousand acres across the family's two ranches and started the first auction." He clapped Dad on the shoulder. "But that didn't seem to matter. She only had eyes for this long drink of water. Lucky stiff."

Dad said something in response to Tommy's praise, but as a pair of cowboys left the sales office, the hairs on the back of Madeline's neck shivered. She glanced up, then desperately wished she hadn't. John David held up a wall and watched the proceedings, a half-chewed toothpick clenched in the corner of his mouth. His eyes pierced her with a sardonic leer. Then he tipped his hat and flashed a one-sided smirk.

Madeline's stomach clenched. Desperate for a solid hold, she tucked her fingers through Dad's belt loop and forced air into her lungs. She would survive this waking nightmare.

Dad's brow furrowed as she tugged on his belt, silently pleading for him to hurry. But Tommy continued to hold court. "John David here's just finished up his business degree at A&M. He's going to run the auction houses next season, and we're planning to expand into central Texas too. Got some strong leads."

Suddenly chilled, Madeline ducked out from under Dad's arm. Muttering she'd meet him at the truck, she pushed through the front exit and didn't stop until she curled into the worn-leather bench seat of Dad's F150.

Surrounded by the quiet comfort, she tucked her head against the window and released a soft whimper. Her body ached. "Daddy, please, come on."

The soft tick of the truck's clock clicked away, but the minutes seemed to stretch to hours. Finally, he opened the driver's side door and sidled onto the seat. "Still can't quite believe it, Pumpkin." With a quick turn of the key, the diesel engine rumbled to life. He grinned at her and shook his head. "Wanna get something to eat? This is a day to celebrate."

Heat rushed to her cheeks. No. She just wanted to forget.

When she didn't answer, his brow creased with worry. "You okay?"

Madeline swallowed hard and forced another lie between her lips. "Think I caught the bug that's been going around school. Can we just go home?"

"You should have said something, Pumpkin. You didn't have to come today."

Oh God, if only she hadn't. Another shudder wracked her body. Bobby had asked her to spend the day with him when he'd kissed her goodbye last night after their date. Why hadn't she said yes to him and no to Dad?

She turned toward the door. *Oh, God. Bobby.*

"We'll go straight home, and you get yourself to bed. Okay?"

※

About an hour later, Dad pulled the truck to a stop in front of the house. "I'll be down in a bit," he said with an encouraging nod. "Gonna get the trailer unhooked and put out some hay."

Madeline nodded and headed inside. The soft whir of the air conditioner pumped out an easy cadence, practice for the summer when it would run full blast just to put a dent in the east Texas heat. Despite her promise to go to bed, she went to the den and curled up in Dad's overstuffed chair. Traces of musk and sweat clung to the smooth, beaten leather. She took a deep breath and released a sob. Another followed. Then another. Until her shoulders heaved and her shirt was soaked.

Madeline wrapped her arms around her chest and

flinched as her hand landed on a tender spot. Turning her arm, she found the first tinges of purple on her bicep.

His handprint.

She leapt from the chair and rushed to the bathroom. Tugging off her clothes, she jumped into the shower shivering as the cold water pelted her like sleet against a winter window. She grabbed the bar of soap and a washcloth. Red chafe marks stained her skin as she scrubbed with fierce intent.

As the water warmed, its soothing stream eased away the remaining pain. But the mark not only remained, it had multiplied. Four long rectangles all darkening to the color of an overripe eggplant now circled her arm.

Madeline choked as memories washed over her.

His hands.

His breath.

She twisted off the faucet and grabbed her towel, burying herself in the softness. Her teeth chattering once more, she stepped outside the shower and shuddered when her foot landed on fabric instead of cold tile.

Her shirt.

A purple tee with a unicorn jumping over a rainbow. It was her favorite. The shorts, cut-offs made from a beloved pair of well-worn jeans.

Tears spilled onto her cheeks as the reminder of her horrors stared back at her. The clothes had to go. She glanced at her trash can. Dad burned their garbage. If she threw them away, he'd find them. And ask questions.

She swallowed hard and searched for the calm again— the void that somehow separated her emotions from her actions. She wrapped her arms tight around her body, rocking, hoping, praying ... until, slowly, emptiness snaked through, bathing her in the welcome sea of nothingness.

When she glanced around the room, it was as if seeing through an antique window pane. Blurred, reality but not. Now numb, Madeline rose and slid through the motions, watching her hands tug the bag from her trash can. They gathered up the t-shirt, shorts, and underwear and stuffed them inside the plastic confines. They tied the ends of the bag together and she walked out of the bathroom toward her bed, no longer at one with her body. No longer a part of this world.

There was only one place she knew the clothes wouldn't be found. One place where they could disappear forever. She felt herself kneel and watched as her hands shoved the bag under her bed. The clothes, the emotions, the memories, they could all vanish there. Out of sight, out of mind.

A manic chuckle tickled the heavy air.

She would move on as if nothing happened.

No one would ever know.

# CHAPTER TWO

*Austin, Texas*
*March, 2011*

"PLEASE, LORD, LET GEORGIA HAVE HAD A GOOD day at school." My twelve-year-old was a happy child, but the transition to her new private school had proven rougher than I'd imagined. Most of Georgia's class-mates had been in school together since first grade. Their familiarity, augmented by their silver baby spoons, isolat-ed her from day one. Tears were a regular and unbecoming accessory to her maroon and gray uniform.

I'd never considered that possibility when I enrolled her at Saint Bartholomew's Preparatory. The school was highly ranked and close to my job at the hospital where I headed the HR department. I thought it would be the best for both of us. But sitting in the pickup line in my BMW X3, surrounded by Mercedes G Wagons, Bentleys, and even a Rolls Royce, I doubted my wisdom. The school's front entry loomed ahead, gothic, cathedral-esque, and quite out of sorts with the casual funk of Austin. Kids of all ages milled on the sidewalks as attendants directed them to their parents' cars.

A whiney beep cut through the radio commercial for a local used car lot, and I jerked my gaze to my rearview mirror. A perfectly coiffed and coutured Austin socialite leaned on the horn of her black Range Rover. The crimson fingernails of one hand shooed me forward. I glanced ahead. A gaping five-foot hole yawned between me and the preceding vehicle. With a snort, I moved up in line close enough to read the make and model of the car ahead. *Porsche Panamera S. Where do they come up with these names?*

I shook my head and crooned along with Brad Paisley as he sang his letter to his seventeen-year-old self on the radio. The DJs mused about their own teenaged mistakes before the news announcer took the mic. Trouble in the Middle East. Threats of government shutdown. *Nothing new.* I tuned out the rest until the announcer transitioned closer to home.

"... and now in regional news, the trial of Blue Springs native, John David Billings, begins Monday."

My lungs seized on their last intake of breath.

"Thirty-five-year-old Billings is accused of raping three local women although he continues to deny the allegations. Prosecutors are confident—"

I fumbled off the car radio with a clammy hand and trembling fingers. Memories pinged me like buckshot. Sharp, stinging.

His hands.

His breath.

I rubbed my arms to smooth the bumps on my skin, but they tightened even further.

My unsteady hands put the SUV in drive as the line

inched forward. I glanced in my rearview mirror and found the socialite taking selfies while perfecting her pout. At least the Kardashian wannabe wasn't beeping at me anymore.

A flash of honey blonde hair snagged my gaze as Georgia raced toward my SUV. My heart sank at her beet-red face and damp cheeks. The Austin heat might have been responsible, but I doubted it. She threw her back-pack on the floorboard, climbed into the backseat, and burst into a fresh round of tears.

*Come on, God. Really?* I took in a steadying breath and forced my own terror aside. "Sweetie, what happened?"

"Mom, it was awful." Georgia wiped her cheeks and grabbed a tissue from the box I kept on the floorboard. "Why do they have to be so mean? I just want to be their friend." She tossed the tissue in the trash bag and tucked her head against the seat.

I'd run out of fingers trying to keep up with the reported incidents. Georgia had begged me to stay out of it, certain the other girls would come around. But I was at the end of my patience for diplomacy. She might be heading into her teen years, with all the guts and impulses of the age, but she was still my little girl. I had made too many sacrifices and told too many lies to have a couple of bullies turn her into a victim.

I pulled out of the pickup lane and onto the highway heading south for Georgia to spend spring break at the ranch with Dad. Glancing in the rearview mirror, I caught Georgia's gaze. Her pale blue eyes and honey blonde hair were so much like my own when I was her age. "Tell me," I said.

Georgia took a sip from her water bottle and cast an irritated glance toward me in the rearview mirror. "We started a new lesson on ancestry."

My lungs hitched.

"The teacher wants everyone to make a family tree poster."

Cold sweat beaded in my palms.

"We're supposed to present it to the class when we get back from spring break."

*Lord. Already?* I forced air into my lungs and wiped my hands on my designer pants.

Oblivious to my rising terror, Georgia continued her recap. "I waited 'til class was over, and I asked if I would get points taken off since I don't know who my father is. Madison and Brianna, they must've overheard."

I took a swig from my water bottle, desperate to ease the tightness in my chest. Those names had become frequent topics of my after-school conversations with Georgia.

"As soon as I got in the hall, they started in on me, saying my dad was a monster and you thought I'd take after him so that's why I don't know who he is." Her voice cracked. "They said it was one more reason I didn't belong at their school."

*Please, God, I can't tell her the truth. Not now.*

Sympathizing with the folktale boy who tried to plug the dam with his finger, I cobbled together an explanation, hoping she wouldn't hear the tremble in my voice. "Sweetie, you are kind, caring, and beautiful. That threatens some girls. So they find weaknesses and use them to make themselves feel better. That's what bullies do." I shot a desperate glance to the rearview mirror and caught Georgia shaking her head.

"I don't understand. Why's it such big secret?" She scowled and looked out the window. "Why won't you just tell me who my dad is?"

*Not yet. Please, not yet.*

I stopped at a red light and desperately wracked my brain for a more pleasant subject. We were spending the first weekend of spring break at the ranch together. On Monday, I'd return to work and leave Georgia to stay the rest of the week with Dad. "You looking forward to spending spring break with Grandpa at the ranch?" When she didn't answer, I glanced back. Earbuds peeked out from between locks of hair and her eyes were closed.

A reprieve. *Thank you, God.* But knowing my daughter, the conversation was far from over.

# CHAPTER THREE

*Blue Springs, Texas*
*May, 1997*

M ADELINE STOOD AT HER LOCKER AND TRIED TO quell her stomach's churning. The bell for second period clanged in the hallway sending students scurrying to class. She should be following them—there was a test today in Algebra—but all she could do was stand stockstill. Leaning back against the locker and closing her eyes, she savored the feel of cold metal against her cheek. She hadn't felt this sick in forever. When she'd returned from visiting Maribeth in Austin last month, she'd been queasy, but nothing like this. She'd chalked it up to sympathy pains for Maribeth's mom and the bug she had brought home from work that weekend. But that was a month ago. No way it could last that long.

Taking in a few deep breaths, her stomach slowly uncurled. Relieved, she studied the hallway and a halfopened locker. Regina Bell would be so mad to see John Watson's name encircled by a red heart. The most popular pair in school had been on and off since sixth grade. But then, if they were off again, maybe she wouldn't care.

Who was she kidding? Regina would—her stomach twisted again and Madeline swallowed hard.

Breakfast must've just not set well. She'd made scrambled eggs. Maybe she hadn't washed the shells enough when she'd brought the last batch in from the henhouse. Madeline glanced up the hall to the water fountains. Hoping the cool water would help settle her stomach, she took a long sip and prayed her instincts were correct.

"First trimester's a beast, but it does get better," a voice said, weary wisdom aging its youthful tone. "And make sure you get a Sprite on your way back to class."

*First trimester?* Madeline choked on a swallow. Releasing the fountain's push button, she coughed until the water cleared then turned. A girl with a very large belly stood waiting for her turn at the fountain. Madeline stared, then caught herself and scrambled for an apology.

The girl flashed a wry smile. "Yeah, I get that a lot these days."

"Sorry. Just not what I expected."

The girl shrugged and moved to the fountain. "S'okay. It wasn't what I was expecting either. But it is what it is." She gave Madeline a long look. "So how far along are you?"

"How far ..." Madeline stared at the girl. The question jumbled with her earlier advice, whirling together in a dirt-devil of confusion and worry.

"You're preggers, right?" she asked with a considering moue. She took a quick sip of water then, cradling her protruding belly, gave Madeline another close look. "Trust me, I know the signs."

Madeline crossed her arms over her flat stomach and

backed against the cinderblock wall. "No, I-I can't be. I mean ... no ... you're wrong."

The girl looked skeptical, but was silent. After a moment, she shrugged. "Okay. But don't forget the Sprite. It'll help either way."

Madeline nodded and watched the girl leave.

She was wrong.

She had to be.

Because she and Bobby had only kissed.

So if she was ... pregnant ... then it was from ... Head swimming, Madeline reached for stability. Feeling the wall behind her, she leaned into it and closed her eyes.

*"How you doin', Madeline?" John David breathed into her ear.*

*Madeline gagged as she inhaled the minty sweet scent of chewing tobacco. A shiver scraped across her skin raising goosebumps in its wake.*

*"You're sure lookin' fine, Madeline." He drew out the last syllable of her name, then released an amused huff at his rhyme.*

*Her heart thudded in her ears. Breath hitched in her lungs. She tried to duck under his arm, but he pulled her to him. He swung open the stall door and pushed her against the wall. A hard click slid the door lock into place.*

*His eyes glittered with leering promise. "You've been flirtin' with me for most of your life," he growled as he pressed against her. "Time to make good."*

*Madeline's eyes widened. "No! Stop!"*

*"No more teasing, girl." He covered her mouth with his lips swallowing her scream.*

Madeline took in a deep breath. A sweet, detached calm

fell over her like a blanket warm from the dryer, smothering the terror back into its tiny, black box, squirreled away in the deepest folds of her brain.

But the girl's words dogged every step.

*You're preggers, right? First trimester's a beast.*

Madeline reached her classroom and peeked through the door's window. The class looked knee deep in the Algebra test.

*A test.*

A pregnancy test would confirm or deny the girl's words.

But what if the girl was right?

No, she wasn't right. Because she and Bobby hadn't ... and the other ... shouldn't have that result. God wouldn't let that happen, would He? But He'd let John David do ... that. Let Mom die in the car accident. He let bad things happen to people all the time. But would He do that to her? Break her heart again? Surely not.

And a test would prove that.

The cool detachment lifted as confidence slid into its place. Madeline squared her shoulders, then pulled open the classroom door and slipped into her seat.

※

The final bell rang, and Madeline shuffled along with the flow of students to the school's front entrance where Bobby stood waiting. Though his blond curls, camo jacket, and beat-up UT trucker hat blended in with fifty-percent of the student body, no other boy could make her heart stampede like a herd of half-wild cows.

They'd been dating for six months and as graduation

neared, his conversations had grown more serious. He hadn't mentioned the word marriage outright, yet it lurked behind the words he did say. Would he still want to marry her if her illness turned out to be something else?

Faking a smile, she accepted his kiss and waited for the customary rush of heat or a flickering pulse, but the gnawing in her stomach overpowered both. She swung her backpack off her shoulder as Bobby planted a quick kiss on her forehead and took the bag from her grasp.

Squaring her shoulders, she focused on keeping up her usual appearance. Thankfully, the huge grin wreathing Bobby's face told her he had plenty to distract him.

"Guess what, Mads?"

She couldn't help but grin at his child-like enthusiasm. "I don't know. What?"

"So get this. Dad woke me up this morning and said he had a surprise for me."

She could picture him as a little kid on Christmas morning practically jumping around the tree eager to open his presents.

Bobby spread his arms wide. "A brand-new crossbow. My graduation gift, but he gave it to me early because turkey season is about over. He wants us to go try it out today." Uncertainty lit his eyes and he sobered. "He took off from the factory. You mind catching the bus or getting another ride home?"

Madeline exhaled. With his new plans, she could slip out to the store, and he'd be none the wiser. She reached for her backpack and lied to him for the first time. "No problem. Matter of fact, um, Dad left me a message at the office earlier. Said he needed me to run errands with him after school."

Bobby nodded and hugged her to him. "All right. Want me to wait with you until he gets here?"

"Nah." The lie curdled in her heart. "He won't be long."

"Call me later?"

She nodded into his chest, gave him a final squeeze, and then watched as he rushed out to his truck.

⁊ઽ

Madeline pulled a bright blue New Holland ball cap out of her backpack. The color was more than enough to catch someone's eye, but it was the best she could do. She piled her telltale chestnut hair into a messy ponytail and tugged the hat low over her eyes. A few tendrils spilled out from the sides, but once she tucked them up under the brim, no one would recognize her. Satisfied, she waited until the last of the students left campus.

Then, she trekked a half-mile, walking past the post office and the old hotel that had been abandoned longer than she'd been alive. The gas station was just ahead.

There wasn't much to it—only two pumps and one of them diesel. But the store carried the bare essentials—lottery tickets, cigarettes, and a hundred varieties of Coke. She hoped somewhere on their shelves she'd find an unexpired pregnancy test.

As she reached the sundries aisle, the cashier watched her with the eagle eyes of one accustomed to nixing five-finger discounts. Madeline hunched her shoulders and continued her search.

She found a row of tests wedged between various necessities and pulled the closest one off the shelf. She ignored the price tag and studied the directions as she walked to the counter. Turning her head away from the store's camera, she pulled the required amount of money from her backpack.

"Bathroom's thataway," the casher said. Her resigned dismissal grated, but Madeline said nothing and headed for the women's restroom.

It took less than a minute to perform the test, but it would be at least ten before she'd get the results. Madeline checked her watch then eased onto the floor to wait. "Please, God," she whispered. "Please. Let this all just be a bad dream. Please, let her be wrong." Trembling fingers pulled her phone out of her backpack and estimated the wait time. A minute passed. Then two.

*Positive. Negative.* The words bounced through her as the clock ticked away.

One would destroy her life.

The other would spare it.

It wouldn't be positive. It couldn't be.

Slowly, a figure formed on the test strip.

A pink plus sign.

Madeline swallowed her gasp and shook her head. "No. No, it's too early." She glanced at her phone. It had only been five minutes. There were still five more to go according to the directions. Still plenty of time for it to change and her to wake up from the nightmare.

The girl from the hallway was wrong after all. God wouldn't allow this. He wouldn't condemn her for someone else's sin.

Madeline sat and stared at the floor, her only movement, the trembling in her limbs. Nothingness slipped over her, now familiar, comforting. She closed her eyes and savored the numbing sensation.

She should check it again. No. She would sit there a little while longer, cocooned in the merciful detachment. Neither here nor there. What had Dante called it? *Limbo.*

Her hands shook tapping the test against her leg jarring her back to reality. She glanced at her phone. Ten minutes were up.

And the pink plus sign had only darkened.

Her lungs seized.

*First comes love.*

*Second comes marriage.*

*Then comes Madeline with a baby carriage.*

Hiccuping laughter gurgled on frenzied breaths. Grim mirth disintegrated into panic. She would be a mother like she always hoped. But not like this—never like this. Snatching her backpack out of the floor, Madeline stuffed the test in the garbage can then rushed out the door, avoiding the prying eyes of the cashier as she hurried past. Outside the gas station, she staggered to a crosswalk sign and sagged against the metal stake as her knees weakened.

Sweat beaded across her forehead. Her breath hitched in frantic gasps for oxygen. "Why?" The question tumbled from her lips. "I was good, God. I was gonna do this right. Why this?" She pulled her knees to her chest, desperate to soothe her trembling.

"Miss, are you all right?" asked a voice, distant and concerned.

Madeline shook her head and tried to focus on the man who suddenly knelt beside her.

His face was dark, lined, and covered with a curly gray beard. He smelled of jasmine and newly mown hay, and his dark eyes were kind. But his clothes were stained and pressed into odd folds—likely the result of park bench sleeping.

A drifter. Blue Springs had plenty of them passing through town. She cleared her throat, but a deep rasp still laced her words. "I need to call my dad."

"Okay, then." His voice was soothing, melodic. "Let's get you up." He eased her to a standing position and lifted her backpack. "You got a phone?"

Madeline nodded and pulled out her cell phone. She tapped speed dial and two rings later, Dad's comforting drawl filled the connection. "Daddy?"

"Madeline? What happened? You don't sound good."

"I-I'll tell you when you get here." She relayed her location and ended the call. Then she glanced back up to thank the man. But he was gone. His sweet scent clung to the air, and her backpack lay at her feet.

She took a deep breath and sank back to the ground. Time passed. Minutes or possibly hours later, the familiar rumble of a diesel truck thrummed her way. Relief pure and heady rushed through her.

Dad jumped out of the truck and pulled Madeline to her feet. "Pumpkin, what on God's green earth is going on?" He wrapped her in a warm hug. "Did something happen with Bobby?"

"No," she mumbled, cherishing his comforting warmth.

They stood silent until a passing car swerved around his truck and honked. "Let's get out of here, Dad."

He nodded and drove to the nearest parking lot. There, he shut off the engine, then turned toward her. His gaze was as soft as his voice. "Whatever it is ... Tell me."

Eyes fixed on the floorboard, she tugged her hair from the ball cap and stuffed the hat in her backpack. "I'm pregnant."

She heard him swallow hard, then clear his throat. "I'm not mad," he said, holding his voice steady. "Promise."

Madeline heaved a quivering sigh. He may not be mad, but he did sound disappointed. She wasn't sure which was worse.

"Have you told Bobby?"

Chin trembling, Madeline shook her head. "We-we've only ever kissed." She risked a glance toward him and found doubt and tears clouding his eyes.

He rubbed the back of his neck and scanned the parking lot as if searching for help. "Pumpkin, kissing doesn't get you in this situation." A sad smile tinged his lips. "I think you've lived long enough on the ranch to know that."

Madeline cringed. She couldn't let him think the worst of Bobby. She would have to tell him the truth. Blood drained from her head. Her throat closed around her breath. "Daddy," she whispered. "I didn't want to."

She watched comprehension darken his eyes to a navy blue. "You mean?"

Madeline nodded.

Blood flushed his cheeks. He sucked in a quick breath. "Who?" He forced the word out between his pursed lips. "Who did this to you?"

Madeline cleared her throat and grabbed the edge of the seat to steady her hands. But the quaking in her voice remained. "You remember that day we took the steers to the auction? And we got that high price?"

His gaze grew distant. His jaw set. "That animal!" Then he shook his head and said, "Why didn't you say anything? We could've gone right to the sheriff. Told him everything."

"I passed out while it happened, Daddy." She bit her lip and cast an uncertain glance his way. "And when I woke up, all I wanted to do was forget it."

He shook his head. "But now, there's no forgettin' it." He fell silent as if embarrassed at stating the obvious. A moment later, he squared his shoulders. "I'll take you to the sheriff's department right now."

Her eyes widened. "No! Daddy. We're nobodies. The Billings ..." She swallowed hard as panicked, horrifying possibilities circled through her imagination. "There's no telling what they'd do. They're the richest people outside of Austin. You heard them at the auction. Everyone's expecting John David to end up governor. And you can bet Tommy won't let anything keep that from happening. They could blackball us at every auction, undersell the cattle. We would go under—lose everything the family has worked for." She shook her head as the possible futures played out before her. "No, I won't let that happen."

"I don't care how much power and wealth he has, Pumpkin. He can't get away with this."

Madeline gnawed on a fingernail and stared back into the past. "Right before ..." Her voice trailed off unable to say the words. "John David said I'd been flirting with him most of the time he'd known me." Her voice softened. A tremble laced her words. "It'd be my word against his. I don't have any proof. And if I did, who'd believe me over Tommy Billings's only child?"

Dad opened his mouth, but Madeline shook her head. "Daddy, you didn't see it—that look he gave me after the steers sold." She rubbed her arms to brush off the memory. Her lower lip trembled as she shook her head. "No, Daddy, I can't go to the sheriff. Please don't make me."

"Okay, then." His voice was low and rough. "But you're gonna tell Bobby, right?"

Madeline bit her lip. A shiver skirted over her skin. "No. I-I can't."

"He's gonna know sooner or later, Pumpkin. And if y'all haven't done anything beyond what you said, he's gonna know it isn't his."

He was right. But how on earth could she tell him? What could she possibly say?

Dad draped his arms over the steering wheel and stared out at the parking lot. A pained grimace etched its way into his cheeks. Her stomach clenched then turned over. He'd worn that same look when he'd told her about Mom's death.

"Well, there's another option—much as I don't agree with it generally." He cleared his throat. "You being in this situation puts a whole different spin on things. I won't say a word, and I won't love you any different if you choose it." His sigh shook with resignation and despair. "It would solve everything."

She fell back against the truck's door. An abortion. The idea crawled through her.

She couldn't.

Could she?

It offered a chance at maintaining the status quo. Bobby would never have to know. Or if nothing else, she would have more time to decide how to tell him.

With no pregnancy to explain, she could go on like nothing happened. Her life would once again be her own. But, could she willfully end the life that was growing inside her? The familiar ache of Mom's absence thrummed through her, opening the hole of missed opportunities and experiences that would forever be empty. Her hands curled into tight fists as she remembered the words ... *car accident ... drunk driver ... Mom ... dead.* Easing her hands open, she stared at the red half-moon welts her ragged fingernails had carved into the sensitive palms.

"I wish your mama was here. Lord knows she'd offer much better advice than I can."

Madeline wished she was as well. As much as she loved him, Jim Williams was no substitute for a female confidante.

Dad tugged his wide-brimmed straw hat low over his forehead, protection too little too late for the creases in his leathery skin. Tired blue eyes stared out at her from a face that was too old for his age. He leaned across the seat and pulled her into a hug. "I'm so sorry, Pumpkin. I never in my life would've thought you'd have to make a decision like this."

She tucked her nose into his chest and took a deep breath. The clean laundry scent mixed with hints of ranch life. "Why did God let this happen, Daddy? Why me?"

He kissed the top of her head. "Growing up I was taught to believe He was good and that He makes things work out for good." His voice cracked under the weight of more than a decade of pain. "But even though I still believe in Him, I sometimes wonder if everything I was taught is true." He pressed a kiss to her hairline then eased back to look her in the eyes. "I can't see anything good in your mama's passing—especially like she did. And now this."

# CHAPTER FOUR

*Blue Springs, Texas*
*March, 2011*

I HADN'T PLANNED ON COMING HERE. BUT FOR SOME reason, I turned left when I would normally go right. Before I realized the error, I'd pulled into the gravel driveway. The former lively auction house was doing a good impression of a Texas ghost town. Tumbleweeds rolled through the parking area that was once lined with dually trucks and cattle trailers.

Signs posted on the door indicated a full demolition was upcoming. Orange highway construction barrels crowded the former feedlot. A few were toppled on their sides, abandoned. Much like the auction itself.

It had been thirteen years since I'd been there. And another thirteen still would have been too soon. But like a homing beacon, it called to me, beckoning me to enter, to remember.

"What are we doing here?"

I pulled my gaze from the past and lifted it to my rearview mirror. Georgia sat staring out at our surroundings, a mixture of confusion and curiosity carving into her forehead. Unable to answer her question, I shook my head and whispered, "Come on."

We reached the main door, and I gave the handle a hard yank. Must and mildew hit my nose as the door's hinges protested their movement. I pushed through a pair of gates, rust flaking through the remnants of green paint. Spiderwebs stretched and snapped, sending their residents scurrying.

Georgia's lips curled as she absorbed the scene. "Seriously, Mom, what are we doing here?"

Still, I had no answer for her. A flock of pigeons, rousted from their contented perches, added a powdery dust to the already stale air and set my nasal passages afire. Like the resident geek returning triumphant to the high school reunion, I stood in my Calvin Klein suit and Steve Madden stilettos and surveyed the filthy surrounds. Images rose like smoke from a forest fire, bringing the past back to me.

The chant of the auctioneer.

The yips of the spotters.

The thunk of the gavel.

I backed up, a vain attempt to evade the onslaught of details, and bumped into the railing around the arena. The gate was an easy, steadying reach, but did I dare? He had held it just so as he'd watched me, warning with his eyes and his winning bid. Would I feel his grip, his fingerprints, melted into the aluminum? I grabbed it anyway, steadying myself and saving my heels from a bad scuffing as the memories continued to crash over me.

Oblivious to my trouble, Georgia slashed at a cobweb then planted her hands on her hips and pierced me with a determined stare. "Mom, you can't keep avoiding me on this. I'm old enough to know. Who is my father?"

*Not yet. Please not yet.* I pulled her into my arms. Maybe, just maybe, I could put the truth off one more time. I breathed in the sweet fruity shampoo that lingered in her soft blond hair and whispered, "Sweetie, you know who your Father is."

Georgia turned her face into my chest and mumbled, "Yeah, God."

I closed my eyes, grateful for her response even if it lacked the enthusiasm she'd shown in her younger years. She still knew who and whose she was. As my counselor, Janine, had said, the rest were details. But those were still awful details. I gave Georgia a gentle squeeze. "That's exactly right. And how much does He love you?"

"Wider than the sky and deeper than the ocean."

"Right again." I kissed the top of her head and said a quick prayer. *Please, Lord, not yet.* "How did I get such a smart kiddo?" I felt Georgia's reluctant chuckle against my shoulder, and I hoped I'd dodged the bullet one more time.

"I know God's my Father. But Mom, who's my biological father?"

I closed my eyes as the blood in my veins thickened with icy dread. The piper had come calling for his payment years earlier than I had planned, and he would not be denied. *Lord, why couldn't You have waited a little longer?*

Georgia pulled away and searched my eyes. I could see all the years of questions, the suppressed hurt.

I'd had thirteen years to ponder, pray, and prepare for this day. And I still wasn't ready. I brushed my fingers through the soft waves of her hair, trying to hold onto these last moments of her innocence, knowing their time was done. *Lord, how can I tell her and not shatter her completely?*

Her earnest gaze stared back. Maybe the best way was to begin at the beginning. Maybe that's why my car turned left instead of right. I cleared my throat and looked around the dilapidated auction arena. "Did I ever tell you about this place?"

Georgia rolled her eyes and huffed. "No. You've never told me anything. That's the problem."

Clearly, she thought I was dodging the question once again. I turned, releasing her just enough to stand shoulder to shoulder, and forced myself to remember the good. "When I was a kid, this was my favorite place. I loved the sounds, the smells, seeing the people. The excitement of the bidding when we brought cattle to sell and the rare occasion when your grandpa was looking to buy."

"Here?" Her eyes widened as she surveyed the ruins. A hole in the ceiling provided enough light to see the bench seats collapsing in place. The American flag was gone, but the old CD player remained, albeit smothered in dust.

"It was nothing like it is now. It used to be spotless," I explained. "The benches were painted red and white, and they were so shiny you could almost see your reflection in them. A huge American flag hung behind the auctioneer's stand. I was eight or nine the first time I saw it. And it was the biggest flag I'd ever seen. I thought there was no way Betsy Ross could've sewn it."

Georgia smirked, but remained silent.

My lips lifted in a reluctant smile as the good memories began to rise from the depths of the dross. "The announcer would always start every sale off by playing the national anthem. Over the years, they had several auctioneers—even brought in some fancy ones for special sales. It was better than a baseball or football game as far as I was concerned."

"You're serious?"

"Very." I smiled. "I'll always remember this one man. He took every bid while smoking a cigar. I don't know how he managed the auctioneer's chant around that nasty thing, but he did. I'd sit on my bench next to your grandpa and watch the ash fall from the end. I was sure it would catch the papers on fire, but it never did."

"Mom, were you a pyro?" Georgia tossed a sardonic glance my way.

I laughed and ruffled her hair. "No, I was not a pyromaniac." With a final glance around the sales arena, I squeezed her shoulder and whispered, "Come on."

We took the stairs up to the open landing and paused at the railing that ran the length of the arena. I leaned back against the rusting metal bars, too lost in the memories to worry about my suit.

"Up here was always like a rancher's version of the mall. Between the buttery scent of fresh popcorn and those nachos with that horrible-for-you-but-oh-so-yummy cheese sauce, it almost felt like a carnival at times." My mouth watered as the tangy memory of bright orange cheese and fiery jalapeños pinged my tastebuds.

"During the bigger auctions, like herd dispersal or breed sales, there would be all kinds of vendors. They'd hang out shirts and hats and sometimes chaps. The chaps were my favorite. I loved the smell of new suede. My heart's desire was to own a pair. But I never would have asked for them."

Georgia's brow wrinkled. "Why not?"

"Well, we never could afford them and even when we had a big sale, I would've felt guilty if Grandpa had bought them for me. Those were for the fancy show riders and full-time wranglers. I was neither. I think to this day he still doesn't know they were at the top of my wishlist for every birthday and Christmas."

We walked a little farther to where the landing overlooked the auction pens. The metal gates clung to the rotting wood looking as if the slightest breeze would pull the limp hinges from their rusted bolts. "I used to love sitting up here and watching behind-the-scenes. Seeing the cowboys herd the lots up. Hearing talk that was, according to Grandpa, 'too strong for young ears.' I felt so grown up, so worldly. From here, I thought I was something."

Georgia sighed, and I could tell her irritation at being put off once again was returning.

My breath quickened. It had been thirteen years since I had spoken about what happened. In that time, I'd buried everything and concentrated on building a new life for the two of us. But there was no avoiding the reality now, despite the consequences. I cleared my throat and inched my way toward the truth. "The auction's owner was a man by the name of Tommy Billings." A tremor laced my words.

Georgia looked up, irritation now replaced by softer eyes, somber concern.

I pursed my lips and swallowed hard. There was no hiding the tremble in my hands. "This place and another about thirty miles further south had been in his family since, I think, his grandpa was a kid. By the time I was about your age, he'd bought up most of the auction houses in east Texas. He also owned a thousand acres between Blue Springs and Fisher City and had as many cattle. Probably ten times that went through these gates over the years, and the Billings family controlled it all."

"Are you okay, Mom?" Georgia's concern now held tinges of fear.

I stayed focused on the story, knowing I had to get the words out now if she was to know the everything. "Tommy had a son named John David, who was a few years older than me. Tommy's plan was for John David to grow up and take over the auctions—maybe even be governor one day. But John David wasn't like his daddy. There was a meanness in him that nobody claimed ownership of, but everyone knew was there."

Georgia eased closer to me, eyes wide. Her cheeks paled as inescapable reality pierced her innocence.

"I don't know what happened to his mama. I never met her. Could be she hightailed it when he was a lot younger. There were rumors she died, but no one knew for sure." I shuddered at the realization. It had never occurred to me we had that loss in common.

"Maybe having her in his life would have made a difference. Maybe she was the reason he was the way he was. All I know is as much as women flocked to him, I only wanted to be as far away from him as possible. He had these hazel eyes that could stare a hole right through you. Some of the girls loved that. They said it was like he could see into them."

We walked a few more feet down the cracked concrete

until we reached the hall that led to the bathrooms and the private horse stalls beyond. The last stop on our tour down memory lane. My breath quickened. I paused.

There was no need for her to see them. No need for her to have that as the final memory of the place that had been so good up until that day. I steered us back to the entrance. When we reached the doors, I stopped and put an arm around Georgia's shoulder, bracing myself as much as re-assuring her. "You asked who your biological father was." Unshed tears clogged my voice. The next words would be ones she'd carry with her forever. *Lord, please.*

"Sweetie, I never told you because he wasn't someone I loved. He was someone I feared. And he did something no woman should ever have to experience."

Georgia lifted her eyes to mine. Widened in horror, their sky blue faded two shades paler. I gripped her shoul-der, the whites of my knuckles stark against my skin. She didn't flinch.

"The last day I set foot in here, I was seventeen. And your grandpa and I had brought a load of steers to sell."

Georgia shook her head slowly. She tried to pull away, but I held her still. As horrible as reality was, I couldn't leave her to her imaginings. "John David cornered me in the back. I never liked him. He always made me feel un-easy, so the last thing I would have ever done was flirt with him. But he accused me of doing just that all those years I'd come to the auction. And he said it was time to ... well ... you get the idea."

Georgia pushed away and stared back at me, mouth gaping. Tears filled her eyes, blurring her shock and disbe-lief. "You mean—he raped you?"

My heart shattered. To hear my twelve-year-old daughter say the words was more than I could bear—not because of the pain I'd carried all those years, but because she would now carry it too. I skimmed a hand across her cheek, wishing I could wipe her reaction away as easily I did the tears. "Yes, sweetie. That's what I mean."

Her childhood innocence lay in pieces before me, all illusion that the world was a safe and beautiful place where bad things didn't happen to good people gone. In one sentence, I would change everything, and she'd never be the same again. But I knew there was no more avoiding reality. Truth was all I had left to give her.

"John David raped me. And yes, he is your biological father."

Georgia yelled, "No!" Then she turned and raced out of the entrance. I watched through the dusty window as she yanked open the SUV's door and threw herself into the backseat. I needed to follow her, to offer comfort. But there was one other thing I had to do first. I had come all this way. I couldn't leave without facing ground zero.

I turned around and walked back to the private stalls bracing myself, certain I would feel something. Grief. Sadness.

But instead, a terrified paralysis gripped my lungs.

Breath disappeared.

Thoughts fractured.

I jerked back and thudded into the concrete block wall, banging my elbows. Stars shot across my vision and a curse cracked the stillness. The blow jarred my logic back into place and the terror slipped away, sinking back into its hole and leaving me with the sensation of whiplash.

I gave my arms a brisk rub. With a final glance, I headed back to the entrance. It was past time to leave.

As I neared the driver's door, I saw Georgia huddled in her seat clutching her backpack. All curled up like she'd do as a little girl when she'd have a bad dream. I wanted to pull open the door and wrap my arms around her. But I didn't. I'd needed time to absorb the truth all those years ago. I understood she needed the same.

Dad, on the other hand, would need a heads-up. I climbed into the SUV and glanced at Georgia in the rear-view mirror. She'd turned her face into the seat, but I could tell by the shaking of her shoulders she was crying. Her silence tore at me. I longed to say something—anything—that could possibly reassure her. But all I could say was, "I love you."

I tugged my phone out of my purse and thumbed the words Dad would understand. Adding I'd fill him in more when we arrived, I put the car in gear and headed to the ranch, my heart breaking with each passing mile. Georgia loved the ranch and adored Dad, which usually filled getaways like these with sweet memories. I shuddered thinking what she would store up from this week.

# CHAPTER FIVE

*Blue Springs, Texas*
*May, 1997*

M ADELINE TAPPED HER FINGERS AGAINST HER leg as she and Dad walked the gauntlet of elders at Blue Springs Baptist Church. She ached for direction, for answers. Hoping to find some sort of guidance, she had dressed that morning with a desperate eagerness that now seeped away with every nod and smile. She was a girl "in trouble." Would they still be smiling, still be so welcoming, if they knew? But then, if she "took care of the problem," would it be even worse?

Sister Beulah Price, the oldest member of the congregation, extended a bulletin clenched in her claw-like hand, jerking Madeline's attention from her thoughts. The woman had to be right behind Methuselah in age, but despite her stooped shoulders and contorted fingers, the light in her eyes radiated unspeakable joy. "Good to see y'all today, Brother Jim, Sister Madeline. Always glad to see the young ones growing up in church. 'Train up a child in the way they should go, and, when they're grown, they won't depart from it.' Proverbs twenty-two, six."

Madeline glanced around. Gray hair topped most of the heads in the congregation. There were a couple of younger families in the membership, but their children were elementary school age. Four months ago, Maribeth Grimes, Madeline's best friend, had moved to Austin with her mother after her parents' divorce, leaving Madeline the lone teen in their small country church.

Bobby's family attended First Methodist along with a few other friends from school. She hadn't minded not having others her age while Maribeth was there. Madeline pretty much kept to herself after all. But Maribeth's absence opened a gaping maw of conspicuousness, which could only grow as her waistline expanded in the coming months.

Dad smiled and accepted the bulletin, leading Madeline into the sanctuary. They paused as families found their customary pews. Looking around, her gaze landed on a man in the brown uniform of the county sheriff's department seated a few rows up. Madeline gulped. Sheriff Grimes, Maribeth's dad.

Why wasn't he on patrol? He'd missed more Sundays than he'd attended since the divorce and Maribeth's move.

Madeline glanced at Dad. She had begged him not to tell anyone, but what would he do now that God had brought the sheriff right to them? "Morning, Sheriff." Dad cast Madeline a sideways look. "You off this morning?"

Madeline flinched. She squeezed his hand, pleading once again for his silence.

Sheriff Grimes stood and extended a hand. The white line on his ring finger glared out from his dark tan, a condemning reminder of what had been lost. "Morning, Jim.

Hi, Madeline." He flashed a smile that bordered on a grimace. "I'm heading out on patrol as soon as service is over. But it's good to be working right now."

As disappointed as she was about Maribeth's move to Austin, Madeline wasn't really surprised. Although Sheriff Grimes had tried to follow Sister Beulah's verse, Maribeth chafed for years under his strict rules. Madeline could still hear Maribeth's childlike intonation of her father's mantra—no smoking, no drinking, home by ten o'clock, and no boyfriends. Each rule had been broken more than a dozen times over the years—at least according to the stories Maribeth would tell on Sundays.

"Madeline said she enjoyed seeing Maribeth when she was up there over spring break. That right, Pumpkin?"

Madeline cringed, but nodded. What was there to say? I'm sorry about the divorce? I'm sorry your daughter isn't who you wanted her to be?

The opening strains of "What a Friend" smothered any further conversation as Brother Jerry's wife, Sister Angela, pounded on the organ. Madeline heaved a sigh of relief and tugged Dad toward their regular pew. A few minutes later, Brother Jerry strutted to the podium as the closing chords of "In the Garden" waned. Sister Angela stepped down from the organ and took her seat on the front row next to her mother-in-law.

Brother Jerry Arnold had shepherded his tiny flock for the last twenty years with a determined eye toward saving the sinner. And the hellfire and brimstone that awaited those poor souls was his favorite topic. But Madeline remembered Bible bedtime stories with Mom. In them, God was a kind, loving provider, saving Daniel in the lion's den, calling to Samuel in the temple, and choosing the shepherd boy David to be king. She prayed Brother Jerry would pause in his customary lecture and offer the comfort and wisdom of her childhood. Since God had answered her other urgent plea, maybe He would do the same with this one.

"It is a woeful thing to fall into the hands of a living God," Brother Jerry said.

Madeline squeezed the bulletin, crumpling it into a faith-filled accordion while stifling a dismayed sigh. *And maybe not.*

"In Isaiah 27:7-13, the prophet tells us that the time has come and judgment begins at the house of God. How and why does he judge his church?" Brother Jerry looked out across the congregation. His sermons usually weren't interactive except for the occasional amen from his mother and wife.

As usual, the question was rhetorical. "In the book of Job, chapter five verse seventeen, Eliphaz tells Job, 'But consider the joy of those corrected by God! Do not despise the discipline of the Almighty when you sin.' God does not judge his bride, but He does use the rod of correction when we stray."

"Amen!" came two cries from the front pew.

"Sometimes His discipline is letting us live with the consequences of our actions."

Madeline winced, but considered his words. Had she sinned? Had she invited John David's actions? Did she allow the rape by not fighting him more and instead passing out? She bit her lip and glanced over at Dad. He sat listening to Brother Jerry's words. Did he think she had sinned?

Was it possible this pregnancy was God's way of disciplining her? Her shoulders sagged. Unable to answer, she closed her ears to the rest of the sermon.

When the service was over, she ducked out of the fellowship and sat in the truck alone. She twisted the hem of her dress, pondering everything she knew about her standing with God. She understood she was a sinner, saved by grace. Jesus had washed her clean and forgiven her sin. But after Brother Jerry's sermon, she felt neither clean nor forgiven.

She couldn't see how she had sinned in this situation, but maybe God saw it differently. She was a human being after all, and sin had been ingrained ever since the fall of Adam and Eve.

Dad climbed into the pickup. A concerned look lit his eyes. "Ready to go?"

She nodded and buckled her seatbelt. Neither spoke, allowing the gospel music from the local country station to fill the silence. She cast furtive glances at him as he drove out of the lot. He seemed sad, almost disappointed. Was it possible he'd asked himself these same questions?

He had said he would support her through this. What if he had changed his mind? What would she do then?

Madeline took a deep breath and glanced his way again. "Dad?" She did her best to hide the tremor in her voice, but failed. "Do-do you think I brought this on myself?"

He braked hard at the stop sign, and disbelief flitted through his navy eyes. "No."

Madeline clenched her dress, creasing the pattern into rough groupings of fabric flowers. "But John David said I had been flirting with him—"

"Madeline Jane Williams." Dad laid a heavy hand over her fidgeting ones and gave her a level stare. His voice carried the authority of generations. "I have been with you every time we've been to the auction. Never at any time have I seen anything from you that would remotely pass for flirting with that boy."

His voice softened as he brushed his knuckles against her cheek. "If anything, you've dodged any interaction with him." He put a finger under her chin and looked into her eyes. "And even if you had flirted, it still gave him no right to do what he did to you. You are not responsible for any of this. It was entirely because of John David's actions."

Madeline nodded, then glanced away. They drove in silence for a while longer. "I just ... I wasn't sure. Not after the sermon today."

Dad sighed and turned into the ranch's driveway. "Pumpkin, I know God speaks through people and He speaks through sermons." He brushed his hair back from his forehead. His eyes held an odd glint. "But I learned the hard way when your mama died that just because the words they say sound Christian, it doesn't mean it's Christ speaking."

# CHAPTER SIX

*Blue Springs, Texas*
*March, 2011*

I TURNED THE SUV INTO THE RANCH'S DRIVEWAY and glanced in the rearview mirror. Judging by the flash of desperation in Georgia's eyes, the familiar bumps of the ranch's cattle guard weren't as comforting as I'd hoped. I barely got the SUV in park before she shot out of the backseat and ran through the front door. Her usual greetings with Dad were filled with long swinging hugs and delighted laughter, but this time she brushed passed him without a second look.

I released a shaky sigh and closed my eyes. *I know there was no other option, but Lord, please help. Surround her and comfort her.* A light tap patted the window. Dad. A sad smile wreathed his lined face. I nodded, opened the door, and fell into his waiting arms. I snuggled closer and took in a deep breath of rancher's cologne, grass, wind, cow. "Daddy, it was awful. I tried to tell her as gently as I could."

"I'm sure you did, Pumpkin. She'll work through it. It'll be okay." He rubbed circles on my back and gave me a long squeeze. "Want some sweet tea?" Without waiting for my agreement, he went to the trunk and grabbed our suit-cases, then followed me into the house. Peace settled over me as soon as I stepped through the door. As Dad told me once before, the ranch would always be home.

He dropped our bags in our rooms while I poured two glasses of tea. We met in the den a few minutes later. I lifted my brows and glanced behind him, silently asking about Georgia.

"She was curled up on the bed with her back to the door," he said with a shrug. "Let's give her a couple of hours."

I took a sip of tea and asked the question that had been hovering in my mind for the last two hours. "Why didn't you tell me John David had been arrested? Surely you know he's on trial."

His shoulders slumped, remorse settling over his rangy frame. "I'm sorry, Pumpkin. I didn't know how to tell you—you're in such a good place right now. I figured it would only reopen old wounds for no reason." He sagged into his armchair, its leather now scarred and scuffed from years of wear and tear. "I just wanted to protect you."

I squeezed his shoulder as I sank onto the ottoman. I could understand that desire. After all, protecting loved ones was how I had gotten this far. I sighed and stared at the closed bedroom door across the hall. "I'd always planned to tell her when she was eighteen. What if I've scarred her for life now? I wish I had talked with someone beforehand, brought in a counselor, something. I mean I had thirteen years to prepare, but—"

"I'm sure you did the best you could."

"How could I have protected her for so long only to ruin it all? If I botched up everything with how I told her—"

Dad leaned forward. "If Janine were around, you could talk to her. Seemed like she always gave you good advice."

I set my tea down on the end table. "You're right. She was a counselor as well as a nurse. Wonder if the crisis center is still in business?"

"Surely, she's moved on from there after all this time."

I grabbed my phone and did a quick web search for the number. "Maybe, but they still might know how to reach her." I read through the listings and clicked on the center's webpage. "Looks like they're still in business. Even have the same address." I tapped on the number and waited for someone to answer.

"Real Choices Pregnancy Clinic. How may I help you?"

"Hi, I know this is a long shot, but I'm looking for someone who used to work there. She was my counselor at the time. A social worker and RN named Janine Reynolds?"

"Ms. Reynolds? She's actually our executive director now. What's your name? I can see if she's available."

I gave my name and agreed to hold. Soothing jazz played on the waiting line. For some reason, I could picture Janine as a jazz aficionado.

A click on the line was followed by a "Hello? This is Janine Reynolds."

"Janine, it's Madeline Williams. You may not remember, but you helped me thirteen years ago?"

"Madeline," she said, her tone warm and soothing. "How are you? I was just thinking about you ... I saw the news."

I sank onto the couch, relishing in the warm embrace

of Janine's kind voice and the familiar leather. "I'm doing well. I'm the Human Resources Manager for SouthSide Medical Center in Austin. I've been there about four years now."

"How wonderful. I always knew God had big plans for you."

I couldn't help but smile at her heartfelt delight. "Speaking of God's plans, you should see Georgia. She's amazing. And the spitting image of my mom."

"With you as her mother I wouldn't expect anything less."

"Georgia is actually the reason for the call. I've never told her the biological story—I had planned to tell her when she turned eighteen. But thanks to a class project, well, it came up much sooner."

"What happened?"

I recounted the story like a bystander viewing a car wreck, helpless to stop it, able to describe even the minutiae in vivid detail. When the whole of it was finally told, I fell silent. The airwaves caught a hiccuping sigh, echoing it between the two of us.

"Madeline. I'm so sorry. I thought I was so wise in my advice and direction to you. I can see now I may have been wrong, and I understand if you're angry with me."

How could she think that? I raised my hand to the phone's receiver in a vain effort to comfort. "Janine, I could never blame you. You were a confidante and a mother when I needed both. You were my safe space when everything around me made no sense."

A tremor rattled over the connection as Janine took a deep breath.

"I'm not calling to vent or to blame you. I'm calling because once again I need help. And I trust your advice."

"I always wondered what happened to you, Madeline."

I closed my eyes to focus on her words, spoken only a hair's breadth above a whisper.

"Clinic rules kept me from calling after you had Georgia, but don't for one minute think you've been out of my prayers."

The years between us disappeared as I said, "Thank you, Janine. I'm sure your prayers are the reason why everything has turned out so well. Now, how can I best help Georgia work through this?"

Janine cleared her throat, and her professional tone returned. "When did you tell her?"

"A couple of hours ago."

"Is she displaying any odd behavior or doing things she hasn't done in years like suck her thumb?"

I thought back over the last few hours. She'd clutched her backpack. Did that count? I shook my head. That was her go-to method of post-school comfort. "No, nothing like that. Thank God. She ran out of the car and into the house as soon as we got back to the ranch. She's been in her room ever since. Hasn't said a word to me or Dad."

"Okay, this will sound strange, but that's actually good. It means she's stunned, but probably not traumatized. And the silence is a completely appropriate response to news like this. Give her space and love. It'll take time for her to come to terms with it. But be ready to talk whenever she opens up. Don't worry if it takes a couple of days for her to broach the subject. I'm assuming she knows about the trial?"

As relieved as I was by her diagnosis, dread crept between my shoulders. "No. At least I don't think so. And I was hoping to keep it from her. She's already had enough of a shock."

"I'm sorry, Madeline, but she's going to have to know. And she needs to hear it from you. Not a radio or TV report and definitely not from someone in the community."

"What do I say?"

Soothing warmth returned to Janine's voice. "Keep it simple and truthful. She's probably going to have a lot of questions that start with why. Don't be afraid to tell her you don't know. There are some things only God knows and that's okay. It's why we're called to trust Him."

Maybe I hadn't done such a bad job telling her after all. "Do I take her dinner in her room or wait for her to come out?"

"She's probably not hungry right now. I'd say keep some leftovers in the fridge, just in case, but don't expect her to eat until she's ready."

I bit my lip as an idea occurred to me. "Do you think it might take longer than a couple of days for her to open up?"

"It's possible, why?"

Leaning my head back against the chair, I wrapped a lock of hair around my finger. "I had planned for both of us to be at the ranch for the weekend. Then she'd stay here with Dad for the rest of spring break while I went back to work. She's always loved coming here. She four-wheels on Dad's ATV, helps him with the cattle, and takes the horse out for trail rides."

I flashed Dad a fond smile, then said, "Do you think

it's a good idea if I stay for the week too? It might be comforting. But then again, maybe I should take her back to Austin. With the trial, being here might upset her more. We don't have to go into town, but there's no avoiding the news and the papers. They're bound to have updates. Then of course, there's always the internet. At least she doesn't have a smartphone, and Dad never wanted internet access even though he has a computer."

"If she feels like the ranch is a safe haven, then that's the best place for her. In fact, it's probably the best place for you too. She'll need you and, in reality, you'll need her and your dad."

I pushed aside her concern for me and focused on the practicalities. "Okay, I'll make arrangements to stay. There are no big plans this week at work, and, if anything comes up, I'm only an hour away."

"How is your dad, by the way?" A curious lilt tempered the question. "I remember him being such a nice man and a very caring father to you."

My brows lifted at the turn in the conversation. She had been married back when I was seeing her—at least I remember she wore a wedding ring. But it had been thirteen years. A lot could have changed in that time. "He's great. Still doing what he does best, ranching and taking care of me. I'll tell him you said hello."

"Please do. And Madeline, please keep me posted on Georgia. I'd be more than happy to talk with her if you'd like." She gave me her cell number, just in case we needed to reach her after hours.

"Janine. Thank you. You're still a safe space for me." I

ended the call and pinched the bridge of my nose as the weight of the afternoon seemed to lift from my shoulders.

"How'd it go?" Dad asked.

Disbelief mingled with relief, and I couldn't help my chuckle at the bemusing blend. "Good. She gave me some great advice on how to handle Georgia's questions. And you know, she asked about you. Sounds like she might have a few fond memories of you too, Dad."

Crimson flushed over Dad's cheeks, and he glanced away.

My lips quirked in a wide, teasing grin. "I'm just saying." I sighed as the rest of the conversation played over in my mind. "She says to give Georgia some space and time. And that it'd be good if we both holed up here for the week instead of me heading back to Austin on Monday. You okay with that?"

Dad's eyes gleamed. "Sounds like a bit of heaven to me, Pumpkin."

"I'll run home in the morning and get more clothes, and I need to call the office to let them know." Fatigue eased through me like a long sigh. I closed my eyes and soaked up the silence and comfort. But my internal list of things to do wouldn't stay silent for long. "What did you plan for dinner? We can get started on it as soon as my call is done."

"I planned to grill out. I pulled some hamburger out of the chest freezer this morning and there's potatoes in the bin we can fry up."

No surprise there. He always was a meat and potatoes guy. "Got anything green laying around?"

He chuckled and shook his head. "Matter of fact, I

picked up some salad fixings the other day. There's practically a garden in the crisper."

I kissed his cheek. "Thank you."

He waved off the thanks and rose. "And there's plenty of hamburger meat left from the last steer. Make sure you take some back to Austin with you."

"Sounds good. I'll go get unpacked and make my call."

❦

Back in my childhood room, I settled on the edge of my bed, suddenly uncertain how to broach the topic of a week off with my boss. Dr. Samuel Kitteridge, or Dr. K as he was known around SouthSide, had been the hospital's administrator for all of my career there, and ten years prior to that. A former internal medicine doctor, he'd brought his caring bedside manner to the boardroom and was possibly the best boss anyone could want.

But no one outside of Dad, Janine, and now Georgia knew the circumstances of her conception. Maybe if I simply stuck to the bullying and needing to be here to help with an unexpected homework assignment? I cringed. The last time I had bent the truth was for Georgia too.

Dr. K picked up on the third ring. "Madeline. Thought you were ranching it this weekend."

"I am, but some things have come up. I'm sorry, but I need to take the week off for Georgia's spring break."

Concern rippled across the phone line. "Is she all right?"

I winced and pushed the crooked story off my lips. "Physically, yes. Emotionally no." I gave him a brief overview of the bullying and then generalized the homework assignment. "Will it be a problem?"

"Well, we are in our Joint Commission survey window."

"Yes, but we're well prepared and talk around town is they'll get to St. Anne's and the big conglomerates first. So I believe we have a bit of breathing room. Plus, I'm just a phone call away if anything changes. I could be there in an hour."

"Sounds like you've got everything ready."

I could hear the relief in his voice. Joint Commission hospital surveys were not for the faint of heart. In fact, half the staff would volunteer for a colonoscopy to avoid one.

"Stay and enjoy the time with Georgia."

I smiled. "Thanks, Dr. K. I'll see you in a week."

After ending the call, I dialed my assistant's work line and left a quick voicemail explaining my absence and asking her to set the out of office reply on my email. I added I was available for emergencies, but requested she hold everything else until I returned.

Bases covered, I kicked off my stilettos. My relieved feet seemed to sigh as they melted back to their God-intended arch. Deciding to put my clothes and toiletries in drawers rather than living out of my suitcase, I went to work unpacking. Arms full of clothes, I snagged my sneakers with two fingertips. Before I reached the closet, the sneakers slipped from my tenuous grip. They landed on the carpet with a muted thud, one rolling under the bed.

I stowed my clothes in their drawers then knelt down and patted around under the bed, searching for the missing shoe. My hand landed on plastic rather than fabric.

Curious, I pulled on the item. A thick layer of dust disappeared in the beige carpet as I tugged it out.

My rear end hit the floor as a shiver whispered over my skin.

It was a white garbage bag.

Blood drained from my head. My skin tingled. My hands shook as I untied the flaps and peered inside.

Denim shorts.

A purple t-shirt with a screen-printed unicorn jumping over a rainbow.

A bra and panties.

Everything I had worn that day.

*That day ...*

I fell back on the floor as the room began to spin. My fingers clenched the clothes. I willed the room to still. Slowly, the whirling eased. But I remained where I was, frozen, paralyzed.

*Why are they under the bed? Why hadn't I thrown them away? Given them to a donation store? Something other than keep them.*

I couldn't remember.

It was a blank.

I shifted the fear to the side and tiptoed through every memory of that time.

My mind skirted all recall of the stall with the finesse of a champion cutting horse and landed on the sale of the steers. Then going home. Then ... I forced myself to focus on any tidbit, any thread of what had happened once we'd arrived back at the ranch.

Thoughts lurched, slowed, then sped. The—the—did I

take a shower? I must have. But there was nothing until ... school, maybe? Or was it the trip to Maribeth's?

Was that how I survived the experience? Had I somehow built a box that would shame the finest Russian artisan and shoved my terrors inside its depths? Had I forced them to disappear until I actually convinced myself that none of it had ever happened?

The room swam. *Lord. Help!*

My thoughts crept back to that morning. Bobby's pleas for me to hang out with him. My excitement as Dad and I loaded the steers. The delight of going to the auction.

If I had I known what that day would bring ...

I adored Georgia and couldn't imagine life without her, but would I have chosen how she'd have to get here?

I never figured myself for a coward. Not with all of the choices I had to make. But maybe when push came to shove, I really was. Maybe that was why I had blocked out the days and weeks afterward. Because I wasn't brave enough to admit it happened. To acknowledge that something very personal and special had been stolen from me.

Still clutching the t-shirt and shorts, I sat up. The time-worn fabric brushed my leg. Repulsed, I hurled them into the bag and shoved it back under the bed with my bare foot.

"Madeline?" Dad called. "You about ready to start dinner?"

Taking an unsteady breath, I balled up the memories and the shame and buried them again. "Give me a minute to clean up," I said and pushed myself off of the floor.

# CHAPTER SEVEN

*Blue Springs, Texas*
*May, 1997*

H EAT FLUSHED ACROSS MADELINE'S CHEEKS AS
Bobby's lips met hers. Her pulse skittered. His eyes
glinted with a teasing light. "I've missed you, Mads."

Madeline rolled her eyes. Still, she couldn't help but
smile. "It's been what, not even four hours since we saw
each other?"

Bobby shrugged and then opened the passenger
door of his Silverado. "Still gotta fix that handle," he said
with a smile.

Madeline tossed her purse on the floorboard. Repairs
wouldn't stop Bobby. Over the months they'd been dating, she couldn't remember a single time when he hadn't
opened a door for her. Truck or otherwise.

He pulled his ratty Chevy ball cap off his shotgun rack,
tugged it low over his blond curls, then hopped in behind
the wheel. "Ready for dinner?"

Madeline hummed her answer and picked up a folder
lying between them on the seat. An Army officer saluted

from one side of the cover while a unit in fatigues ran some sort of obstacle course on the other. "What's this?"

Bobby glanced over as he put the truck in gear then snorted. "Dad ran to Austin to look for parts for the 'vette he pulled out of the junkyard last month. Of course, he somehow found time to stop by the recruiter's office. Guess, it wasn't enough he talked about it most of the hunting trip." He fell silent then heaved a frustrated sigh. "There are times when I wish he hadn't blown out his knee in high school. Maybe if he'd gotten his dream of becoming a Green Beret, he wouldn't be pushing the military so hard on me."

Madeline patted his arm. "He does it because he wants better for you than the factory where he ended up. You know that."

Bobby pursed his lips and nodded. "Yeah, I know. I can't see myself making detergent for the next twenty years either."

Madeline winced at Bobby's dry tone. She flipped through the pages and began to read. "He circled options? Infantry ... Combat Engineer ..."

"Yeah," Bobby replied with more interest in the oncoming traffic than the folder. "He says I can put my hunting and tracking skills to good use. Apparently, those guys work in rough terrain. It sounds interesting, but ..."

Brow furrowed, she studied him as he drove. "But what? Sounds like it's right up your alley."

He darted another quick look to her then returned his eyes to the road. "I've got you." He paused and glanced her way again. "You've heard what military life is like. Moving from base to base every few years. Long deployments. I'm not sure I want to do that to you—to us."

Madeline remained silent. What would he do if he knew there was one more person in his us? Would he love and support them, claiming the child as his? Or would he see her as damaged goods? Her virtuous pedestal shattered at his feet.

But if she didn't keep the child, she wouldn't have to tell him anything. Wouldn't have to deny his dreams, his plans for their future. It would be her secret. But would that secret, that act, haunt her? Could she sacrifice a life to save a dream that might not come true anyway?

"Hey, you okay? You got all quiet on me."

Madeline swallowed hard. "Yeah. Sorry. So any plans for the weekend?"

Bobby's lips lifted in a fond smile. "Mom's got another makeup party at the house. I swear she's bound and determined to get that pink Escalade."

Madeline had attended his mom's parties twice to be polite. Never one to pour over fashion magazines or wear cosmetics, she'd nursed her sherbet punch and hid in the background while the others oohed and ahhed over the latest skin care products.

She bit an unpolished fingernail. "Do I need to be there? Lisa Jean already wants us to get our nails done next week." While going to a nail salon wasn't her first choice, it was an olive branch Madeline could attempt. Bobby's sister had yet to warm up to idea of him and Madeline as a couple—Madeline secretly swore even Miss Texas would have difficulty getting Lisa Jean's approval.

Bobby flashed a reassuring smile. "Nope. Mom says her

entire Sunday school class is coming. It'll be fine. Hey, if you're not helping your dad, how 'bout catching a matinee movie Saturday?"

Madeline grinned. "Sure. But I know you're really wanting an excuse to avoid a houseful of women talking about makeup."

Bobby chuckled. "Guilty as charged."

Madeline shook her head in wry amusement then watched the passing scenery blur into lines of browns and grays as they left ranchland and entered the Blue Springs city limits. A sheriff's cruiser screamed passed them, brimming with urgency and flashing lights as it headed out of town.

"He's in a hurry," Bobby muttered.

"Oh, speaking of sheriffs, I got a postcard from Maribeth yesterday." Ignoring Bobby's unenthusiastic grunt, Madeline soldiered on. "She wants me to go back to Austin for another visit. She hates that her mom was sick the last time I was up there, and I know she's not coming back here any time soon."

Bobby shook his head. "You ask me, that divorce was a long time coming. Dad grew up with them both and said he'd never seen such a mismatched pair. And you and Maribeth are total opposites too. Never could see how y'all were friends."

Madeline wished she hadn't brought up the subject. Maribeth's impulsivity and risk-taking personality had long marked her as a wild child, ostracizing her from the more conservative natures of the townspeople, but she'd been a good friend. Madeline turned her gaze to a line of trucks rolling down the cross street. Most were wrapped in blue and white streamers and covered in chalk paint-ed jersey numbers and well wishes. A few even boasted replicas of Blue Springs High's mascot, the stampeding bull. Friday night home games pretty much closed down the town.

"I'm sorry," Bobby mumbled. "I know her moving has to be hard on you."

Madeline felt his warm hand engulf her own. She gave it a quick squeeze silently accepting his apology and said, "I know you've never liked her." She watched the trucks begin to move again. "But you are right about one thing. She didn't fit here in Blue Springs. Hopefully a bigger city will be better."

A few minutes later, they found a parking spot. Bobby cut the engine and leaned across the seat. His callused thumb scraped the soft skin of her cheek as he pushed her hair back behind her ear then brushed a light kiss across her lips. Warmth flooded her. Madeline savored the sensation.

"Love you."

"You too." She smiled and ruffled the blond curls that peeked out from his hat. With another quick kiss to his cheek, she hopped out of the truck.

���

The tangy combination of oregano and garlic wafted through the door as Bobby held it open. Glancing around, Madeline found most of the tables filled with couples, families, and the occasional singleton. As she started to ask him about placing a to-go order, a familiar voice bellowed from the open kitchen.

"Bobby, Madeline!" Uncle Richie waved from behind a rack of pizzas warming under a heat lamp.

"Hey, Uncle Richie," Bobby said as he tugged Madeline through the crowd. "Any chance we can get a table?"

Bobby's uncle tossed a towel over his burly shoulder and squeezed his bulky frame around the counter. Flour dust, remnants from tossing pizza dough, clung to his dark hair lending a bit of salt for the pepper of its jet black color. He swiped a beefy hand through its short length as a pleased grin lit his face. "You know there's always room for you—even if I have to kick out a few of these chuckleheads." The brusque nasality of a native Chicagoan was softened by the slightest hint of a Texas twang, compliments of thirty years of marriage to Bobby's aunt.

Uncle Richie slung an arm around Bobby's shoulder and gave Madeline a wide smile. "I know this guy wants a large meat lovers with extra cheese. You want your usual too?"

Madeline's brow furrowed. "Pepperoni Stromboli with—"

"Extra sauce, I know." Uncle Richie chuckled. "You did work here every day this summer. And you never tried anything but the Stromboli." He glanced around the restaurant and pointed to a booth covered in cups and plates. "Y'all go grab that one by the window. I'll send Jenny over."

Bobby grabbed Madeline's hand and led the way. Jenny appeared with a tray of drinks. Flashing a teasing smile, she gave the table an efficient clear-and-clean. Then she smiled and said, "I'm sure Richie wouldn't mind if you helped a girl out."

Madeline laughed. "Maybe next time."

Jenny set their drinks on the table. "Gonna hold you to that."

As they settled opposite each other, Bobby relinked their fingers across the table top. A small smile teased his lips and a mischievous glint lit his eyes.

Accustomed to his teasing, Madeline groaned and shook her head. "This is gonna be good."

"So I have been thinking about another career option."

"Like?"

"Ranching."

Madeline rolled her eyes and huffed. "You do remember what happened to those goldfish I gave you for Christmas? Bobby, if you can't keep fish alive, how in the world do you think you'd do with cows?"

He chuckled, but there was hesitation lurking in the lilt.

"It's too bad there's not much else to do around here." The only other employers in the county were the school system and a few doctors' and lawyers' offices. Madeline had no idea what she would do after graduation. Prior to dating Bobby, she'd always figured she'd end up a rancher's wife.

As her father's only child, she'd inherit her family's three hundred acres. Her great-grandfather had dug the family out of the ruins of banking during the Great Depression and invested every penny that remained into the land. Dad had told her over and over, *Money and people come and go, but the land remains.* Responsibility weighed heavily on her shoulders. She was destined to continue the family legacy, but to do that, she'd need someone to help.

But if Bobby chose ranching and stayed with her, would he end up hating it? Would it be fair to expect him to change his entire life just because of her? Was that right?

A teenaged boy stood by Uncle Richie's beloved juke-box splitting his attention between DJing and a girl who looked vaguely familiar. The pair flirted and smiled through one country song and into the next. The sweet strains of "Yellow Rose of Texas" broke through the din of conversation. Bobby squeezed her hands and cocked a teasing grin. "Hey, that's our song."

Madeline watched the boy tug the girl into a swaying armhold the might pass for dancing if there was a dance-floor. "Yeah, I remember."

That song had been playing on the jukebox the day Bobby asked her to be his girlfriend. He'd come to the pizza parlor bearing a red rose after the lunch crowd had thinned out. When she agreed, he'd swept her up into a long hug, swinging her around. Their delight was conta-gious, spreading to the rest of the staff who laughed and clapped celebrating with them. Everything had seemed so perfect. But that was months ago, and as happy as she was to be his girlfriend, reality was a sobering antidote to joy.

Jenny reappeared with their orders and set the dishes down with a quick, "Y'all good?"

At Bobby's nod, she hustled away, off to check on oth-er customers. He slid a slice of his pizza off the stand and held it toward Madeline. Sauce dripped from the tip onto a thick crumble of sausage.

Madeline shook her head. "I'm not taking food out of your mouth. I can barely get around half of my Stromboli as it is." She cut into her meal revealing the usually tasty combination of pepperoni and marinara. Steam rose wafting the savory scents in the air around her.

A family at a table across the room caught her attention as they broke into peals of laughter. Her gaze turned to the other patrons and sorrow slipped through her like a watery sigh. Over the chaos, parents chatted, kids giggled, and couples flirted. Life for them was good. Nice, sweet. Normal.

Why couldn't she have the same? She and Bobby could have gotten married and then had kids. Just like regular people. Just like all their family and friends. She glanced back at her Stromboli, now cool enough to eat, but no longer appealing. "I may take mine to go."

Bobby inhaled his second slice. "You okay?"

Closing her eyes, Madeline turned her head into the back rest.

Bobby put down the third slice and cast a concerned gaze toward her. "Mads, are you crying?"

Madeline wiped the back of her hand across her eyes. "No, I just—"

"Mads, honey." With eyes wide, he cast a desperate glance around the restaurant then scooted out of the booth and quickly returned with two boxes. "Let's get out of here. You want to go to the park? You love the swings."

Madeline nodded and watched Bobby pack up the food. "I'm sorry," she said again. "I don't—"

"Hey, shh. It's no problem." He tucked her under his arm, tossed two twenties on the table, and grabbed the boxes as they left the booth. They wound their way between the tables passing the open kitchen as they headed back toward the door.

Uncle Richie was arm deep in pizza dough, hurling it into the air and catching it on the downward spin. He dropped it on the metal counter and asked, "Everything okay?"

Bobby nodded and held up the to-go boxes. "We just need to run."

"It was good to see you both," Uncle Richie said with a wink.

Madeline flashed a wan smile, and soon they were outside.

Bobby stashed the food in his truck, then curled his arm around her shoulders as they walked toward the park. She leaned into his chest, savoring the musky blend of his aftershave. Cupping her cheek, Bobby pressed a soft kiss to her lips and then tugged her toward the swings. His hands slipped around the chains while pulling her gently backward. Holding her steady against his chest, he leaned down and whispered, "I love you, Mads."

The words warmed her even as his breath tickled her neck. She closed her eyes and relished the sensation as he released her swing. A slight push on her return and she began an easy glide. Remorse pricked at her. He really would be a perfect husband.

# CHAPTER EIGHT

*Blue Springs, Texas*
*March, 2011*

E VEN THOUGH I WAS AN EARLY RISER, I FOUND
Dad already in the kitchen lingering over a cup of coffee. I had tiptoed past Georgia's closed door, deciding to let
her sleep. We grabbed a quick and quiet breakfast, then I
headed back to my house for more clothes.

About thirty minutes later, I reached the outskirts of
Austin. Our first home there had been the tiniest of apart-
ments, tucked just a few miles off I-35. I'd landed my first
grownup job at a temp agency nearby, and they'd kept
me hopping all around the city with a series of short-term
gigs. But somehow, I'd earned enough to cover rent, childcare, and groceries without having to ask Dad for any financial support.

That agency opened the door to a life I would never
have imagined. Eventually I was assigned to cover a ma-
ternity leave for the assistant to SouthSide's HR Manager,
Linda Carmichael. When the new mom decided to stay
home with her baby, Linda hired me away from the agency.

I passed the exit for SouthSide just as my phone rang.

With a glance at the caller ID on the car's display, I smiled at the timing and tapped the button to accept the call. "Hey, Linda. I was just thinking about you. How are you?"

"Good morning, Madeline. I'm well. Just calling to see if you have time to grab lunch this week."

I glanced at the date on the display and swallowed a curse at my forgetfulness. On March twentieth, a year after Linda hired me full time, she'd asked me into her office and proceeded to turn my world upside-down. She'd said that when she retired, she wanted me to take over the department—and we had three years to make that happen. But first, I'd need to earn an advanced degree and upgrade my wardrobe.

I was not excited. As much as I enjoyed my classes, getting my associate's degree had already been harder than anything I'd done in high school, and I couldn't imagine putting myself through more college classes. Then there was the whole dressing up thing. Boots? Yes. Heels? No way.

But Linda looked me in the eye and told me HR wasn't about grades. It was about heart, and she knew I had more than enough for the job. It turned out, she was right. I absolutely loved running the department. Human Resources allowed me to work with people and help them be the best employees they could be. And in time I even learned to enjoy the suits and heels.

Every year since that March twentieth, we'd met for lunch and discussed my career and plans for the future. How could I have forgotten? "Linda, I'd love to, but it's Georgia's spring break at the new school, and we're at the ranch all week." I gave her the same story I'd told Dr. K and apologized for forgetting our anniversary.

"Oh, no, poor thing. Yes, definitely stay with her. And let me know if I can help at all. I may be out of the game, but this old dog keeps up with the trends. And the workplace is no different from a school when it comes to personal interactions."

"Thanks, Linda. I appreciate that. I'll give you a call once I can meet with the principal. I'm done waiting for diplomacy to start working."

"Perfect. Talk then."

I ended the call and pulled into my driveway. The single-story colonial was perfectly situated in an up-and-coming neighborhood near the hospital. Dad had been so proud the day I signed the closing papers. Four years had disappeared in a breath.

꧁

It had been a while since I'd spent more than a weekend on the ranch and my collection of Calvin Klein and Kate Spade wouldn't survive a day there, let alone a week. I pulled some old jeans off a shelf, adding a few t-shirts from various hospital-sponsored events. Tossing in a couple of dresses for church, I grabbed a casual work outfit, just in case I was called into the hospital. I gave the plants a quick drink of water and threw the bread into the freezer. Then, with a quick scan, I locked up. Suitcase loaded, I hurried back to my driver's seat and told the car to "Call Dad."

He answered as I backed out of the driveway. "Hey, Dad, I'm on my way back. How's Georgia?"

"I haven't seen hide nor hair of her." He paused and then continued in a lower voice. "But I heard the water run in the shower, so she's at least up and around. I think we should take that as a positive."

The on ramp for I-35 was just ahead, and I glanced in my rearview mirror before changing lanes. "Yeah, I think so too. Hey, I know you weren't expecting both of us for the week, so I'll swing by the grocery. Anything in particular you need?"

"Don't worry about that. I'd already planned to make a run in a couple of days."

"No, it's only fair. Let me treat you a little bit." Small time ranching still paid more in self-fulfillment than folding money, and picking up groceries was the least I could do.

"Well, all right," came his reluctant reply. "But just so you know, it bothers my raisin' to have my daughter paying for me."

I smiled at his mock indignation. "I love you, Dad."

"I love you too, Pumpkin."

I asked about perishables, adding them to my mental list, and ended the call as I turned onto the interstate.

Over the last ten years, the community of Blue Springs had ballooned to a hair over three thousand residents, two-thirds more than when I was little girl. Though it still bore the name, it was no longer the same small town I'd known as a child—thanks mostly to the death of a rancher who owned about two-hundred acres north of town. A bachelor with no family, the gentleman willed his land to a television evangelist who promptly sold it to a developer out of Dallas. Despite the ranching community's disappointment, the sale ended up being a boon for the town.

On half the land, the developer built high-end houses for those seeking a peaceful haven from city life. The other half he held onto for future growth. The combination of the dot com boom and being tapped as the headquarters for a presidential candidate had turned Austin, a town known for its thriving music scene, into a bustling cornucopia of industries. And Blue Springs, with its easy commute, became the perfect bedroom suburb.

Christened as Twin Lakes, the developer's billboard boasted that only five lots remained. No base price was listed, which brought Dad's dry wisdom back to mind: *If you have to ask, you can't afford it.*

I took the Blue Springs exit about twenty minutes past the billboard and drove until I reached a stately brick and mortar building. It was one of the first new additions after Twin Lakes had begun construction. A county courthouse annex built to ease the lives of our new wealthy neighbors who saw no sense in driving an hour out of their way for licenses, tags, and property issues. The ranching community grumbled. But once again, its benefit was soon realized. More jobs were added to the area and kids who might have moved away stayed a bit closer to home.

A sign up ahead prompted drivers to choose either the bypass around the business district or the route straight through it. It had been almost a year since I'd seen the downtown area. With a glance at the clock, I opted for the direct route.

The last time I'd driven straight through, the old movie

house had been undergoing extensive renovations. The socialite wife of one of those Austin executives had set out to restore it to its 1940s heyday. With one glance, memories surfaced, returning me to my first date with Bobby—dinner and a movie, right there at the old theater.

As I stopped at the four-way stop, I studied the renovated theater. The freshly painted cream exterior was offset by the marquee listing a movie title I didn't recognize and two old favorites. I decided to cruise around the square to get a better look.

A coffee shop and a ladies' boutique had replaced the bank. The old shoe store had been given a new façade. The community park was still in the middle of the square, but a smattering of black cherry trees had been added to the canopy of hundred-year-old live oaks. I pulled into an empty space and turned off the engine, admiring their blooms.

Across the way, a teenager sat on a bench with one eye on two kids and the other on her cell phone. The younger children soared and twirled on the swing set. A wave of sadness trailed my amusement.

The playground equipment had gotten a much-needed upgrade since Bobby had brought me there on our last date. He'd pushed me on the swing and spun me so fast I got dizzy. We laughed a lot, but then the conversation turned deeper. The hunting trip with the crossbow his dad had bought him for graduation. The military versus ranch life, tiptoeing around the idea of a future together.

My chin trembled as I watched the kids launch themselves off the swings. I made all my choices to protect my own child. To ensure she grew up knowing only love. But sometimes at night, when the house was quiet and Georgia was asleep, the loneliness crept under my well-maintained armor and I wondered ... What would life have been like if I had told Bobby the truth? If we had married? Would we have been better off together?

I shrugged off the questions. With a press of a button, the SUV's engine turned over, and I headed to the grocery. What was done was done.

⁂

About ten minutes later, I pulled into a parking spot at Whitlock's where an abandoned buggy sat in the middle of a nearby slot. Taking pity on it, I tossed my purse and reusable bags in the child's seat and headed to the sliding doors. Flyers covered the glass—a local band performance, weekly grocery specials, and the second annual Blue Springs Honey Festival.

I skimmed over the schedule of the festival's events. One called a "honey drop" caught my eye. It could be anything from a giant replica of a beehive lowered like the New Year's Eve ball to a dunk tank dousing someone in the gooey mess. Either way, it sounded like something Georgia might enjoy. I made a note of the date, the third weekend in April. *Please, Lord, let her be talking to me by then.*

With a sigh, I pushed the buggy through the doors. A quick glance at the overhead signs gave me an idea of the layout. The store's small-town square footage made it easy to navigate, so I opted for starting in aisle one and making my way to the end. Soon enough I'd checked off a third of my mental list. Next stop, cereal on aisle five. I didn't let Georgia eat it often, given the added sugar, but once in a while wouldn't hurt. And Lord knows she deserved something special to help lift her mood.

I turned at the end cap, and then wished I had stuck to my ban. One of Dr. K's favorite four-letter words slipped off my tongue. I'd spent years ducking Bobby's sister, Lisa Jean, and for the most part had been successful. There had been a few near misses in stores and at restaurants, but I could thankfully count the number of actual run-ins on one hand.

Make that two now.

As if alerted by some internal sensor, Lisa Jean looked up from her study of kids' cereals. Her glossed lips curled, radiating the revulsion I had come to associate with our encounters. "Well, well. Look who's back in town."

Purple eye shadow and neon pink fingernails had been trademarks of the younger Lisa Jean Poteet. As Lisa Jean O'Dell, the polish had changed to red and the eye shadow to a tasteful green. But each were still perfectly applied. A long tunic draped over yoga pants managed to accentuate rather than hide the extra pounds she still carried five years after her son's birth. Her once golden hair had darkened to a light ash. Whether from a bottle or hormones, the color was becoming against her complexion.

Tucking a lock of hair behind my ear, I squared my shoulders and pushed the buggy forward. As much as I dreaded the conversation, I wasn't about to turn tail and run. "Hi, Lisa Jean. You're looking well. How's your son ..." I wracked my brain and found his name before the pause was too noticeable. "... Caleb?"

"He's fine." She shrugged. "Growing like a weed. And going to be meaner than a snake if his daddy doesn't stop letting him get away with everything."

She gave me a long once-over, sizing up my jeans and UT alumni shirt, making me wish I'd opted for my work clothes. My college education was high up on her log of my offenses—something about rising above my raising. I waited for her comment and was surprised when she didn't mention it.

"I don't guess you've heard the news, what with being all snug up in Austin." Lisa Jean worked at the new annex, and I'd take even odds that the courthouse gossip started right at her desk.

"John David Billings was arrested. For raping three women."

I clenched the buggy's handle and prayed she didn't check the color of my knuckles. Clearing the tightness in my throat, I managed a response better than the squeak I feared. "I heard about it on the radio."

"I know one of the women," Lisa Jean continued, lowering her voice. "And I'd believe her over him any day of the week and twice on Sunday. Trial starts Monday over in Red Lick. The prosecutor's hoping for the max." Her jaw clenched. Disgust rounded her lips. "But ol' Tommy bought a fancy attorney who's known for dancing around courtrooms all over Texas. Bets are John David gets little more than time served. Doesn't seem fair to me. But you know as well as I do, money talks."

Gossip for Lisa Jean might be like money to a wastrel, but her openness was confusing.

Come to think of it, the encounter itself was the mildest

to date. Was it possible Caleb and motherhood had mellowed her hatred of me? Perhaps given her some perspective on my situation?

But then she gave my t-shirt a second look. "Don't suppose it means all that much to you, what with you hightailing it out of here and leaving all the rest in your dust."

And there it was. I sucked in my sigh.

The implication hung as it always had, accusing, berating. I had betrayed her beloved brother. Thrown him and all he'd offered me out the window. And if all that weren't bad enough, I'd broken his heart. Though she'd always been a frequent churchgoer, those were unforgivable sins in her Bible.

But in truth, I didn't blame her. She was exactly right, minus one important detail.

"So in case you're interested at all, Bobby's out of the Army. Discharged for medical reasons. He's not right in the head anymore, something called PTSD."

Stunned by the thrust of her verbal knife, my throat closed.

*No. He was supposed to be successful. To thrive in the Army.*

My fingers clenched the buggy's handle even tighter than before. The cracked plastic covering, which thanked me for shopping at Whitlock's, bit into my sweating palms. I tried to swallow my shock, but I was too late.

A maniacal glint lit Lisa Jean's eyes as she watched her words inflict their intended damage. But beneath her delight in my pain, I saw true sorrow. "He's staying with our parents, but he never wants to leave the house. The slightest noise sets him off—and the other night, he woke up screaming about terrorists." She twisted her weapon deeper, gutting me and my good intentions. "War changed him. He doesn't say a word about it, but I know he saw things over there no man should have to see."

*Oh, Bobby, I'm sorry. I'm so sorry.*

"Never would have happened if not for you." Lisa Jean crossed her arms over her chest and shook her head. "You know, he never got over what you did to him. It destroyed him. He's never married, not even had another girlfriend near as I know. I'll never understand how you could throw all he offered away."

I forced myself to breathe. What could I say? That it was never my intention to hurt him? That wouldn't fly. And I certainly wasn't about to tell her the truth. All I could do was forgive her and get out of there as fast as I could.

"I'm sorry to hear about your friend. And about Bobby. I'm so very sorry." I took in a quick calming breath as the fire in Lisa Jean's eyes dimmed a bit. "I hope he gets the help he needs to heal." Somehow, I managed to keep my voice steady. I searched the aisle for any excuse to leave and my gaze caught on the row of brightly-colored cereal boxes.

Georgia.

"I'm sorry but I have to finish my shopping, Lisa Jean. Need to get back to my daughter. She's at the ranch with Dad." I eased around her, grabbed a box of the marshmallow laced cereal Georgia had been wanting to try, and forced my mind to focus on the rest of the shopping list. By the time I was in the checkout lane, Lisa Jean was nowhere to be seen. Hands still trembling, I loaded up the SUV and headed back to the ranch.

# CHAPTER NINE

*Blue Springs, Texas*
*May, 1997*

M ONDAY AFTERNOON, MADELINE SIGHED AS SHE closed her locker door. Only two more classes before Bobby would meet her at the entrance to drive her home, and she still had no idea how to tell him. She slung her backpack over her shoulder and spotted Regina Bell, the most popular girl in school, lingering near a classroom door. Her clique circled, their perfectly coiffed heads tucked together as a hushed, but urgent, discussion was underway.

Madeline rolled her eyes. She had dealt with more than her share of whispered comments in the weeks after Mom's death. While those words were more pitying than judgmental, they'd still stung. Gossip was stock and trade in a small town, so she brushed off their blather and walked toward the classroom. But as she neared the girls, she realized they were looking at her. No, more than that. They were looking straight at her stomach.

She stopped mid-stride.

They couldn't know. No one knew. No one ... except

... the pregnant girl from the water fountain. She thought back to her response to the girl's diagnosis. No, there was no way she could do anything except suspect. Unfortunately, suspicion was a hair away from truth and often much headier fodder. It wouldn't be long before the whispers would become accusations, and accusations, truth. She was running out of time to make a decision. If word got to Bobby ...

Staring down their whispers, she adjusted her backpack on her shoulder and slipped through the door into her classroom. Mrs. Hastings, her English teacher, moved from her desk to the whiteboard. "Good to see you, Madeline." A slow, thick Alabama drawl slathered her words with more honey than a plate of chicken and waffles.

Madeline offered a slight smile and slid into her desk. It wouldn't be long before the fit was much tighter. Sighing, she pulled a mint out of her backpack along with her Bible and her English notebook. Giving her mother's copy of the New Living Translation a soft caress, she opened the cover and flipped through the pages. The margins were dotted with little notes scribbled in her mother's cramped hand-writing. Legible or not, every word was precious.

"All right, class," Mrs. Hastings said. "Let's get back into our literary study of the Book of Job. Remember we're dis-cussing character traits before we move into the poetry found in the text. Last week we learned about Job and his friends. As a quick review, who can tell me about Job?"

A hand shot up from a desk in the front row. Madeline smiled as Jessica Chambers, who was in the running for class valedictorian, gave a full description. They'd been in class together since first grade and 4-H up until high school when Jessica's penchant for academics overtook her love of horses. "He was selfless and faithful even though his life was falling apart through no fault of his own."

"Yes, exactly right," said Mrs. Hastings. "Now, let's talk about God's character. Based on what we've read so far, if you didn't know anything about God, how would you expect He'd react to Job's questioning?"

Jessica's hand shot up again, but Mrs. Hastings looked around the classroom. An emo transfer student pushed his bottle-black bangs out of his eyes and raised his hand. In his quiet twang, he offered his thoughts on God's likely response including reasons why He might be angry with Job. Madeline's brows lifted in surprise. That was the most she'd ever heard him say in the weeks they'd been in class. As if feeling her stare, he glanced over his shoulder and flashed a wry smile.

"Nice job, Anthony," Mrs. Hastings said. "You're right. Job had been questioning everything that God allowed to happen to him. His friends offered their opinions as to why he's suffering, but no one seemed to have the right answers. Job had come the closest, when he said back in chapter two, verse ten, 'Shall we receive good at the hand of God, and shall we not receive evil?'"

Mrs. Hastings flipped a few pages in her Bible. "Now, let's read how God reacts and see if it's different from the interpretations Job's friends have offered thus far. We're at chapter thirty-eight, verse one. Remember I'm in the Revised Standard Version so the wording may be different from yours."

As Mrs. Hastings read the verse aloud, Madeline listened to the words God said to Job—"Who is this that darkens counsel by words without knowledge?" She grimaced. God's question to Job sounded more Shakespearean than biblical. Finding the verse in Mom's Bible, she read, *"Who is this that questions my wisdom with such ignorant words?"*

The words seemed to glow, reaching into the depths of her uncertainty. She read the verse again. Was God asking her the same question? Was He astounded by her doubts and questions just as He had been by Job's? Something inside her clenched.

All the questions replayed in her mind. *What did I do wrong? Why me? Why did God let this happen, Daddy?*

Ashamed, she bowed her head.

Yes, she was just like Job. Questioning God's actions in her life. Wondering why the turmoil and tragedy had come upon her, why God hadn't spared her from it.

And like Job, she couldn't do what God had done. She wasn't there when He'd laid the foundation of the earth. She didn't know how He'd planned for it all to turn out. So who was she to doubt God's wisdom?

She believed nothing happened without God's knowledge or planning. Yes, He could have kept John David from raping her. And yes, He could have kept her from getting pregnant. But truthfully, the idea He was using the rape and pregnancy to punish her didn't feel right.

She loved God. She honored her parents. She'd wanted to remain a virgin until marriage and had made that plain to Bobby. So what happened had to be for God's purpose and reasons.

But what if He never told her what they were? Could

she learn to live without answers and simply trust it would all be okay in the end?

Madeline bit her lip and studied the pages of her Bible. If she couldn't trust God, what did that say about her faith? Did she believe He was good only when good things happened? Or like Job, could she say, "Shall we receive good at the hand of God, and shall we not receive evil?"

God help her, she didn't know.

#### ✌ॐ

Madeline snapped a green bean and tossed it into a pot to wash. It splashed and then sank to the bottom to join "his brothers," as Gram would have said. She cracked another and watched it, too, descend the watery depths. Dad had picked up the beans from a neighbor down the road on his way home from running errands.

Now he sat at the kitchen table and flipped through the mail, finding his favorite ranching magazine. Tommy Billings's smiling face radiated from the cover, bloated with ego and pride. Dad frowned and tossed the magazine face down on the table.

Madeline had read the cover when she'd brought the stack in from the mailbox. The headline coiled in her stomach. Tommy's plans for John David were going smoothly. They were opening a third auction building in central Texas, and John David would run it. The governor's mansion might not be far behind.

She waited for Dad to finish sorting the stack then asked, "Do you have anything you have to do tomorrow afternoon?"

He cast a curious glance her way. "Why?"

"I've got so many questions. Someone, somewhere must have some answers."

Dad searched her face. "Well, I know you don't want to ask anyone around here."

"That's for sure." She snapped the last bean then dried her hands on a dish towel. "Would you take me Austin if I found someone there?"

Dad stood and threw the magazine into the garbage. "I'll take you wherever you want to go."

✍

The next afternoon, Dad checked her out of school during study hall. She had told Bobby Dad needed her to run errands, sticking to the lie that had worked before. Still, she'd cringed as the words had left her mouth. Would the stories get even easier to manufacture as the months went on?

About an hour later, they pulled into a parking lot. The Yellow Pages had shown two listings for crisis pregnancy centers in Austin, New Life for Crisis Pregnancies and Real Choices Pregnancy Center. Though the idea she had choices was appealing, New Life was a closer drive.

Dad chose an empty spot between two other cars parked facing the white-brick building, then cut the engine and unbuckled his seatbelt.

Madeline sat in silence and studied the pots of cacti and other succulents that framed the entrance, all easy keepers in the Texas heat. A discreet bronze sign hung to the right of the door, giving no real clues to the turmoil that led most people through it.

"I'll go in with you if you want," Dad said. A game, if uncomfortable, grimace twisted his lips.

She turned in her seat and put a hand on his arm. "Would you mind if I did this on my own? I mean—I know you know what happens, but—"

He patted her hand and nodded, almost looking relieved. "Sure, Pumpkin. I understand. I'll go across the street to the diner and get a drink. Meet me there when you're ready."

"Thanks." She took in a steadying breath and headed for the front door. Hand on the pull, she glanced over her shoulder. Maybe it would be better if he did go. But Dad had already crossed the street heading for the restaurant. Forcing a sigh through her tight chest, she grimaced and tugged opened the door.

A brunette woman sat behind a counter reading a book, but at the soft ding of the opening door, she looked up and smiled. "How can I help you?"

Madeline squared her shoulders. "I, um, I need to talk to someone."

The receptionist's smile filled with sympathy. "Well, you've come to the right place. Gretchen is our counselor on call today. If you have a seat, she'll be right with you."

Madeline surveyed the options—a blue leather love seat, a couple of side chairs, or a bench by the door. She opted for the loveseat and sat on the edge, her feet tapping against the tile floor. She closed her eyes, willing her emotions to settle.

A few minutes later, the receptionist jostled her shoulder. "Gretchen's ready for you now. You'll like her. She's got a wonderful heart."

Madeline nodded and rose.

A plump, middle-aged woman with pinched eyebrows creased in unspoken judgment escorted Madeline to an office. "I understand you have some questions?"

Madeline nodded and dropped into one of the two armchairs in front of a desk.

Gretchen settled into the other and pulled a clipboard and pen off the desk. Her thin-lipped smile looked painted in place. "Well, don't you worry," she said as she uncapped the pen. "I'm here to help." She turned an expectant gaze Madeline's way. "So how did this come about?"

Madeline gulped. "I-I didn't want to."

"You mean, you were raped?" Gretchen's brusque tone cut through the quiet as she made a note.

Unable to find words, Madeline nodded.

Gretchen reached over and squeezed Madeline's forearm a bit too hard. "Did you report it?"

Madeline shook her head. "No. I-I can't."

Sensibilities ruffled, Gretchen straightened in her chair and made another note. "Well, then. There are other ways he can be held accountable."

Madeline's brow furrowed, hoping Gretchen would explain.

But Gretchen merely pierced her with a questioning gaze. "Now, before we can go any further, let me ask you." She paused. Her tone turned more serious. "Have you confessed Jesus Christ as your Lord and Savior?"

*What does my salvation have to do with anything?* Bewildered by the question, Madeline sat forward, again hoping Gretchen might expand on her reasoning.

"Well? Have you?"

Madeline nodded.

"Well, good, I thought so." Gretchen looked pleased. "I can always tell when a sister in Christ walks through those doors." She smoothed her skirt. "That'll make what comes next make sense."

*That would be a good start.* Madeline tamped down the instinct to leave this odd interview. Even though nothing about this visit had made sense, she still needed answers. She'd give it a few more minutes. Maybe Gretchen was new at this.

"Now, dear," Gretchen said, her voice filled with certainty. "First, you'll have to forgive the man who did this. You won't be able to make wise choices until you've done this." She gave a short, decisive nod. "Why don't we start there? Can I pray with you?"

Madeline shook her head, even more confused by the turn of events.

Gretchen's eyes darkened. She straightened in her chair, and a thin layer of ice sharpened her tone. "Well, then. You need to think about your refusal. It will have a huge impact in how you move forward."

Madeline opened her mouth to respond, to explain her reaction, but Gretchen had already moved on.

"Now, let's talk options. You're keeping the child, of course."

"Is that my only option?" The question left her in a rush, desperate to be answered.

Frost chilled Gretchen's icy tone to something colder than snow on an iceberg. She closed the file with a snap. "This is your child. Killing it wouldn't please God. And you will regret that choice. Everyone does." She squared her shoulders and lowered her voice to an urgent whisper. "I can assure you it haunts them."

Madeline shook her head, uncertain if she'd heard the older woman correctly. She tried once again to respond, but Gretchen had already risen from her seat and walked to the door.

She shot Madeline a perturbed glare, her lips pinched in distaste. "Why don't you come back when you're ready to move forward." She glanced down at Madeline's stomach and added, "You have a few months." Gretchen opened the door. "God be with you."

Stunned by the sharp dismissal, Madeline made her way to the waiting room and nodded to the receptionist.

"Can I set up another appointment time for you?"

Madeline's cheeks burned. She ducked her head under the clerk's curious gaze. "Um ... not right now," she said and slipped out the door.

Head spinning, she hurried across the street and found Dad in a booth at the diner. Relieved, she slumped into the bench opposite him and stared at the table.

"That was fast."

Her mind still whirled. "You're telling me." She reached for his Coke. Taking a steadying sip, she leaned back in her seat.

He shot her a concerned look. "Did you get your questions answered?"

Madeline recounted the experience in a whisper. By the end of it, Dad was equally dumbfounded. She pulled a napkin from the dispenser and began to fold it. When it formed a tiny diamond, she laid it on the table and gave a helpless shrug. "An abortion isn't my first choice—I don't think I'd feel right doing it. But all the stuff she said I would feel ... how I would regret it and it would haunt me ..." Madeline shivered. "It felt like she was pushing me to choose what she thought was right."

With a sigh, she leaned back against the booth and continued, "If I get rid of the baby, I can pretend every-thing that happened was a nightmare that went away." She picked up the diamond shaped napkin and twirled it against the table top. "But if I don't, then my whole life changes. Who I am. Who I wanted to be. Who people see me as. I'm seventeen. I should be worrying about what dress I'll wear to prom and if Bobby will get a matching cummerbund." She snorted. "Guess now I'll have to won-der if I'll go to prom at all—especially with Bobby."

"I'm so sorry, Pumpkin." Dad gripped her hand. "You know I'd do anything for you. But I can't make this deci-sion for you." A sad smile lifted his cheeks. "It doesn't mat-ter that you're not eighteen. It's not my life that's going to change so much." He gave her hand a squeeze. "What I can do ... what I *will* do ... is be with you every step of the way. No matter what you choose to do."

# CHAPTER TEN

*Blue Springs, Texas*
*March, 2011*

I PULLED TO A STOP IN FRONT OF THE RANCH HOUSE and cut the engine. Buddy, Dad's cattle dog, trotted toward the chicken coop, nose down, tracing the scent of something else four-legged. Though the hens terrified him, his protective nature kept a vigil eye out for anything that didn't belong near them. I dropped my head to the steering wheel and closed my eyes. Maybe I should take him with me next time I ventured into town.

My door handle clicked open. "Lisa Jean?" Dad asked.

I turned and found his eyes watching me with a soft sympathy. "How did you know?"

His cheeks crinkled in a reluctant half smile. "You were wearing the same expression the last time you saw her."

"Dad, that was two years ago." I shook my head, dumbfounded by his insight.

He clicked his tongue. "It's memorable to say the least. Let's get the groceries in, and you can tell me about it."

I climbed out of the SUV, grabbed my suitcase, and followed him into the house. My quick glance toward

Georgia's room found the door still closed. "Any more movement on that front?"

Dad glanced over his shoulder. "Maybe she'll come out for lunch. So what'd you get?" He unzipped a bag and whistled, low and impressed. "Are the shelves bare at Whitlock's?"

I snorted, unzipped another bag, and began stocking the cold items in the freezer. "I left a few things for Lisa Jean."

"Yeah, so what happened there?"

Though the drive had calmed my nerves, it couldn't erase my memory of the run-in. "Oh, you know, the usual recriminations. Leaving Blue Springs, getting a degree, breaking Bobby's heart. But she did have some information on the trial. Her job at the new courthouse must be paying off in spades for inside scoop on the community."

After I unloaded the grocery bag, I folded it up, steamrolling out the creases with my palms. My fingers caught on the zipper, nipping at the soft skin. Soothing my injured digits, I leaned against the counter and watched Dad sort through his bags. He shot me a delighted smile at the sight of the pork roast and chops—his favorite splurges at sit-down restaurants.

"She said she knows one of his victims—make that two now." I huffed. "But the worst of it was what she said about Bobby. He's been medically discharged with PTSD, and it sounds bad." My voice cracked. "If I'd known it would end like this—"

Dad pulled me into a comforting hug. "Hush, Pumpkin. No one knows the future except God. And somehow, someway He'll make it all work out." He gave me a long squeeze. "Don't you start blaming yourself for something that wasn't your fault. Bobby's daddy was pushing the military long before you told him your story about Georgia."

He was right, but the guilt still felt appropriate. Pulling the last of the groceries from my reusable bags, I tried to accept his reassurance.

"So what did she say about the trial? Between working at the annex and having her fingers on everyone's pulse, I'm sure she knows something." His wry bark of laughter crackled the air between us. "Whether it's accurate might be another thing altogether."

"She thinks John David'll only get time served. Said Tommy found him an attorney with a reputation for fancy footwork."

Dad looked up from stocking the canned goods and grimaced. "Think it would make a difference if you came forward?"

I pushed off the counter to pace the kitchen as the first twinges of panic flickered through me. If I came forward, Georgia would be dragged through the mud by a defense attorney. I would be labeled a rape victim. The people who looked at me with confidence would only see what happened. Everything I had built for me, Georgia, and Dad would be gone.

It was bad enough we'd had to leave Blue Springs in the first place—and that Georgia learned the truth years before I'd planned. That was not a way I wanted to live—and definitely not how I wanted Georgia to welcome her teens. I had nothing to gain by testifying. In fact, I could lose more than John David would get in years.

I didn't realize I had spoken aloud until I caught Dad's

doubtful gaze. Though he'd always supported my decisions, his ingrained honesty was often scraped raw by my choices. Sometimes, though, I wished he would have said something. I'd decided so much on my own. Maybe if he had simply told me what to do, then everything would have turned out better.

Another wave of guilt slid over me. If I had admitted what happened thirteen years ago, I might have stopped John David from hurting others. Those women might have been spared the traumatic experience. I had been so sure of my decision at the time, but was I selfish in choosing to protect Dad and Georgia instead of coming forward?

"Pumpkin, you could worry the warts off a frog."

"So you've said once or twice." A weak smile lifted my lips as I returned to my pacing.

"And you're gonna wear a hole in the linoleum if you keep that up."

I stopped mid-stride and looked down at the floor. He was right on both counts.

Dad grabbed my hand, tugged me closer, and cupped my cheek. "Go on, get out of here and clear your head. Princess is desperate for a long ride. I haven't had the time with all the early calves this year. Never expected the new bull to be so good at his job."

Trail riding had always been my outlet. I'd done a lot of it those first few weeks after telling Bobby. I glanced down and considered it. I was already wearing jeans and it would be less than a minute to switch my sneakers for riding boots. It would be an easy escape. Maybe Georgia would want to go. Janine had said to give her space, but I couldn't help but want to at least check on her.

On the way back to my room, I tapped on her door and eased it open enough to peer inside. Book in her lap, she sat curled into the rocker I'd held her in when she was a baby. She didn't look up.

"Sweetie, I'm going to head out for a ride. Want to come?"

Georgia shrugged off my offer with a pained glance and returned to the magazine.

I sighed. *Lord, please help her.*

It took less than fifteen minutes to catch Princess and tack her out. Dad was right, she was desperate for a ride, butting her head against my hands eager to accept the bit and bridle. She nudged me as I lingered over the saddle pad and girth as if to hurry my work. Giving her a fond pat, I swung up into the saddle and found my stirrups. One cluck and we trotted out of the barn. Bright blue skies tufted with cottony clouds and golden sunbeams greeted us in a postcard-perfect hello.

Once we cleared the barn door, I let Princess have her head, trusting her to choose the path. The cows had learned to associate her presence in the field with round ups for vaccinations or sale, so they gave us a wide berth. The world around me glowed. It had showered while I was in Austin and drops still clung to the grass, creating prisms in the early afternoon sun. The crisp air was saturated with the blend of fresh grass and the earthy, acrid mix of fertilizer and clay. I took in a deep breath and savored the aroma. Dad said he had put out the phosphorous and nitrogen a few weeks ago. The rain must have drawn the odor back up. Princess picked her path through the field while I looked for clarity.

"Lord, I know none of this caught You by surprise, and everything happens on Your schedule. But between the homework assignment, the bullying, and now John David's trial, it seems like awful timing."

Helpless to stop the coming storm of the situation, my shoulders slumped, the burden almost too heavy to carry. I glared up at the sky, trying to look God in the eyes. "Why couldn't You put it off a few more years? Georgia would have had a bit more time and innocence before she knew the truth. You know I'd planned to tell her when she was eighteen. She would have been an adult with adult understanding."

Princess reached a patch of bright red Indian paintbrushes, one of my favorite wildflowers, growing along the fence posts. Up ahead, I could see the purple blooms of bluebonnets poking their heads up amid the shorter grasses. The lilies of our fields. The cows had wintered in that pasture, and the grass was only beginning to grow back making the ground clearer for Princess's hooves.

I hopped down and unlatched the gate, its links worn smooth by the elements. Still, they held strong and moved freely in my hands as I worried them like rosary beads. "And what about Bobby? Why does he have to suffer because of my choices? All I wanted was to protect him and allow him a life of freedom. Why didn't that happen? Maybe Lisa Jean was right and all this is my fault."

Dad's earlier caution echoed over my rising guilt. No, he was right. Bobby's dad had been encouraging military service. But it was my choice, my lie, that thrust Bobby into it as a career. Princess tossed her head, jingling her bit and bridle, ready to continue our ride. I wrapped my arms around her neck, steadying her and myself. Her soft coat still held traces of downy winter undergrowth. She calmed and, giving her a fond pat, I led her through the gate. A quick flick of the snap and the gate was relocked—I'd learned the importance of closing and re-chaining gates at an early age—and swung back up in the saddle.

We loped among the bluebonnets and paintbrushes relishing the wind in our faces and the possibilities that lay before us. Straight through the flat land? Right toward the low hills? Or left toward the bog and loblolly pine grove? Any route I chose offered its own avenue of escape. But true flight was impossible. My secret had come calling and there was no avoiding its ramifications.

A couple of hours later, the rumble in my stomach and the lowering sun told me it was time to turn back. I had no answers, but at least, the questions had calmed.

When we reached the barn, Princess was soaked and I was dripping. Hopping off before we headed back inside, I wiped my forehead while Princess took a long drink from the cattle trough. Idly, I gazed around the barn and found Georgia perched on a bale of straw, petting Buddy. They both looked up as I tugged Princess back inside and began untacking her in silence. Georgia's contemplative stare told me she wasn't quite ready for conversation.

A handful of sweet feed and a thorough rubdown thanked Princess for the lovely ride before I released her into the small pasture Dad kept for her and Charlie, an old pony he'd gotten when Georgia was learning to ride. She'd outgrown Charlie after a few years, but Dad kept him as company for Princess. Charlie looked up from his grazing and nickered. Princess returned the sentiment then promptly laid down and rolled. I shook my head. At least she missed the mud and manure so my grooming efforts weren't completely destroyed.

"Mom?"

Here it came. Despite her long silence, Georgia had all the hormones and angst for an above adequate pre-teen tirade. I could already hear it. How could I keep such a secret? How could I tell her and ruin her life? Why was she even born? Or any other reasons a twelve-year-old could create to hate her own mother. Turning, I leaned back against the gate and studied her. Hoping to gauge her mood, I asked, "Penny for your thoughts?"

She smiled a bit.

*Thank God for small mercies.*

Her hand paused in Buddy's thick fur, and he rolled on his back, eager for a belly rub. Georgia obliged. "How did the girls at school know?"

I shook my head, uncertain if I'd heard her correctly. "How did they know what?"

"That my father is a monster." By the sound of her voice, she was on the verge of tears. "Who told them?" She looked at me, eyes wide and pleading. "And if *they* know, why didn't you tell me? Does Grandpa know? He must hate me."

I pulled Georgia into my arms and poured every ounce of love I felt into my grip, held her with every bit of love a mother can offer. Whispering, "I love you, Georgia," I rocked her slowly, allowing her time to cry out as much pain as possible. When the tears slowed, I tried to find the right words, praying they'd do more good than harm.

"First off, Grandpa adores you. He always has. There was never any question in his or my mind about that, so don't you let it be one in yours. Okay?" I kissed the top of her head and felt Georgia's nod against my chest.

"Secondly, there's no way those girls knew, sweetie." I paused and gave my words time to sink in. "I didn't tell anyone the truth except for Grandpa and my pregnancy counselor who is required by law to keep that secret. No one else knows."

"Then why would they say my dad's a monster? They have to know."

"Oh, honey. They don't know anything about us. It's just bad timing and a terrible coincidence. But no matter what awful things they try to make you believe about yourself, you can't let them shake you from the truth. Grandpa loves you, I love you, and most of all, God loves you. There's not a moment you've been in this world that you haven't been loved. So let go of their lies and hang onto the truth."

Confusion clouded her eyes. "But how could you keep me? After he did that to you? Every time you look at me, I'm a reminder of what happened."

"No." I shook my head and put a finger under her chin holding her gaze to mine. "What I see when I look at you is your grandma—my mom. You were named Georgia, after her, and May, after her mother. Having you in my life every day is like having a part of my mother here with me again. And that is a tremendous blessing. You, Georgia May, are a blessing."

Georgia's eyes pooled with unshed tears. "Really?"

I nodded. "Really."

We fell silent, and I prayed this was the end of the discussion. I should have known Georgia was just getting started.

"Was this how you thought your life would turn out?"

*Nothing like going for the jugular.*

"I mean you never got married, and you don't even date."

I grimaced. While she wasn't wrong, perhaps this was not an answer she needed. Of course, I'd wanted a partner in my life, some days more than others. But that would have meant telling them the truth about her at some point. And I couldn't risk any father figure looking at her in any way other than with love and acceptance. But even more, I didn't think I could bear to be seen as a victim instead of a woman loved and cherished.

Sighing, I shook my head and told her a truth. "No, it wasn't how I saw my life going." I paused knowing I should tell her I made the choice to believe God would bring good out of what happened. That He would redeem the action for His purposes. It would provide her more comfort, but I wasn't one-hundred percent certain of that—especially not after everything that had happened that week.

"Don't you hate him for stealing your life?"

I pursed my lips, giving her question serious consideration. "You know, I can't say I ever hated him. I was so focused on protecting us I didn't have the opportunity. The Billings were a powerful family. I was terrified of what they would do to Grandpa, me, and even you. They could've blacklisted us in the ranching world, bankrupting our family and robbing you of the legacy your great-grandparents sacrificed to create. As it was, Grandpa chose to haul the cattle further away for sale just so he wouldn't be supporting the Billings auction houses, which ended up being a financial setback."

"What about now?"

Did I hate John David now? He had done plenty to warrant the emotion. As I searched for an answer, terror, fear, desperation bubbled in the bottom of my heart. But was there hate? I had no idea. Janine had said it was okay to not have an answer. "I honestly don't know, sweetie."

Georgia's shoulders stiffened. A low growl darkened her voice. "Can I hate him for you?"

I kissed her forehead and pulled back to look her in the eyes. Anger and hurt flashed in their depths. I needed to quench both in a hurry. "No, sweetie. I don't want you to hate him. Especially not on my behalf." I gave her a weak smile and shook my head. "Hating him would only hurt you. It makes you a hostage to what happened. And I've fought too hard to keep that from happening."

Georgia's brow wrinkled. Her gaze grew distant. "Hmmm."

"I do need to tell you something. You're bound to hear about it soon, and I want to be the one to tell you." Janine was right, but I worried how much earth-shattering revelation my twelve-year-old could realistically handle. "When I picked you up from school the other day, there was a report on the radio. John David has been arrested. He'll be on trial this coming week."

"This keeps getting better and better." Georgia snorted and ran a hand through her hair. "What did he do? Rape someone else?"

Her tone—jaded, resigned, and so unlike my hopeful and positive child—crushed my heart. Georgia's eyes widened as she studied me. "He didn't, did he?"

I could only nod and watch her resignation turn to horror and then something more appalling, self-loathing. "Sweetie, his actions are his alone. They have no bearing on who you are as a person."

She buried herself back in my arms. Whispers of the breeze, low moos of the cattle, even the soft munching of the horses, the sounds of the ranch surrounded us in a hug of their own, grounding me in the timeless comfort of my heritage.

Knowing she would need space to mull over our conversation even as I needed time to recover from it, I exhaled and asked, "Ready to head back to the house?"

She looked up at me with a thoughtful frown, but nodded. With a snap of her fingers, Buddy jumped up and trotted along behind us. I threw an arm around her shoulders and heaved a relieved sigh. There would be more questions, and possibly more for which I had no answer. But she was talking to me again. And that was enough.

# CHAPTER ELEVEN

*Blue Springs, Texas*
*May, 1997*

M ADELINE SAT ON HER BED, MOM'S BIBLE OPEN
to Job, and tried to answer the homework questions
Mrs. Hastings assigned. But her conversation with Gretch-
en mixed with her questions for God, turning her concen-
tration into a bowl of pea soup.

*"This is your child. Killing it wouldn't please God. And
you will regret that choice. Everyone does. I can assure you,
it haunts them."*

*Why did God let this happen? Why couldn't I just forget
it and move on?*

She stroked the passage of text. There were no words of
wisdom scribbled in the margins, no helpful hints printed in the footnotes. The decision was hers alone. She had
told Dad the truth when she said abortion wasn't her first
choice. And she had a feeling Gretchen was right about the
likelihood of the act haunting her. After all, Mom's death
left a huge ache in her soul, aborting her child couldn't be
any better.

But could she really do this? Could she survive the

judgment, the heartbreak she would face if she kept the child?

*Shall we receive good at the hand of God, and shall we not receive evil?*

What if this was actually a good thing? God could have stopped John David. He could have not allowed the pregnancy. But He'd permitted both. And the Bible was telling her that God used bad things to create good outcomes. Was this a test of her faith? Could she trust Him to use this pregnancy for good?

Searching for answers, Madeline closed her eyes and felt the slightest tug on her heart. *Only believe.* The words whispered through her, hushed, easily missed in the turmoil of her emotions. But she heard them.

She opened her eyes, drawn to the heading *Job Responds to the Lord* above chapter forty-two. She read verses two through six.

*"I know that you can do anything, and no one can stop you. You asked, 'Who is this that questions my wisdom with such ignorance?' It is I—and I was talking about things I knew nothing about things far too wonderful for me. You said, 'Listen and I will speak! I have some questions for you and you must answer them.' I had only heard about you before, but now I have seen you with my own eyes. I take back everything I said, and I sit in dust and ashes to show my repentance."*

Job had apologized. He had repented from his lack of faith. She read back over Job's words: *"Things far too wonderful for me."*

*None of this feels wonderful to me, Lord. I don't understand why Mom had to die when I was so young. I don't understand why You let John David rape me. I don't understand why You allowed me to become pregnant from his actions.*

*But I do understand Your thoughts aren't like mine, and this may all be wonderful to You. So I'll accept I may never have answers. And that You have a plan. I'll put my trust in You. I'll see the pregnancy through. And I'll love this child.*

Confusion and guilt lifted away as the responsibility of becoming a mother settled over her. It was a heavier weight and yet, somehow, it felt right. Madeline nodded her acceptance. She could do this.

The savory scent of bacon wafted through the air vent above her bed. Dad had said something about breakfast for dinner when they'd gotten home from Austin. Filled with a new resolve, she moved the notebook and Bible to her dresser, and headed toward the kitchen.

"Hi, Pumpkin. Get your homework done?" Dad's soft greeting was almost lost in the sizzle of bacon frying.

She joined him at the stove and took over scrambling the eggs. Toast was already buttered and on the table. Dad forked several slices of bacon onto their plates and they moved to the table to eat in silence. Madeline waited for him to scrape the last bits of eggs onto his toast before opening the conversation. "I was wondering if you might go with me to Austin again. I had a revelation of sorts just now. This baby must be God's plan for my life—no matter how it came to be." She glanced over to him and nodded. "So I want to keep it, but now I have different questions."

Dad scratched his forehead. "You want to go to the same place as before?"

"Definitely not. I'd like to try the other one. But it's a bit farther away and traffic may be bad getting home."

"How 'bout I pick you up at lunch and we get something on the road. It's been a while since we treated ourselves to a Daddy-daughter date."

She smiled. "I'd like that."

Dad's voice warmed. "Then that's what we'll do."

⚮

Wedged between a decaying service station and a car lot advertising "buy here, pay here" financing, Real Choices Pregnancy Center looked to be a standalone former box store. Hard lines and a prickly stucco exterior radiated a clinical detachment. Harsh reality seemed promised to those who entered.

Concern pricked at her. Madeline was just about to tell Dad to take her back to New Life, but then she saw it. Under the business name was the verse Matthew 11:28. *Then Jesus said, "Come to me, all of you who are weary and carry heavy burdens, and I will give you rest."*

Rest for her mind and her heart was what she sought. Not a pretty façade and potted plants. The concern slipped away and peace filled her.

"Want me to come in this time?"

Madeline shook her head. "I've got a good feeling about this one. Will you hang out here?"

He glanced around. There were no good places to wait. "Why don't I run to the hardware store and come back in a bit?"

She nodded and leaned over to kiss his cheek. "I'll see you in a little while."

Despite her initial peace, her gut clenched as she climbed out of the truck. She squared her shoulders as she pulled open the center's door. In the lobby, a pregnant woman with a toddler sat on a low couch playing together. The mother held a block out of his reach and shushed him as he squealed. "You gotta play quiet, Brady. Anna is on the phone."

Madeline followed the woman's gaze and found the receptionist listening to a caller and taking quick notes. Anna flashed a welcoming smile, and Madeline nodded. A row of business cards and flyers sat on one corner of the counter. Madeline picked up one for a Janine Reynolds, LCSW, ABECSW, RN. Madeline recognized the letters her mother had used: RN.

A few minutes later, Anna asked, "How can I help you?"

Madeline glanced up. "I, uh, need to talk with someone." She fiddled with a stack of the cards, tapping them straight in their boxes. "I'm pregnant, and I need some help."

The receptionist eyed Madeline's choice of cards. "Janine is available if you'd like to talk with her."

Something felt right about that. Madeline nodded.

Anna smiled and picked up the phone. She told the person on the other end about Madeline's presence then hung up. "She's on her way. Would you like something to drink while you wait?"

"Water would be great, thanks."

She accepted the bottle then settled on a floral couch and picked through the stack of magazines on the coffee table. Before she could select one on babies, the young mother asked her how far along she was.

Startled, Madeline scrambled for an answer. "Oh. About two months."

"You're almost through the rough part." The mother nodded with remembrance. "The morning sickness can be a pain. And of course, the swelling isn't a picnic either."

Madeline followed the woman's hand as she pointed to her ankles. They did look a little puffy.

"With Brady here, it kicked in when I hit third trimester." She gave her protruding belly a fond pat. "But with this little one it was much earlier."

Madeline nodded and returned her focus to the magazines, hoping the other woman would take the hint. While she needed to talk with someone, she wasn't ready to bond over shared pregnancy experiences. They fell into a companionable silence punctuated by the boy's giggles as he tossed and dropped the block again and again.

By the time Madeline finally selected a magazine, the other woman was called to the back. She collected her purse and Brady and offered a sympathetic smile. "Don't worry. This is a good place. With good people."

Madeline heaved a sigh and flipped through the pages chronicling a baby's first year. She had heard something similar about the other place.

"Madeline Williams?" A tall brunette woman stood at the same door the young mother had just walked through. Madeline nodded and rose.

"Hi, I'm Janine Reynolds." Clad in pink scrubs and matching crocs, hair tied back in a practical pony-tail, Janine was the picture of a healthcare worker. She extended her hand and smiled. Her bronze eyes were kind and her grin, genuine.

Madeline followed her to a cheery lounge where she eased into a deep loveseat. Janine took an armchair and turned a soft gaze toward Madeline. "So tell me what's going on."

With hiccups and tears, starts and stops, Madeline recounted the whole story of the rape, the discovery of the pregnancy, and the realization she had while doing her homework. Throughout the tale, Janine remained silent, but attentive.

When Madeline finished, Janine handed her a box of tissues. "I'm sorry, Madeline. I am so very sorry that happened." She shook her head. Her lips flinched in a sympathetic wince. "I won't begin to tell you I have any idea why this happened. But like you, I do believe God is trustworthy, and He is in control." She paused while Madeline blew her nose. "I'm glad you've reached the same conclusions. And I'm glad you want to keep this baby. I can tell you'll be a wonderful and loving mother."

Madeline bit her lip and pulled another one from the box. But instead of using it, she began to fold it into a small square. "Even though I know that's what God wants, I'm scared. I mean, everything is going to change. And I'm just not sure I'm ready to do this. I mean, it's just me and my dad. Mom died when I was young."

"I'm sorry to hear that. It sounds like you've already had to handle a lot of hard situations."

Madeline shrugged.

"You know, keeping the baby doesn't mean you have to raise it." Janine lifted her eyebrows as if encouraging

Madeline to think beyond the obvious. "There is another option."

"You mean adoption?" Madeline's brow furrowed at the thought.

"Yes." Janine added an affirming nod. "It's an alternative you should consider. There are many couples who can't have children and would provide a good, loving home for the child. Some would even allow you to remain a part of the baby's life, on terms that felt comfortable for you."

*Lord, I'm so confused. Just when I thought I had the decision made, here's another option. What do You want me to do? Carry the baby, but then give it to someone else?*

Madeline pursed her lips. "I hadn't thought about adoption." She fell silent, contemplating the idea. "I'd still have to go through seven more months of rumors and snide comments. And then, will I regret not keeping it and raising it?"

She stared at her stomach, picturing the baby growing inside her. The questions fired rapidly now, louder. "But then, if I keep it, won't it be a constant reminder of what happened? And what if the baby looks like its father? How could I love and raise it then? And what will I tell it when it asks who its father is?"

Janine placed a steady hand on Madeline's arm. "Okay. I want you to take a breath. These are all valid and scary questions, but you can't let them overwhelm you."

Madeline followed Janine's suggestions until she felt settled. A moment later, she nodded.

Janine smiled. "Good. Now, let's get some perspective. I know women in your situation who have had children who look dead-on like their fathers, and yet, they can still see themselves or other family members in them. The key is they see the baby through their hearts. I can't explain the sensation to you—it's something that has to be experienced—but I will promise you there's nothing quite as powerful as love."

She paused as if considering Madeline's other concerns. "As for what to tell the child? You tell them the truth. You tell them God is their Father. That's the truth. And then one day, when they're older and emotionally equipped to process the specifics, then you fill in the details."

Madeline chewed her lower lip. If she gave the child up for adoption, she could avoid all of those problems. The adoptive parents wouldn't care who the child favored. And they would be the ones to tell it the truth when the time came—if they chose to reveal it at all.

She puzzled through the alternatives. Keeping and raising the child by herself would be hard. So much of her life—the future she thought she'd have—would change. She'd raised enough animals on the farm to know the toll on a mother. Bottles, diapers, and sleepless nights were only the beginning.

But giving it up and possibly never knowing how its life turned out? Never seeing it smile, feeling it snuggle in her arms? Not knowing if the child graduated, or married, or had children of its own? And what if this was her only chance at motherhood? What if, for some reason, she'd never get pregnant again? A deep ache welled in her stomach.

She shook her head. "I'm sorry, Janine, but adoption doesn't feel right."

"That's fine, Madeline," Janine said with a supportive smile. "I'm not pushing adoption, but I want you to know if you do change your mind, we have plenty of time to put a plan in place."

Madeline appreciated Janine's forthrightness. But as the ache ebbed then disappeared, she knew her decision was correct. *Okay, Lord. As much as it scares me, this is the right thing to do.* "My dad is okay with whatever I choose. He'll help support us."

"I'm glad you have him for a support system. Do you have any other family? What about a boyfriend?"

Madeline sighed. "No other family, but yeah, a boyfriend. His name's Bobby. And that's a whole other ball of wax." She couldn't quell the shiver. "I can't tell him what happened. I just ... can't."

"So what *will* you tell him?"

"I don't know." She flicked a quick glance toward Janine. "It ... um ... There's no way it can be his ..."

Janine would have to know everything in order to fully understand. Taking a deep breath, Madeline barreled through the explanation. "We ... we ... I never ..." She swallowed hard. "We were waiting."

Janine offered a sympathetic wince. "I am doubly sorry, Madeline." She eased back in her chair. "Madeline, can you tell me what happened that day ... when you were raped?"

Madeline's throat closed around her last breath. Blood rushed from her head leaving her gasping and grasping for purchase. She mentally reached for something, anything to steady her drowning as memories buffeted and overwhelmed.

His hands.

His breath.

Invisible doors slammed shut in her mind trapping the memories behind them, silencing their cries and easing the instinctive rush of pain. "No!" Was that her voice? Distant, strained? "I just want to move on. Focus on the child. Nothing else."

"Okay then." Concern laced Janine's words, but she said nothing more.

As if looking through blurred glass, Madeline watched Janine pick up a clipboard from her desk and make a few notes on the papers.

"While you're here, would you like to hear the heartbeat? At eight weeks it may be faint. But it's there."

Her muffled words thudded against Madeline's internal wall, but Janine's encouraging smile drew Madeline out of her cocoon.

"You-you can do that?"

"Our ultrasound room is down the hall. It won't take but a few minutes."

Madeline stared at the clipboard. Hearing the heartbeat would make the surreal even more real. "Can I call my dad first? I think I want him to be here. He's not far away."

"Absolutely," Janine said. "And, while we're waiting, we can talk about getting you set up for prenatal care. If you don't have insurance, that's no problem. There are a few free clinics in the area. And of course, you can always come back to us if you don't mind driving in each time."

Janine slipped papers and flyers into a plain white folder while Madeline called Dad, appreciating Janine's discretion as much as the information.

He joined them in the office about a half hour later,

looking uncomfortable and out of place among the soft feminine colors and baby magazines. Madeline couldn't help but smile. She'd bet he'd worn that same look at Mom's first prenatal appointment with her.

Janine escorted them to an exam room and gave Madeline a paper-thin gown. "Go ahead and get changed. Your dad and I will come back in a minute. Do you want another bottle of water?"

Madeline shook her head. "I'm going to need the bathroom soon enough as it is."

"Perfect. That will help with the ultrasound."

Madeline nodded as Janine closed the door. She looked at the gown and decided to put it on with the ties in front then laid back on the bed and covered up with a light sheet. A slow sigh slipped between her lips as she melted into the exam bed. The ultrasound's soft hum and the steady tick-tick of the wall clock blended into a soothing white noise. Tears pricked her eyes. *Lord, Janine has a point. What do I tell Bobby?*

She twisted her trembling hands in the sheet and stared at the ceiling. *Why couldn't the baby be his? If Your plan was for me to get pregnant, having it be Bobby's would have made everything so much easier.*

Smoothing the sheet over her flat abdomen, she closed her eyes as visions of a different future wafted through her mind, ethereal gauzy. *We would have been just another teenaged couple who got caught by their hormones and had to pay the piper. Bobby would have been such a great dad. Kind and caring.*

A light tap on the door pulled her thoughts away from their downward spiral.

"Madeline? You ready?" Janine asked from behind the door.

She cleared her throat and said, "Come on in." Her gaze searched for Dad and found his quiet, comforting eyes. An unexpected peace fell over her. It would be all right.

Janine lifted the sheet from her abdomen. "This may feel a little weird."

A warm gel hit Madeline's stomach. She flinched then shivered at the odd sensation. Janine spread the gel with a tool that looked more like a concert prop than medical equipment. Moments later a rapid *thump-thump-thump* filled the air. Madeline's eyes widened. She gasped and looked from Dad to Janine. "Is that ..."

Janine beamed and nodded. "Got a very strong heartbeat there."

Madeline stared transfixed by the image on the ultrasound monitor. A tiny kidney bean reflected out of a pool of black. Little flickers of movement matched the audible thumps. A tear slid down her cheek. "Wow," she whispered as laughter tumbled from her lips. "My baby."

※

Later that afternoon, Dad pulled the truck into a gas station on the north side of Blue Springs. Madeline sat and stared at the black and white ultrasound photo Janine had printed. Though they'd left Real Choices over an hour ago, she still couldn't put the photo down. The slick paper caught the sunshine as it faded into dusk. Moving her hand a bit, the golden glare disappeared. She traced the tiny white bean, barely able to discern the bumps that would be arms and legs. This was her child.

Dad cut the engine and Madeline scooted across the bench seat, leaning her head against his shoulder. She'd never thought much about her future, even with all of Bobby's waffling over his possible military life. Everything seemed too nebulous. Too many possibilities, too many decisions. But the pregnancy narrowed those possibilities exponentially, providing an odd clarity. "It's really real now."

"Yep. That it is," Dad said with a kiss to the top of her head.

"Are you okay with this? I mean really okay with me keeping her?"

He nodded. "It's not how I wanted your life to turn out, but yeah, Pumpkin. I'm really okay with this." Dad climbed out and began to fill up. A moment later he leaned through the driver's side window. "Look who's here."

Madeline glanced up. Brow furrowed, she scanned the gas station, seeing only the expected cars and trucks. "Who?"

Dad pointed to a cherry red F350 tucked in between the diesel pumps. Madeline could just make out one side of the ranch logo decaled on the passenger door. Billings Ranch. Eyes wide, she turned back to Dad.

"Think I'm going to stop over and have a chat with Tommy about life and kids, and—"

"Daddy, no." Madeline reached across the front seat and grabbed Dad's wrist, staying him. "Please, no."

"He needs to know what his boy did. Someone needs to

be held accountable—especially now that there's a child involved."

Madeline's heart clenched. She glanced back at the truck, its polished chrome gleaming in a taunting reminder of the Billings's wealth.

"Daddy, we can't tell them. You know how connected they are. Tommy and John David would destroy us. Besides, you heard Tommy. He's got his eye on the governor's mansion for John David. You can't tell me he wouldn't do anything to protect that dream. Can you imagine the smear campaign they'd create?" She rubbed her arms trying to still their quivering, but she shivered again.

Concern carved a ravine in Dad's forehead. "I don't know if he'd get away with that. We've got enough friends in the county."

Madeline laughed. "You don't think? Dad, he could ban you from the auction houses. They own every one of them in the surrounding counties. They'd drive you out of business in no time flat. And no one would take our side over theirs, even if they did believe us."

Her throat closed as a horrifying thought occurred to her. "Or ... they could take the baby. Oh, God. Daddy, we can't let them do that. Not now. This baby is mine."

They stared at the sonogram photo together in silence, then over to Tommy, watching as he climbed into his truck. A moment later the big red diesel rumbled to life and eased back onto the main road.

Only when Tommy was long out of sight did Dad finally clear his throat and speak. "What are you gonna tell Bobby?"

Madeline sighed and laid the photo on the seat. She

folded her hands as if she were about to pray. "I'm not sure. I mean I can't let my child grow up knowing this. What kind of childhood would that be? I can't tell anyone the truth—especially not Bobby. I'm sorry, Dad. I just can't."

Dad sat back, stunned. "But you love him, and he loves you. I really don't think he'll abandon you in this."

She bit her lip. "Maybe, maybe not. But I know one thing for sure. Telling the truth is a no-win situation. Can you imagine what Bobby would do? He'd probably run straight to John David, try to protect me. If they had any kind of confrontation, Bobby would be the one to get arrested 'cause we both know who has the power in this town. Any kind of trouble could keep him from joining the military."

She shook her head and pressed on. "Even if there was some way I could convince him to stay away from John David, he'd tell his family. He wouldn't—couldn't—lie to them. And Lisa Jean can't keep a secret to save her life. She'd spread it all over three counties before I even gave birth, which means the child would grow up with everyone knowing how they came to be. What kind of life would that be? To grow up with people already judging you based on something you'd had no say over? The baby would be marked from the start. That wouldn't be fair."

There was another option, though. She'd told Bobby early on she wanted to wait for anything more than kissing, and he'd respected her stance. But some of those kisses sorely tempted her resolve. It wouldn't take much to cross the line. Bobby would marry her in a heartbeat then she could pass the child off as his. They could just be another teenaged couple who'd gotten caught up in their hormones.

Shame stole over her. She couldn't do that to him. Live as his wife with that lie forever between them. Take his future from him. No, he was too honorable to cheat him like that.

Dad nodded, reluctantly. After a few beats, he lowered his voice and asked, "So you'd rather go through the wringer yourself?"

"To protect my baby and our family?" Her brows lifted as surety stiffened her shoulders. "No question, yes."

He remained silent though it looked like he wanted to argue.

Madeline lifted pleading eyes to his.

The fuel pump clicked off, cutting the air between them. Dad sighed. "Okay then."

# CHAPTER TWELVE

*Blue Springs, Texas*
*March, 2011*

SUNDAY MORNING DAWNED BRIGHT AND CLEAR. Cup of coffee in hand, I headed out the front door in search of the peace that beckoned. The ranch house was set about a mile back from the main road. When I reached the mailbox, peace remained elusive, but my coffee was gone and the Sunday paper was stuffed in the mail slot. At least I could accomplish one productive thing.

Dad preferred the paper from a town the next county over rather than from San Antonio or Austin. He considered news reports—especially national stories—mostly sound and fury, signifying little, and figured reading it once a week was plenty. If there were anything urgent, the radio would carry the details. He had a TV, but it came on for the nightly game shows and maybe a Western every so often. He was more piddler than sitter when it came right down to it.

I tugged out the paper, bracing myself for the likely headline, but I couldn't quell my shiver as John David stared at me from full color ink. His hair was darker, thinner, but the hard cheekbones and piercing appraisal in his hazel eyes remained the same. Below the fold was a picture from a society event of him accompanied by a strikingly beautiful woman. Inset further below in the full-page story was a candid of Tommy at a cattle sale.

My pulse pounded in my ears, and I forced myself to focus on the woman. Olive-skinned with dark wavy hair and exuding a regal elegance, Maria Castilla Billings had been John David's wife for a time. The daughter of a wealthy San Antonio businessman, the pair had married at Christmas a year after I left Blue Springs. Georgia and I had come home to the ranch only to see a huge spread in the Life section of the San Antonio paper.

Matter of fact, it wasn't long after that when Dad started to subscribe to the smaller local paper. *Hmmm ...*

I skipped to a paragraph with her name. According to the reporter, they'd been married for just three years, but had no children. Apparently, she'd divorced him after he was arrested for embezzling. My eyebrows lifted as I read the details. He had skimmed from the livestock auctions Tommy had set him up to manage and spent two years in jail.

More Texas anachronism than ruthless antihero, I couldn't see Tommy as a party to John David's actions. At least, not the Tommy I remembered. He had been the stereotypical good ol' boy rancher, full of bluster, ego, and patriotism while lacking John David's cunning. But maybe he, too, had changed over the years. Maybe he wasn't as blind to John David's faults as I thought.

I folded up the paper and began the walk back to the house. Despite my apprehension, the enigma of Maria

Castilla and her marriage to John David tumbled around in my head. Why hadn't they had children? Had he told her what he'd done to me? Had she known the type of man he was when they married? Or was this more of a merger than a marriage?

I reached the house and slipped back in the door, surprised to find Georgia in the kitchen with Dad. Last night's sleep shorts and shirt were already replaced with a buttercream and pink sundress and a pretty braid. She flashed me a welcoming smile as she pulled plates out of the cabinet.

Dad was also dressed and ready for church, sporting his Sunday-go-to-meetin' khakis and a western dress shirt. I felt conspicuously behind, but also very grateful Georgia had rebounded so well. Tossing the paper on the counter, I caught Dad's eyes and pushed the paper under a stack of magazines. Georgia pulled eggs and bread from the fridge. "You go get ready," Dad said. "Georgia and I will throw some breakfast together."

I mouthed my thanks and headed off to my room to find my own Sunday best.

ॐ

Sister Beulah Price stood at the door from the fellowship hall into the church sanctuary and extended a bulletin, welcoming us to Sunday service. Of the older members of their congregation, Sister Beulah had been the only one to embrace me after word of the pregnancy filtered through town. Our first day back in church after the birth, she'd grabbed Georgia out of my arms showering her with undisguised affection. During the first years of Georgia's life, she had been a balm and source of many an old wives' tale. I took a bulletin and wrapped her in a tender hug, grateful for the angels like her who had been placed in our path from the start.

"Madeline, dear, look at you. And look at little Georgia growing by leaps and bounds. I'll blink and you'll be all growed up." She gripped Georgia's shoulder and gave her a wide grin. Georgia returned it, but I could see the question in her eyes.

*Does she know?*

I gave the barest shake of my head and pulled Georgia into a side hug. Her stiff shoulders relaxed. One day she would ask what story I'd told if no one knew the truth, but now was neither the time nor the place.

"So good to see the younger ones growing up in the faith," Sister Beulah said. "But it's been Christmas since we've seen you ..."

I took no offense at the admonition—shirttail kin had every right to question behavior. I smiled. "It's been hard to get back what with work and all, but Georgia's on spring break, so we're here for the week. You'll get to see us two Sundays in a row."

Her delighted cackle turned multiple heads in the crowded fellowship hall. "Bless my soul, that does this old body a world of good to hear. Now, y'all go get yourselves settled."

We sat on the same pew I had grown up occupying most every Sunday morning. Warm smiles and welcoming embraces reestablished long-standing familiarity. The first tones of the organ brought the fellowship to a halt, calling the congregation to focus their hearts for worship. I closed my eyes and savored the peaceful serenade.

As we sang hymns and listened to the announcements, contentment eased into my bones. The homey feel of faith rooted in tradition and ritual were the complete opposite of the megachurch we attended in Austin. The simplicity of the gospel was sometimes lost on giant projector screens and pre-planned, fill-in-the-blank note pages. By the time Brother Daniel rose to begin the sermon, my heart and questions had found peace, if only for a moment.

Brother Jerry Arnold, my childhood pastor, had retired a few years ago and taken his fire and brimstone preaching style with him. When Brother Daniel asked the congregation to open their Bibles to Luke chapter ten, I fully expected to hear about the sweetness of life in Christ.

"Who is my neighbor?" Brother Daniel began. "It's a question posed to Jesus by the self-righteous lawyer and the beginning of the parable about the Good Samaritan. Like other parables, there is much wisdom in it for today. 'Who is my neighbor?' is a question we should all be able to answer."

I considered his words and nodded. The sermon would be uplifting and supportive. Just what the doctor ordered.

"Jesus calls us to look beyond the obvious. Beyond physical addresses, neighborhoods, and cities. To widen our viewpoint beyond the idea of property ownership and consider character and life situations."

Something pricked at my heart, stealing my peace and disturbing my contentment. Uncertain if it was a forewarning or conviction, I shifted in the pew and glanced around. Dad listened and nodded from time to time. Georgia doodled on the bulletin. Sister Beulah sat rapt by Brother Daniel's words. All were oblivious to my difficulties.

I tried to shrug off the feeling as he continued his sermon. "To Jesus, a neighbor may look completely unlike you. A neighbor may be someone you would duck or avoid when you passed them on the street or in the grocery store. A neighbor may have made mistakes you haven't made or don't believe you would make in their situation. A neighbor may be someone you encounter at an inconvenient moment. And a neighbor may even be your enemy."

He was absolutely right about every example. And really, Lisa Jean would have benefited from sitting in the next pew and listening for herself. But still, my discomfort remained. Unable to put a finger on why his words ruffled my calm, I picked up the bulletin. There were a few names listed under the prayer requests. I decided to distract myself by adding my petitions on their behalf.

Peace restored, I looked up and found Georgia staring at me in odd consideration. Figuring she was merely questioning my inattention, I smiled and gave her a wink. The furrow in her brow remained. Knowing her, she would get her thoughts together and then broach whatever was bothering her. But my stomach clenched as a shiver slipped through me. I put my arm around her shoulder absorbing the comfort of her presence and listened as Brother Daniel wound up the sermon.

That afternoon, Georgia drove Dad's old New Holland tractor, a roll of hay speared on the front. Intent on Princess and Charlie's field, she rolled by and waved gleefully. The tractor lurched and the roll thumped against the ground.

"She hit the brake too quick," I mumbled under my breath.

"She's got it. Don't worry, Pumpkin." Dad jerked his thumb up, miming directions to raise the prong so the roll wouldn't drag the ground.

Georgia's brow wrinkled. A moment later, her eyes lit up again as she found the right lever and raised the front end. She bounced along the rough pasture until she reached the gate. Then, she slammed on the brake again. The tractor lurched, throwing her against the steering wheel.

"Dad!"

He placed a calming hand on my shoulder. "She's okay. Even if she runs into the gate, it'll still be okay. You can't hurt that old tractor, and hay is hay." I could feel his amused grin.

I didn't take my eyes off Georgia as she raised the prong higher and lifted the roll over the gate. A quick tilt from another lever, and the roll slid off. Princess and Charlie trotted over to their meal and began to chomp.

Dad cheered, then said, "Remember when I taught you how to drive the tractor?"

I blushed. "I did run over the gate, didn't I?"

Dad smiled.

*Point taken.* During my first turn at the wheel, part of the herd had bypassed the hay roll and lumbered past the tractor, the taste of freedom much more enticing than that of sweet grass. It had taken the better part of an hour to get them all back in the pasture where they belonged.

Georgia backed up the tractor with a finesse that belied

her previous troubles, then returned to the row of rolls ready to put one out for the yearling steers.

I heaved a sigh. "Dad, have I ever told you how much I appreciate you? I could never have raised her without you."

Dad scratched his forehead, a denial forthcoming.

"I'm serious. You've been the absolute greatest through it all. I want to make sure you know how grateful I am for you."

"I wish I could have done more," he mumbled. "Should have done more." He shook his head as pain filled his blue eyes.

I stared at him, stunned by his admission. He had been with me every step of the way, supporting every choice I made even when he didn't agree with it. What more could he have done?

"You know I love you, Madeline. But I should have done better by you when all that happened." He removed his straw hat and wiped his brow. "When your mama died ... I just didn't know what to do with a child—especially a girl. So I just let you grow up." His words faltered. Even more than twenty years later, he still couldn't talk about Mom.

He pursed his lips and nodded. "I see now I was wrong. You shouldn't have had to make all the decisions by yourself. Yes, it was your life, but you were seventeen. And I was your daddy." He stared off into the past and blinked the extra moisture from his weary eyes.

I always knew he loved me. But there had been times when it would have been nice if he would have told me what to do.

"I wanted to make everything better. But I couldn't change anything." He turned a pleading gaze toward me.

"So I watched from the sidelines. And I am sorry for that. Sorry I wasn't the daddy you needed."

I pulled him into my arms and tucked my head into the crook of his neck. "I love you, too, Dad. I know you did the best you could."

Georgia rolled up a few minutes later and cut the engine. I released Dad as she hopped out of the cab. A huge grin wreathed her face.

"Grandpa, that was the absolute best. Did I do okay?"

Dad picked her up and twirled her around. "You did great, sugar pie."

"You sure did, sweetie," I agreed with a pat to her back. "Much better than my first time. You want something to drink?"

Georgia nodded and followed us into the barn office. A window AC unit tried its best to displace the stuffy air with something a bit cooler. The local FM station belted out an old Garth Brooks hit. Papers and cattle magazines were scattered across the desk. The place hadn't changed from my childhood—except for the addition of the dorm-sized fridge. I opened it and found three bottles of water next to a couple of glass containers with rubber stoppers in the lids. A box of syringes lay open on top of the fridge.

"You going to start vaccinating early?" I asked.

Dad glanced over as I handed him and Georgia each a bottle of water. "No, but that reminds me, there's a cow with a new calf I need to check out. Her udder looked pretty swollen when I saw her out in the field the other day. Think she may have mastitis, and I don't want that calf to suffer."

I nodded and took a long sip of the cool water.

The song ended, replaced by the DJ's voice. "Top of the hour; time for our local news."

I cringed as I waited for the lead story. There was no doubt what it would be.

"Over in Red Lick, the trial of Blue Springs native, John David Billings, gets underway Monday. Testimony is expected to last three days with each victim taking the stand. The prosecutor's office says they hope for a quick convict—"

Dad cut off the radio and cleared his throat. "I've got some fence on the back forty that needs mending. Lots of deer running around back there this spring looking for love."

I gave him an absent nod. My mind was still absorbing the update, but I could feel his concerned gaze.

"You going to be okay?" Dad asked.

I shook my head to clear the news report from my thoughts and flashed him a weak smile. "Yeah, you go on ahead and get your work done. We'll be fine."

He nodded and picked up a pair of heavy leather gloves for protection from the barbed wire. When he turned to gather the other equipment, I placed a hand on his shoulder needing to say something, but not certain what. "Um, Dad?"

He turned back, a question in his gaze.

I found the word and smiled. "Thanks."

# CHAPTER THIRTEEN

*Blue Springs, Texas*
*May, 1997*

M ADELINE JERKED AWAKE. THE SHRILL RING sounded from her phone, not her fitful dream as she'd first thought. The last vestiges of the nightmare lingered like mist in the morning sun. John David stood to her left and Bobby to her right. A light gleamed before her, coaxing her nearer. But as she looked between the two men, the urge to run overshadowed everything else.

She grabbed her phone off the end table and focused on the number. Bobby. She fell back in bed and covered her eyes. Last night, she'd barely made it to her bedroom with her eyes open. But once she'd climbed under the covers, she'd tossed and turned for hours. She had to tell Bobby soon. Between the rumors beginning to circulate and the impending changes to her body, she didn't want anyone to out her before she could tell him. He deserved to hear it from her.

The phone rang again. Guilt pricked at her. She sighed and answered the call. "Hey."

"Hey, yourself." Bobby paused. "You okay? You sound like you just woke up."

She couldn't help but smile. He was the kindest person she knew after Dad. "Yeah, 'cause I did." She yawned. "Sorry. I wasn't feeling well. Went straight to bed after school yesterday and forgot to call."

"How're you feelin' now?"

Madeline didn't answer. It was the perfect opening. The phone offered safety. She could spill everything and not have to watch him absorb the impact. But that would be the coward's way out.

"Mads?" he asked.

"Sorry. Kind of dozed off for a minute," she said. "I'm still not feeling great. Looks like I'm going to miss school. Haven't felt this bad since I got back from visiting Maribeth."

"I'm sorry. Want me to bring you anything?"

"You're sweet, but no. I would like to see you though. Can you come over after school?"

"Sure. I can bring your homework if you want."

"Sounds good."

"I love you, Mads."

"You too," she pushed through her tight throat. She tossed the phone on the bed and covered her eyes with her arm. She had to tell him. But what? A thought flickered through her. She'd been up in Austin with Maribeth right before John David raped her. It would be perfect timing.

Madeline lowered her arm as an idea began to form.

ॐ

Later that morning, Madeline found Dad up in the barn attaching their flatbed trailer to the truck. He nodded to her and tossed her the electrical plug. She flipped open the outlet cover and connected the plug.

"I'm going to start stocking up on hay rolls so we're ready for the summer drought." Dad tied up the straps that would hold the huge rolls in place. "You want to go?"

She shook her head. "Bobby's coming over this afternoon. I'm telling him today." Her heart clenched. "I've decided to tell him I cheated on him when I went to see Maribeth a few months ago."

With a glance around the barn lot, Dad shook his head. "I don't have to tell you this isn't a good idea, do I?"

She winced. "No, I know that. But it's the best of a whole pile of bad options." She covered her mouth with her fingers and studied the dusty truck bed. "Now, I just have to figure out what to say."

She felt Dad's steady hand on her shoulder and glanced up.

"I'll stay. The hay can wait."

"No. You're doing enough as it is."

He sighed, squeezed her shoulder, then climbed into the truck. "All right, then. Promise you'll call if you need anything?"

She nodded and watched until the truck disappeared from sight. Squaring her shoulders, she headed back to the house. Time to put pen to paper.

Unable to stomach the thought of an actual meal, Madeline grabbed a package of crackers in the kitchen. She crossed her fingers there was some nutritional value in her food selection. But she figured actually keeping something down was a higher priority at this point. She also picked up a pen and notebook on her way to the den and settled on Dad's overstuffed leather armchair.

Her stomach churned. She was about to craft a life-changing lie to the boy who wanted to marry her. Tucking her feet up under her, she snuggled into the comforting leather, wishing she was an undiscovered princess somewhere in a forest or working as a housemaid. That any moment a fairy godmother would appear, wave her wand, and everything would work out. But she was no longer a child. Fairytales were simply that. There would be no riding off into the sunset with her cowboy.

She wanted to be everything Bobby believed her to be, not who she had to become. But there was no avoiding it. She sighed and started writing.

No matter what else, the story had to be believable. "Maribeth," she murmured as she wrote her friend's name down. "You're the only person who could lead me down this path." She studied Maribeth's name then pursed her lips and shoved the guilt aside. Now was not the time for remorse. Now was the time for a plan.

But she needed something else. It wasn't enough to have Maribeth as the instigator. They'd been friends a long time, and Maribeth's inclinations hadn't rubbed off on her. She tapped her pen against the paper. What would remove her inhibitions and make her act out of character?

Alcohol.

It changed people. Impaired judgment and lowered inhibitions.

She swallowed hard.

Her stomach twisted again. This story would be

believable. Or would it? She loathed the very idea of alcohol although she'd never outright said as much. A drunk driver had killed Mom. Richie, Bobby's uncle, was in AA—ten years sober. But out of all the options, it made the most sense. She gripped the pen and wrote the word letter by letter, forcing her hand to form the shapes.

But once chosen, the rest of the lies tumbled from her mind. Maribeth was into the Austin music scene. They had gone out clubbing. Maribeth got her a drink—said she knew the bartender. Told her it was just one to loosen her up so she could have fun. Madeline didn't want to disappoint her, so she drank it. They danced to the live music. Two guys came up to them. They were cute. Madeline was caught up in the music, the drink, and the attention. When the music slowed, she couldn't help but respond to her guy's touch.

It was done.

She shuddered. Her hand trembled. She didn't want to know more. Surely, Bobby wouldn't either.

❦

A light breeze waltzed with a pot of geraniums hanging from the porch's whitewashed trim. Guttural cries of cattle bellowed over the low rumbles of thunder a few miles away. The heavy scent of ozone saturated the air. Around her, the dusty expanse of ranch land seemed to strain toward the impending storm. Madeline sat on the front porch and chewed on her cuticles. Her nails had been nibbled to nubs an hour prior, and three o'clock was still ten minutes away. Wide-rule notepaper lay in her lap. Lies bled from the page.

She read them for the fifth time. Maybe a sixth reading would force them into truths.

Maribeth. Clubbing. Alcohol. A cute stranger. Losing herself in the drinks and emotions. Temptation accepted. Each word soured her stomach.

Dust swirled at the end of the drive. She balled up the paper and shoved it between the bench's cheery red cushions. Time was up.

Bobby pulled to a stop in front of the house and hopped out of his truck. Arms loaded with textbooks and papers, he met her on the porch with a quick kiss. When he pulled back, his easy smile battled the worry in his eyes. Worry won. "You still not feeling better, Mads?" He reached to cup her cheek, and she forced herself to take a step back. "What's wrong?"

Longing to bury herself in his arms and push the encounter to another time, Madeline instead took her homework. The longer she waited, the worse it would be. "There's something I have to tell you."

Fear flooded Bobby's eyes, turning their coppery depths to a molten gold. "Mads, you're scaring me. What's going on?"

She took a deep breath. "There's no good way to say it."

"Mads. Don't, please. Are you ending this? Us? I love—"

Madeline shook her head and stopped him. "I'm pregnant."

Color leached from his face. His mouth worked around silent words. He shook his head and backed away. "When?

Who?" he managed to choke out, his usual baritone pinched and pained.

Her heart lurched. The truth slipped to her lips. She could still tell him. Dad might be right. Bobby would understand. It would all be okay. She opened her mouth.

In the distance, thunder rumbled. A cow mooed.

Images flashed through her mind.

The child.

John David.

Bobby's future.

Dad.

The ranch.

Losing everything.

Yanked back to her reality, she blinked. She swallowed and forced herself to proceed with the plan. "Remember when I went to see Maribeth that weekend a couple months ago? Well, we went clubbing and she got me a drink ... there was this guy ..." She let the explanation dangle, ready with the details, but prayed he would fill in the gaps on his own.

"So ... what? What are you telling me?" Shock abating, a hard edge creased his bark of laughter. His eyes narrowed as he considered her. "You get drunk, and you jump the first guy you see?" Arms spread wide, he shook his head. "Was that why you were upset that night at dinner? I thought you were just getting sick or something. But it wasn't that at all. It was guilt. I can't believe you. You sat there and flat-out lied to my face."

Guilt roiled through her stomach. She closed her eyes as he hammered away at her, pain lacing each word with heated agony. And who could blame him?

"I was happy to wait for you." Hurt shadowed his eyes. His voice dropped to a pained whisper. "I thought you wanted to wait, too. To save it ... for the wedding night ..."

Madeline turned away hugging her belly and clinging to the only solid piece of ground she had left. Cheeks burning and chin trembling, remorse crashed over her. She should have listened to Dad. He was right. Bobby really did love her. He probably would have stood by her. Maybe have taken the baby as his own and kept her secret from his family.

Everything could have been okay.

"I can't believe you would do this—throw everything we had away. I thought our relationship meant more to you than that."

The words tugged at the lie, taunting and tormenting her resolve. How could she have been so blind? She had brushed aside his serious looks and conversation at every turn. Yes, she was inexperienced and scared, but he'd seen a future for them. It wasn't idle talk or pipe dreams. When he wrestled with enlisting versus staying, he truly had been struggling to decide what would be best for them. She hadn't trusted him—hadn't believed the depth of his love for her.

Now it was too late.

She turned back and opened her mouth, wanting to take back every word she had said. But seeing his devastation, there was no way she could tell him the truth. Not after such a brutal lie.

His eyes glistened, but his jaw still clenched. "I guess you were right all along. There isn't anything for me here."

He gave her a long look then turned away. He didn't

look back. The truck door slammed. She flinched as the wheels spun in the gravel. He was gone.

❦

Two days later, Madeline shuffled into the school gym with the rest of the juniors. The assembly was the traditional gathering for yearbook signings and gag awards on the last day of school. The freshmen and sophomores were already seated, hooting and hollering, passing yearbooks and trading hugs. The seniors jumped and jostled in through the opposite door. They clambered up to their section of bleachers celebrating their impending launch into the real world.

Madeline clutched her own yearbook and leaned around a taller classmate trying to see if Bobby was among the group.

"You floozy!"

Madeline froze. Blood drained from her head as she recognized Lisa Jean's voice.

Cheeks as pink as her Mary Kay eye shadow, Bobby's sister elbowed and pushed classmates out of her way as she clambered down the bleachers hurling five-letter insults.

Madeline's classmates backed away, abandoning her in the middle of the sideline. Conversation died. Each student leaned forward, ears and eyes fully open, eager to witness the latest school drama. Lisa Jean landed right in front of her and shoved her to the middle of the basketball court.

"My brother is on his way to boot camp right now because of you!"

The entire school took a collective breath. Hushed whispers filled the room.

"How could you? How could you cheat on Bobby?" Lisa Jean stabbed a finger in Madeline's chest. "He's the best guy in the world. And he loved you. I knew you were no good from the start." She lowered her gaze to Madeline's stomach as disgust wrinkled her features. "Serves you right you got knocked up from it too. That child is your punishment for breaking his heart."

Madeline paled. The yearbook slipped from her grasp landing with a splat on the shiny wood floor. The low rumble of voices turned into gasps of surprise as all eyes locked on her.

Two teachers raced into the gym. One grabbed Lisa Jean, trapping her arms and dragging her out of the gym as she continued to spew invectives, insulting Madeline's dad and her deceased mother. Her tirade echoed as the door latched behind her.

Madeline's gaze roamed the room, unseeing. She tried to think, tried to feel ... anything. The gym began to spin.

A teacher's voice somehow cut through the muffled roar. "Let's get you out of here."

$\mathcal{S}\mathfrak{D}$

Still reeling from Lisa Jean's outburst, Madeline spent the evening in Mom's old craft room. Over the years, it had become a catch-all room of sorts, safely storing boxes of family history. Though it brought back painful memories for

Dad, it was the one place she could hide when the world seemed too much to bear. Tucked away between year-books and photo albums, she found her beloved childhood book, *The Fuzzy Duckling*. She pulled a pale green hardback off the shelf. The pages cracked open, falling to her favorite scene of the duckling and the colts. She'd snuggled with Mom at bedtime with soft conversations as they looked at the pictures and made animal noises. But though cherished, it was like most memories of Mom, vague and sporadic.

Sliding the book back into its spot on the shelf, she pulled the photo album down. The cellophane had lost its stickiness long ago, and the photos now lay in random fashion. She smiled and tucked an old Polaroid of the three of them back between the yellowing clingfilm. Taken at the county fair, they had poked their faces through a ply-wood board to become a family of clowns for the camera. She figured she had to be three or four-years-old in the picture, but only the vaguest of memories sifted through the fog of childhood.

How had they decided to take the picture? Had Mom pleaded and tugged on Dad's arm, dragging him to the photo area? Had Dad blushed mightily at the thought, but agreed because his wife was adamant? Or maybe Madeline was the first to spy the clown board and towed her parents over to it?

She smoothed the cellophane covering the photo. What would life have been like had Mom lived? Would they have had more moments like this? More photos of a smiling, happy family? Who would she have been with two parents instead of one? Would she have grown more feminine and learned more ladylike ways?

Dad had taught her about women's issues, but it had been done in cow speak. Maribeth had shown her how to shave her legs and apply make-up—not that Madeline wore it. And the local hair salon had taken care of her hair for years. The stylist taught her how to do a simple braid for times when she wanted to pull it back. She was never one for curls and frills ... but maybe that was because Mom had died early.

She closed the album and pushed it back into its slot. A photo slipped from the pages fluttering to the floor. Knowing it would leave evidence that would only hurt Dad if he found it, she leaned down to retrieve it and slide it back into place. As she reached it, something caught her peripheral vision. A square shadow tucked into the deepest recess of the closet.

Madeline knelt on the floor and peered inside. A small cardboard box sat snug in a corner. *Aldridge & Williams Family History.* That was Gram's shaky scrawl. How had she never seen it before? She pulled out the box and tugged the loose packing tape off the cardboard. The flaps eased open with a worn sigh revealing a trove of family gems. Photos of people she didn't recognize, locks of hair tucked in envelopes, even a worn piecemeal quilt. She lifted the quilt and felt something shift within its folds. Frowning, Madeline eased the cloth out of the box and found a pair of framed pictures.

Smiling infants stared out of the black and white gloss. "Baby pictures?" She traced the edges of the plain frames then tugged the cardboard backing out of one of the frames. *6/5/46.* Dad's birthday. She flipped over the photo. It was Dad. But were those dimples in his chubby cheeks? She chuckled and returned the photo to the frame, then to the box. Easing the backboard out from behind the second picture, she again found Gram's unmistakable scrawl, faded, but still readable. *Georgia Lynn Aldridge, born 7 May 1947.* Beneath the biological details was a Bible verse, Psalm 127:3.

Curious, Madeline slipped back into her room and found Mom's Bible. She turned to the verse and read, "Children are a gift from God; they are a reward from him." Tears sprang to her eyes. Madeline rubbed her stomach and studied the verse. Gram had thought of Mom as a gift from God. But how?

Gram had told her many times about how she'd fallen hard and fast for the handsomest boy at a county dance. Knowing little about him, they'd married a month later. Two months into the marriage, she had learned to duck his fists and hide his liquor. He died from drinking when Gram was pregnant with Mom.

How had Gram done it? How was she able to see her child as a gift from God instead of a constant memory of an unhappy marriage? Madeline remembered her as a tiny wisp of a woman, part-steel, part-Texas wildflower. A woman who fiercely loved and grieved Mom, dying herself just two years later. Somehow, she'd accepted Mom was more than a responsibility.

Closing the Bible, she sank down on the edge of her bed. What if it was simply a choice? To see the child as a gift. After all, it wasn't the child's fault how they came into being. If Gram could do it, maybe she could too. Madeline bowed her head. "God, please help me see this baby as Your gift, Your reward rather than just a responsibility or a choice."

Warmth skimmed over her like the first rays of the sun as it crept over the horizon. The world around her seemed to slow. Each breath she took tingled in her lungs as she inhaled in a new awareness. She could do this. Just as Gram had done, she could see the child as a gift.

Madeline sneaked into the kitchen and pulled her sonogram photo out from under the magnet for Uncle Richie's pizza parlor. With a slow caress of the glossy film, she flipped it over, grabbed a pen, and wrote the full Scripture on the back.

"My little gift."

※

Later that night, she pulled open her bedroom door and slid out into the darkened hallway. Planning to drown her restless thoughts with warmed milk, she tiptoed toward the kitchen, careful to not wake Dad. But the light glowing in the den told her that wasn't an issue. Low mumbles drifted from the room. Brow creasing with concern, she eased closer.

His familiar voice was choked by low moans. But who was he talking to? And ... was he crying? Reluctant to interrupt an obviously private moment, her heart tugged at the sound of his grief. The only other time she had heard her stalwart father cry had been in the days following Mom's death and funeral. And even then, those tears were blotted and swallowed before they could cause too much commotion.

Heart pounding, she edged closer to the doorway. If he saw her, he'd be embarrassed by his weakness. But she had to know. Willing her pulse to calm, she leaned against the wall and took slow deep breaths. Soon, Dad's voice was louder than her heartbeat.

"Lord, I don't know sic 'em from come here about raising a girl. But I've always tried to do my best, especially after You took her mama. Did I fail to protect her? Is all this my fault? Did I mess it all it up somehow?" Sorrow, guilt, and despair soaked his words.

Madeline swallowed her instinctive reassurances.

"Lord, she's having to make awfully grownup choices, much too early. But she's Your child."

He paused and Madeline could hear him clear the remaining tears from his voice.

"Please give me the wisdom and strength to support her in this."

Madeline had never heard Dad ask God for anything other than a blessing for their food. Surely God would answer such a desperate prayer. His heartrending request eased her roiling emotions. No longer in need of warmed milk, Madeline crept to her room and slipped back into bed.

# CHAPTER FOURTEEN

*Blue Springs, Texas*
*March, 2011*

M ONDAY MORNING, GEORGIA AND I SCOOPED
up grain while Dad called the cows with calves in
for feeding. The pasture was coming in well, so the grain
was more about checking on them than filling bellies. Dad
climbed up on the gate and gestured for Georgia to join
him. "See that gal over there?" he asked pointing to a black
cow with a huge white spot on her flank.

I watched the pair of them and listened to Dad's soft
drawl. Georgia sat enthralled by his words. When I was
her age, Dad and I would sit just like that. We'd talk about
God, the ranch, the herd, anything really.

"She has a new calf," Dad said, "but it's still too young
for her to bring it up with the herd."

Georgia raised her hand to shade her eyes and searched
the field. "Where is it?"

Dad shook his head. "She's got it hidden somewhere,
probably under a tree, to keep it from getting too hot."

Her shoulders sagged. "When will she let it join
the herd?"

"Probably a few more days, but not usually above a week."

"What if the calf died?" Worry creased her brow. "How do you know it's still alive?"

Dad put an arm around her shoulder and pointed. "See the way she's hanging back from the trough? She wants to eat, but she's also keeping an eye out for the calf."

Georgia smiled her relief then turned her attention to another cow. "Grandpa, look at the udder on that cow. It looks like it's going to explode it's so big."

Dad nodded. "She'll be calving in the next few days I'd say. Her milk's come in, and it'll be ready and waiting for the little one."

"What about that one? Hers don't look the same."

Dad hopped down from the gate and whistled for Buddy. "That's the one I was watching for. We need to get her and her calf up in the barn. Madeline?"

I nodded and climbed over the gate, muscle memory kicking in from years of the practice. "Georgia, sweetie, you stay here. Grandpa and I'll get her up."

"Can I close the gate after her?"

"Only if there are no other cows around," Dad said.

Three cows and two calves lumbered into the barn, prompted by Buddy's careful herding. Dad and I pushed everyone out except the cow and calf Georgia had pointed out. Georgia's concern was warranted. I recognized the signs of mastitis in the cow's swollen front teats.

"You got a good eye, Georgia," Dad said with a proud smile. "Her back quarters are also big, but that's more from age than infection. We call 'em 'Coke bottles' when they get like that."

"'Cause they look like those old-fashioned glass bottles?" Georgia asked.

I caught Dad's wince at her description and hid my smile.

"Just so," he said with a nod. "The calf won't latch on well and might not get enough milk. Plus the mama is in pain. I'll need to start her on some antibiotics."

Worry furrowed Georgia's brow again. "Will the calf get poisoned?"

"No," Dad shook his head. "They sense something's not right with the milk in that quadrant and they'll avoid it. But with the back area being so large, the calf runs the risk of starving unless we help out."

"You mean bottle feeding?" Georgia asked, her eyes dancing at the prospect.

Dad smiled and nodded. He readied the oversized bottle and handed it to Georgia. "This old gal is pretty tame, but you'll still be near her calf so keep your eyes open. Hold the bottle just so and the calf will smell the formula."

Within minutes, the calf had latched onto the plastic nipple and sucked enthusiastically. Dad sighed and ran a hand along the back of the cow. "This'll be the last calf for her. She's getting too old for this."

Georgia looked up from the calf and surveyed the cow. "How old is she, Grandpa?"

"Well, it's hard to tell since there's not a record of her birth. But this is her fifth calf, so she's closing in on seven or eight, I'd say."

I watched the pair from my perch on the barn gate, unwilling to interrupt their time and marveling at their bond. I never gave much thought to Georgia being raised without a dad. I had grown up without one parent, and while there were times I wondered what I'd missed, I was as loved as one person could be.

But I thanked God every time we came back to the ranch, and I saw Dad and Georgia together. In Dad, she had a grandpa and a father all rolled up into one. Between his physical presence and God's spiritual one, it was little wonder she hadn't missed having a father figure. *Up until now, that is.*

The calf butted the bottle, knocking Georgia's arm into the barn wall and nearly toppling her to the ground. She giggled at his enthusiasm and concentrated on holding the bottle with two hands, as Dad had directed. "Grandpa, what's the oldest cow you've ever had?"

"Well, I can't rightly say I know which was the oldest of all." Dad scratched his head and gave her question serious thought. "But the first cow I ever got lived to be seven years old. My daddy gave me her as a newborn. She was born on my birthday and she died when I was fourteen. Got hit by lightning in a big storm. Might've lived longer if it weren't for that."

"Were you upset?" she asked. The Lord sure had given her the kindest spirit.

"Sugar pie, I cried like a lost little boy up here in the barn when no one was looking. Tore my heart to pieces."

"Did she have a name?"

"A name? No, I can't say she did." Dad paused and smiled. His eyes gleamed with a fond memory. "But she did come when I called her. Every time, no matter how far back she was in the field. I'd holler at the top of my lungs, 'sook-sook' and it wouldn't be long before I'd see her running up."

Georgia glanced over her shoulder, and I hopped down from the gate. The wariness in her gaze stopped me. She had questions. And didn't want me to hear them. Thoughtful and considerate, I could well imagine she would be reluctant to broach sensitive issues in front of me. I busied myself with stacking feed buckets, but kept an open ear to their conversation.

"Grandpa?" she asked in a quieter voice. "Mom said you know the truth ... you know ... about me. And that you're the only one here who knows it."

Georgia paused and looked uncertain. The calf finished the bottle and went back to his mother. Georgia leaned against the barn wall and Dad, bless his heart, gave her time.

"So," Georgia said, "What did she tell everyone else? No one at church has ever said anything. Why don't they ask who my dad is?"

"Well, sugar pie, that's a question for your mama. It's her story."

"Grandpa, I can't ask her. I don't want her to feel bad. Or be embarrassed."

I caught Dad's eye and nodded. She deserved to know.

"All right, then," Dad said and leaned back against a post. He stroked his chin as if thinking how best to explain my choices. "Well, I'll tell you it doesn't paint her in such a good light. And she took a lot of flak for the story she decided to tell. But she made those choices for good reason, trying to protect the people she loved."

Georgia continued to watch him in expectant silence.

She would wait for hours if needed. She'd been waiting years, after all. Dad wiped his brow and winced. Having been on the receiving myself, I sympathized with his discomfort.

"Sugar pie, I don't know how much she told you about her life around the time you were conceived. But she was dating this boy, Bobby. He was a year older'n her and a good boy. Had a mind set to marrying her."

Georgia's eye's boggled. I guess it hadn't occurred to her that I might've considered marriage at one point.

"But when it happened, she decided it would be best if he went on and lived his life. The life his daddy wanted for him in the Army." Dad paused and lowered his voice though there was no one other than the cow and calf to hear him. "She also didn't want you growing up knowing … well, what you know now. So she did something I wasn't fond of, but I understood she meant well."

Georgia still watched him quietly.

"She, uh." Dad cleared his throat and shot me a pleading look.

I gave him a sad, but encouraging nod. *In for a penny, in for a pound.*

"Well, she never wanted to give you up for adoption or have an abortion. Those weren't paths she was going to choose. But telling the truth about John David wasn't a good option either, for many reasons. So she made up a story. She told Bobby she'd cheated on him, and that, of course, spread like wildfire through the county."

Georgia sneaked a glance my way, and I turned my attention to opening the packages of mineral blocks to put out for the cows. She was already seeing me in a new light, but she needed to know everything for the full picture.

Dad laid a comforting hand on Georgia's shoulder, drawing her gaze back at his. His lips wrinkled with encouragement. "She kept her head down and worked hard, always wanting better for you. And she was sure you were only going to know you were loved. So as soon as she could, she took y'all to Austin for a fresh start. And she's built a really good life for the both of you. I'm proud of her, and I know you are too."

Georgia's eyes narrowed as puzzle pieces of our lives seemed to find their homes. "Is that why she doesn't have any friends here? And why she doesn't really have any in Austin either?"

"Yeah, but everything she's done has been about giving you the best life she could."

Georgia's shoulders slumped. My heart clenched. I could read the guilt she felt as plain as day.

Dad tucked a finger under her chin and pulled her gaze to his. "I know your mama. And I know she would say you were worth putting up with every bit of the talk and the getting out of Dodge." He smiled and nudged her cheek. "I'll never forget the look on her face when she heard your heart beating and saw you on the ultrasound for the first time. Your mama loves you from the bottom of her feet to the top of her head, sugar pie. And don't ever let anyone make you think otherwise."

The calf returned to sniff the empty bottle. Georgia's brow furrowed as she stroked his head. "Mom's kind of like that cow you said had hidden her calf, right? The cow wants to keep the calf safe until it's ready, and Mom did the same thing with me."

"That's exactly right, sugar pie."

Georgia glanced over her shoulder and watched me. "She gave up her whole life to protect me, Grandpa. Doesn't seem fair."

Dad threw an arm around her shoulder and walked her toward me, leaving the cow and calf penned up for monitoring. "Well, maybe that wasn't the life she was supposed to have. Maybe this one is."

Georgia nodded, but I could tell she wasn't convinced. Dusting my hands on my jeans, I decided we needed a change of subject. "Y'all ready for some lunch?"

Dad shook his head and took the bottle from Georgia, giving her an encouraging push my way. "Why don't you two go on up to the house. Found a bit more fence to fix when I was out yesterday. I'll be back before dinnertime."

Georgia grabbed his hand. "Won't you get hungry before then?"

Dad smiled and brushed her cheek. "Breakfast filled me up pretty good. But I've got a few protein bars stashed up here. I'll take one with me."

Georgia looked doubtful, but after a quick glance to me, headed back to the house. Buddy moved to trail her, but Dad's quick whistle pulled him up short. "Come on back, boy. You need to go with me." The dog trotted back, more eager for work than attention.

I watched Georgia walk away and tucked an arm around Dad's waist, leaning into his side. "Thank you. I know that wasn't easy. But I'm very glad you were the one who told her."

Dad kissed my temple then gave me a long squeeze. "I'll be back after a while. Call me if you need anything."

૪જ

When I reached the ranch house, I found Georgia in the kitchen organizing vegetables for a salad. I ruffled her hair and pulled out the leftover steak to add some protein to the light lunch. She selected a chef's knife from the block and started to chop the carrots. She loved building salads and often came up with some creative and tasty combinations. Her cranberry, walnut, and sliced parmesan was my favorite.

"Mom?"

I gave her a sideways glance. Figuring she was curious about what ingredients I wanted in my bowl, I continued to slice the steak. "Hmm?"

"Can we go watch the trial tomorrow?"

My heart skipped, and I barely missed cutting my index finger. Laying aside the blade, I turned and faced her. "Why on God's green earth would you want to do that?"

Her gaze flicked to mine, then returned to the chopping. Loud pops echoed as the carrots fell under the knife's edge. "Grandpa said what happened with John David might have been how your life was supposed to turn out." Her words rushed together like ripping off a verbal Band-Aid. "But what if it really wasn't?"

She paused and took in a short breath.

"What if I wasn't supposed to be here? What if John David stole the life you were supposed have?" She pushed the carrots to the edge of the cutting board and grabbed the celery. Her normally precise dicing turned abrupt and uneven, creating ragged cuts. "So I want to see him."

*See who? John David?* Feeling exposed, as if I had unknowingly stepped into a spotlight, I managed to push "Absolutely not" between my clenched teeth. I hadn't laid eyes on him since that day at the auction. And I wouldn't see him ever again if I had a choice. Which I did.

Georgia's eyes lit with fire and determination. "It's not fair what he did to you, Mom. You don't have any friends. You don't date. That's all his fault."

The pounding in my ears grew louder. Unable to find words, I shook my head.

Georgia put her knife down and crossed her arms. "I mean, you have to be angry at him on some level. If nothing else, don't you want to make sure justice is done? He's not going to stop unless someone stops him."

Surely, she was joking. Had she forgotten her whole conversation with Dad? All the choices I'd made so she wouldn't have to grow up with the world knowing her father was a rapist?

Her eye glinted with confusion. "What about those other women? Don't you want to help them?" Georgia had the bit in her teeth and launched full tilt into her argument. "Aren't they our neighbors—like what Brother Daniel said yesterday?"

The sermon echoed in my mind. *A neighbor may be someone you would duck or avoid when you passed them on the street or in the grocery store. A neighbor may be someone you encounter at an inconvenient moment.* The pounding turned deafening. I grabbed the edge of the counter to steady myself.

"He said we're supposed to care about them and help them." She gestured widely. "John David stole their lives just like yours. You could put an end to this and get your life back. You could help put him away so he never does this to anyone else."

Words disappeared. I stared off, desperate for distance from her argument.

She paused and shook her head. "Wouldn't you have wanted help back when it happened to you?"

Panic clenched my throat, paralyzing my lungs. I fought for breath. Oxygen scraped through the constricted spaces, forcing my lungs to expand against the paralysis. "No!" The word torn from my lips instinctive, guttural. "Stop it."

Georgia's eyes widened; her chin trembled. Her anger and outrage evaporated. And for the first time in her life, she backed away from me.

Still, I couldn't keep my denial silent. I had to stop her. "I am not going, and neither are you."

She cringed, and her eyes filled with tears.

Fight or flight ricocheted through my senses. My mouth was parched, and yet words continued to pour from me, hot, panicked. "I will not throw away everything I have done to protect you just because three other women had my experience. I don't care what you or Pastor Daniel think. There is no debate, no discuss—"

Horror etched into her brow. Georgia ran from the room, leaving me with my terror.

Guilt crashed over me. I had never yelled at her before—had barely raised my voice even when she misbehaved. What was wrong with me? My whole body shook. My teeth chattered. I couldn't understand ... anything.

I had no idea how long I sat in the floor. But when Dad opened the back door, I could tell it had been a while. He called to both of us, then looked down. I couldn't let him see me like this. Not after I had been strong for so long. I tried to turn away, but I couldn't move. Tears coursed down my cheeks, and shudders wracked my body.

I heard a vague soothing noise. But nothing could calm the whirling emotions inside me. Terror, panic, fear, they dipped and eddied, gripping me in their storm.

A moment later, a familiar voice. "Madeline? I need you to breathe."

Janine. But how?

I turned my head and felt the cool exterior of my cell phone.

"Madeline," she said again. "Listen to me. Take a slow deep breath in."

I tried to do as she asked, but my breathing continued panting, staccato.

"Madeline. That's not breathing. That's hyperventilating. Focus on my voice and match my breathing."

I clung to her words like a life preserver, willing my ears to hear her steady breathing rate. Slowly, the pants eased to hiccups and then to actual breaths.

"Good. Very good, Madeline. Keep breathing and when you can, I need you to tell me what happened."

*Oh, God, no!* My lungs caught.

"Slow and steady, Madeline. I know you're terrified, but we have to figure out why."

I nodded even though she couldn't see me. I felt a warm hand on my shoulder. Dad. Wiping the tears that blurred my vision, I looked up. The sight was enough to tumble my emotions back into the whirlwind.

He was scared. Maybe even panicked.

"Jim? Are you there?" Janine asked. Dad had put her on speakerphone.

He coughed, but couldn't ease his pained response. "Yes, I'm here."

"I need you to get a cool rag or towel, and put it on the back of her neck. Can you do that?"

Dad hesitated then said, "Yes. Just a moment."

A few heartbeats later, a cool dampness engulfed my neck. Water dripped down my back soaking my shirt. But the sensation calmed my terror. I took in a deep breath and heard Janine's pleased reply. After a second one, my pulse eased.

"How's she doing, Jim?"

Dad offered a wan smile. "Better, I think."

I nodded and closed my eyes.

"Okay, good," Janine said.

I could hear the relief in her voice.

"Madeline?"

I tugged the towel off of my neck and wiped my face. "I'm here."

Janine's relieved sigh floated between us. "Yes. Yes, you are. That's good."

She paused, and I waited for her to reiterate her earlier request.

"Tell me what happened."

I leaned my head against the wall and thought back over the morning. "We-we were all up at the barn. Georgia is learning how to drive the tractor—and doing a good job."

I couldn't help my proud smile. Dad's lips lifted as well.

"When we got back to the barn office, the radio was on. The announcer mentioned the trial started today. Georgia heard it and while we were making lunch, she told me she wanted to go. Said I needed to help the other women find justice. Stop him from hurting more people."

My heart lurched. I still couldn't believe I had yelled at her. I told Janine as much.

"Okay." She sighed. "Was your reaction over the top? Yes and no. But I don't think now is the time to talk about why. Right now, you need to check on Georgia and repair that relationship."

A shaky sigh slipped between my lips. "Right. Of course. What on earth do I tell her?"

"The truth. But first, you apologize," Janine said.

"And what's the truth? I'm not sure I know at this point."

"Tell her you're scared. And that you reacted badly to her request. I think she'll understand that."

"Okay." That sounded reasonable. As for the rest ...

"Mom?"

Georgia stood in the doorway. Dad helped me to my feet, and I ended the call with Janine thanking her for talking me down and promising to keep in touch. "Hi, sweetie."

Hesitant, she hung back until I reached toward her. Then she took my hand and buried herself in my arms. "I'm sorry, I'm sorry, I'm so sorry."

I held onto her as fresh tears fell. Giving the top of her head a kiss, I pulled back enough to look her in the eyes.

Their sky-blue depths darkened to a pained cornflower as fear warred with—was that shame? My heart clenched.

"Mom, I'm sorry I got angry. I'm not mad at you—I could never be mad at you. I-I didn't mean to push, and I won't mention anything about it again. We can go on like nothing happened, right?"

I shook my head. "No, sweetie, I'm sorry. I reacted badly. And to be honest, I don't know why. You didn't do anything wrong." I tucked her head under my chin and gave her a long squeeze.

"Every choice I made and every lie I told, I did to protect you. To give you the opportunity to grow up without this hanging over your head. I wanted to make sure you knew you were loved and wanted. And I needed you to know who you were in God's eyes."

Georgia sniffed and snuggled closer. "You've done a great job, and I couldn't ask for a better mom." She reached out and pulled Dad into our hug. "And you are the best grandpa a girl could want. I'm sorry. I won't mention John David or the trial again."

I pulled back and looked at both of them. "No, you're right to ask. Whether I like it or not, he's a part of this. It's only natural you would be curious about him."

But curiosity and actually laying eyes on her biological father were two different things. And while I could brace myself for the first one, it was much too soon in my thinking for the second. I stared into Georgia's sorrowful gaze. There had to be a middle ground in this somewhere.

Squaring my shoulders, I exhaled and offered the best compromise I could make. "While I won't let you go, I will ... go ... to the trial. Tomorrow. I won't talk to anyone while

I'm there, but I will see what's happening. That's the least I can do."

Georgia's eyes lit with worry, but she offered an encouraging smile. I pulled her into my arms and sighed. "And again, whether I like it or not, there has to be a reason that everything has come up now."

# CHAPTER FIFTEEN

*Blue Springs, Texas*
*June, 1997*

T UESDAY MORNING DAWNED RED AND CLEAR, staining the grasses and trees with pinks and crimsons. Madeline savored the sun's brushstrokes across the range as she walked up to the barn for her morning chores. She tossed grain to the horses and snagged five eggs while the chickens pecked at their meal. Tucking them into the empty feed bucket, she ran back to the house and made a quick breakfast before Dad left to work on fencing and she started the laundry.

A couple of hours later, she heard the crunch of gravel under tires as she folded the last pile of clothes. She peered out the window and up to the end of the drive. A dark sedan slowly ate up the gravel on its way to the house. The ranch was off the main road by a little ways, so the likelihood of it being someone looking for directions was slim. Maybe it was another rancher. Or some salesman.

But when the car pulled to a stop in front of the house, she was even more confused. Madeline stepped out the front door to find Bobby's pastor, Mike Hastings, and her

English teacher, Mrs. Hastings, seated next to her husband. From behind the steering wheel, he looked over at Madeline. Mrs. Hastings waved and opened the passenger side door.

"Hi, Madeline. I hope you don't mind us dropping by your house." She gave a smile that seemed a little too friendly. "How are you doing? Are you feeling okay?"

Madeline sensed there was more to the visit than a general check of her health and gestured for them to join her on the porch. Pastor Mike leaned against the railing while Mrs. Hastings sat on the bench next to her.

Leaning back on the bench, Madeline studied the young couple. "Look, I don't mean to be rude, but ... may I ask why you're here?"

Mrs. Hastings blushed then paled. She cast an uncertain glance to her husband. Pastor Mike clasped his hands together as if he were about to lead them all in a prayer.

"Madeline." He lowered his voice. He needn't have bothered. The closest ears were attached to cows. "I want to tell you something that not many people here know."

Madeline waited.

"Mrs. Hastings and I, well, the doctor says we can't have children."

"And we really want them," his wife said. Urgency clipped her usual Alabama drawl. She squeezed Madeline's forearm as if to emphasize their determination.

"Okay." Madeline nodded. "But what's that got to do with me?"

Mrs. Hastings glanced over to her husband then back. "I heard what happened at school yesterday, and I'm so sorry it came out that way." She paused and offered a wan smile. "But your life doesn't have to change. You don't have to take on this responsibility. Because we want to adopt your baby."

Madeline shook her head, trying to clear her ears, certain she'd heard her teacher wrong.

"It can be our secret." Mrs. Hastings continued, gripping Madeline's arm harder. Her drawl ran faster than a Derby winner. "And you could have as much or as little contact with the baby as you wanted." She fell silent, then her eyes brightened. "You could babysit if you wanted. No one would have to know. You could live your life, and we could have a child to love and raise as if it were our own. We can make this work."

Madeline glanced from her teacher to the pastor. He fidgeted with his shirt cuffs and glanced around the porch, but when his gaze landed on her, it was steady. Mrs. Hastings was a different story altogether. Gone was the cool, collected, knowledgeable teacher. In her place sat a young woman who had suffered great disappointment and heartbreak. Madeline dipped her head, unable to meet their eyes any longer.

"We don't want to push you, Madeline," Pastor Mike said. "But we want you to realize you have an option. You know both of us in one way or another. We would give the child a good home."

Madeline tried to swallow the lump that crowded her throat. She nodded and managed, "I'll think about it."

Warmth filled Mrs. Hastings voice and the drawl returned to its normal honeyed rate. "Oh, thank you, Madeline. Thank you."

Madeline glanced up as Pastor Mike tugged his wife

from the bench. He nodded and said, "We can help each other. Let us know when you make your decision." They got back in their car and drove away.

Madeline bit her lip and squirmed as guilt slipped over her. Janine had talked adoption at their first visit. Pastor and Mrs. Hastings were right. Why was she really keeping the child when there were options? Not to mention opportunities to help a couple who longed for a child and could give it something she hadn't had, two parents. Though there was no guarantee, of course—she had started out life with both—but starting out with two was still better than only one.

Despite what she'd told Janine, maybe this child was a gift for someone else after all. Maybe God had sent the couple here as a sign that they were supposed to be this baby's parents.

❧

Dad tugged open the wooden door to church and ushered Madeline inside. Conversations stopped mid-sentence. Gazes that ranged from judgment to worry to smugness lasered in, searing her with self-righteous condemnation. Whispers, hushed but just loud enough to pass off as misheard words, scurried around her as she and Dad made their way into the fellowship area.

"Always knew that Maribeth Grimes was a bad seed that would lead others to ruin. Despite her daddy, God bless him, sometimes bad seeds take root in a family and no amount of steering keeps them from their nature."

"Would never have thought Madeline would have such a fall."

"So glad her mama isn't alive to see this."

"How can her daddy be so calm? Surely, he doesn't approve."

Madeline stumbled and glanced up at Dad. He offered a supportive smile and laid a comforting arm around her shoulder.

"Don't pay them no never mind."

"No, indeed," a soft voice said.

Madeline looked around and found Sister Beulah's kind, mysterious eyes gleaming with love. Madeline swallowed her sudden tears as the old woman pulled her into a long, warm hug.

"Oh, sweet girl. Praise God for a new little one coming into His kingdom." Sister Beulah sent a speaking glare around the rest of the room. Madeline watched as the others blushed, looked away, or echoed the sentiments. Their searing condemnation eased to an indignant simmer.

"You hold onto Jesus' hand, and He'll guide you through this. I lost my Will when we had three young'uns still in diapers and two barely able to keep up with their own selves. I held tight to Jesus and every single one of those kids turned out just fine."

The church door opened and silence fell like a heavy fog in the fellowship hall. Madeline didn't have to guess the person's identity.

"Sheriff Grimes," Dad greeted as he held out a hand.

Maribeth's dad flashed a pained smile and grasped the offered hand, releasing it a second later like a hot branding iron. Pink seared his cheeks as he cleared his throat and glanced around. Dozens of curious gazes stared back, eager to absorb the fallout of the biggest scandal since little Timmy Jones was caught stealing from the offering plate. "Jim. I'm, um—"

Guilt crashed over Madeline. She hadn't considered the ripple effect of her lie, its impact on others outside her immediate circle. Sheriff Grimes was a good and honorable man. He shouldn't have to bear the weight of his daughter's presumed actions. Madeline stepped forward and forced a smile. "Sheriff, it's good to see you this morning." She had no idea what else to say, but thankfully, the words she'd chosen seemed to be the best. The congregation returned to their coffee and conversation, and the sheriff offered a genuine smile.

"Thank you, Madeline. I'll have to leave the service early to start my patrol."

"Well, we're glad you're here for at least a bit," Sister Beulah said with a fond pat to his arm. "Won't you all sit with me this fine Sunday?"

Sheriff Grimes and Dad gestured for the older woman to lead the way. Madeline swallowed a relieved sigh.

❦

Madeline sat on the examination bed ready for her second prenatal appointment. It had been a month since hearing the baby's heartbeat and a week since the awkward run-ins with Lisa Jean and the Hastings. After reviewing all the paperwork Janine had given her, Madeline couldn't think of going anywhere else for her care.

"How have you been feeling?" Janine asked, as she looked up from Madeline's chart.

"Okay, I think. The morning sickness is still pretty bad, but from what I've read, it should pass in the next month or so." She watched Janine pull on latex gloves and begin taking her vitals. Her wedding band gleamed in the fluorescent light. Madeline idly wondered if she'd ever wear one herself.

Janine smiled and stuck a thermometer in Madeline's mouth. "I'm very glad your father has been so supportive. You'll need him as time goes by. I know you said you don't have any other family, but do you have any girlfriends? You'll need some female support too." She pulled the thermometer out and logged the results.

Madeline leaned over and read the entry upside-down. It looked normal to her and, judging by Janine's calm, she was right. "Living on the ranch doesn't give much opportunity for friends outside of class. And I don't think the girl I've thought of as my best friend will be talking to me any time soon."

Janine lifted her brows in a silent question as she tugged off her gloves. She sat on the rolling stool across from the medical bed settling in for the counseling portion of the visit.

"Maribeth and I went to the same church for years. But her parents divorced recently, and she moved to Austin with her mom." Madeline fell silent as memories of her visit came to mind.

They'd gone to dinner and then a movie. At the restaurant, they had fallen back into their customary roles of Maribeth talking and Madeline listening. Though her topics focused more on the Austin music scene and Maribeth's dreams of fronting for a band, Madeline took comfort in the easy familiarity. But the movie gave her pause.

Maribeth had been dying to see the latest Ben Affleck film, so of course they went. Two guys who had been best friends forever found their friendship changing after one met a girl. Madeline laughed at times, but when the movie ended, sadness and a bit of regret sat uneasy on her heart. She hadn't been able to shake the feeling even as they walked back to the apartment. With the move and Maribeth's head-first dive into Austin's music scene, the girls seemed to be starting on separate paths, too.

"Madeline?" Janine asked.

Pulled from her musings, Madeline said, "Sorry. It's just that I think our friendship was already starting to change. And now ... you know I couldn't tell the truth about the baby. So ... I blamed Maribeth. Telling Bobby she took me to a bar, and I met a guy. When she finds out, well, I can't imagine that will help." She rolled her eyes and forced a pained smile as another loss occurred to her. "Last summer, I waited tables at the pizza place. Guess that's over, too."

"I don't see why. You're healthy, and as long as you take some precautions, you'll be fine."

"It's not that." Madeline shook her head. "Bobby's uncle owns the restaurant. That's how we met. I can't bear the thought of Uncle Richie's reaction—if he would even rehire me."

Janine studied her as the silence stretched between them. "Do you regret deciding to keep the baby?"

"No, but ..." Madeline glanced away. "Remember how you said, keeping the baby doesn't mean I have to raise her?"

Janine nodded.

"Well, something happened that's making me wonder if raising her myself is the right choice."

"What was that?"

Madeline relayed the Hastings's offer.

"Well, it happens. Couples desperate to have children will sometimes promise anything. How did that make you feel?"

Madeline shrugged. "I don't know. Sad for them— they're really not much older than me. Maybe a little guilty ... and ..." She bowed her head and mumbled, "And selfish."

"Selfish? How?"

"Well, if I keep the baby, then they'll grow up with only one parent." Her voice dropped to a whisper. "I know how that feels. And here they are, desperate for a child and not able to have one." Tears gathered in her eyes as the couple's desperation warred with her own protective nature. "This is an opportunity for the baby to have two parents instead of one. And to give a nice couple something they really want."

"What did you tell them?"

Madeline sighed. "I didn't want to hurt their feelings, so I told them I'd think about it. And that's all I did for the rest of the weekend."

"Did you tell your dad about their visit?"

Madeline shook her head. "No, he was out working the fence when it happened. And ... I don't know ... I guess I didn't want him to tell me to do it." She stuck her hands under her thighs and returned her gaze to Janine, uncertainty and shame hunching her shoulders. "What do you think I should do?"

Janine flashed a sympathetic smile. "I remember we talked about adoption at our first meeting. Do you recall what you said then?"

"That keeping the baby felt right. Like it was God's plan for my life."

"Hold on to that and don't let guilt or shame steal your peace."

"Then why would God let them come to my house and offer adoption?"

"Madeline, God gave His children free will. He didn't create us to be robots. He wanted us to be able to choose to follow Him—out of love and a desire to be with Him. So that means He allows options. I think this is a choice He's given you, and it's up to you to decide which one to take. No matter what you choose, this won't be an easy road. Thankfully, you have your dad to support you, but there are still hard times ahead."

Janine paused. Her gaze sharpened and warning laced her words. "Both paths will require you to trust Him. But I think God is giving you an option."

"Even though He already knows which one I'll choose?"

"That's the mystery of following an omniscient God."

Madeline smiled in spite of herself. As much as she hurt for the Hastings, her heart told her the right choice was to keep the child. "Thanks, Janine. I really appreciate having a girl—I mean a woman—to talk with."

"Any time," Janine said.

"Do you think you could do me a favor?"

"Sure."

"Will you contact them—Pastor and Mrs. Hastings—if someone else comes in here and wants to give up their child? I think they really would be good parents."

Janine's smile warmed and pride lit her eyes. "That I can definitely do. There may be a possibility even now."

Madeline sighed in relief. She hated to disappoint someone truly in pain, but maybe telling Janine was all God wanted her to do with their request.

"Now, what are your plans for high school?" Janine asked. "I would encourage you to finish and get your diploma. You'll have much better options for jobs if you have that degree."

Madeline nodded. "I definitely want to finish high school. But I never really thought about anything beyond that. Really, I always figured I'd be a rancher's wife. Guess that's out of the question now."

She stared at the floor and silently bid goodbye to the future she thought would be hers. "But to finish high school, I'm going to have to transfer."

"Why's that?"

"The other school has a program for pregnant teens—all the girls who get pregnant move there. I hear they have a daycare and the girls have to spend part of their day in there, taking care of the kids." Madeline paused as she considered the likelihood. "As much as I hate the idea of transferring, it might end up being for the best. It's on the other end of the county, so there's a fair chance no one will know anything. It could be good to have a fresh start."

Janine's brows lifted. "I'd say give it serious

consideration. Having your childcare covered will be a big help so you can focus on finishing school. Do they offer parenting classes for the new moms?"

Madeline nodded. "I think so. And that would be good too. A real-life *What to Expect When You're Expecting*. Dad knows plenty about cattle and calves, but not so much about raising little people."

Janine smiled and reached over to pat Madeline's arm. "I don't know about that. I'd say he's done a pretty good job with you."

Madeline blushed at the praise. She couldn't think of any response that wouldn't sound egotistical, so she held her tongue.

"So what's keeping you from transferring?"

"I guess with all the other boxes ticked off, it's down to transportation. Their busses don't run where I live, and Dad can't take me and pick me up every day. Half of his day would be gone."

"Do you have a driver's license?"

"Yeah, I've been driving since I was eight. Just the tractor up until I was sixteen and then Dad's truck every now and then. It's easier for me to ride the bus to school and Bobby—well, he always wanted to drive me home once we started dating."

"A friend of mine has a son who is deploying to Germany for two years and wants to sell his car. I could ask how much he wants for it, if you're interested. It runs fine, but I've got to tell you, it's not much to look at."

Madeline shook her head. "I don't care about looks. I only need something that'll get me from point A to point B."

"All right then, I'll give her a call."

# CHAPTER SIXTEEN

*Red Lick, Texas*
*March, 2011*

FIGURING COURT WOULD CONVENE AROUND NINE, I left the ranch right after breakfast and prayed the hour drive to the courthouse would calm my nerves. I'd pulled off a convincing performance for Georgia, but I knew I hadn't fooled Dad. He'd walked me to the SUV then patted my window after shutting the door behind me, concern narrowing his eyes and blanching his cheeks.

I checked the highway sign and confirmed the Red Lick exit was just ahead. Smoothing my trembling hand against my khaki pants, I once again willed my nerves to steady. *I can do all things through Christ who strengthens me, right?*

I made it to the courthouse by eight-forty-five and spent ten minutes hunting for a parking place amidst the mass of parked sheriff's cars. *Of course, they get all the good spots.*

As the headquarters of the county sheriff, it was still surprising to see all the designated places filled. Usually the deputies were out cruising the more than thousand square miles of the rural county. I finally found a space down from the lone diner in town. A beat-up Ford truck whined its way out of the spot, and I sneaked in before an Austin news van could cut me off. The vultures were definitely circling. And the Austin group was playing catchup. I had already counted two news crews out of San Antonio cluttering up the fire lane near the courthouse.

The trial had become big news fast. I hadn't heard word one about it in the months leading up to it, which made me wonder what had happened to raise its importance in the news cycle. Perhaps some enterprising soul had made the connection between John David and his former in-laws. It was possible, given the recent cover story in the local paper. And if the Castilla family was as prominent in San Antonio society as I feared, the story could grow salacious and wide-reaching.

Why hadn't I thought to bring a hat and sunglasses? I hauled in a deep, unsteady breath, easing my galloping pulse to a bumpy trot. I wished the tremble in my hands would have the same response, but one out of two wasn't bad.

I hurried toward the crosswalk and distracted myself with a look at the town square. If Blue Springs was the town new money had saved, Red Lick was the town that same money forgot. Nearly an hour west of Blue Springs and centrally located in the county, Red Lick was a bump in the road with a state championship football team.

Despite its preeminence as the county seat, one was more likely to see a tumbleweed blow through the square than a street full of cars—except for trial days. During a trial, the town roared to life with spectators ready to reminisce about good old-fashioned hangings in the square. I shuddered at the thought. But those old offenders would have at least had a lovely view for their sendoff. The county courthouse was a stately pink granite building with a copper dome that had turned a milky shade of green over the past hundred years. The manicured lawn and precisely trimmed hedges suggested a priority in upkeep over the rest of the downtown.

I passed a gaping hole in the row of historic buildings. Black soot coated the interior brick walls, suggesting a fire had caused the ruin. But despite the fresh appearance, it had to have occurred several years prior. A sapling oak tree and several bushes now grew in what would have been the main floor.

The next storefront over was the local diner. Paint peeled from the sign, but the place was packed with people. *Vultures and rubberneckers.* But what did that make me? I was certainly no innocent bystander.

I shook off the feeling and crossed over to the courthouse. The heavy wooden doors were propped open to reveal a black and white letterboard that presented the various departments and their locations. The air was still and heavy with the musty smell of plat books and fresh ink, combined with the tang of perspiration. Someone ahead of me complained about the AC and another person replied it was broken.

I didn't need a sign for the courtroom. The odd mix of people gathered around the doors up ahead provided plenty of direction. Journalists in their Oxford button downs and rolled-up sleeves. Cowboys in their western shirts and dusty jeans. Legal teams in suits and ties.

I hung back by the entrance to the sheriff's office and listened to the drone of conversation. A few minutes later, a bailiff opened the doors and the horde rushed in to claim the best seats. I followed, hoping to blend in with the crowd on the off-chance anyone would recognize me and question my presence. Wanting the option of a quick escape, I settled on the back bench near the aisle.

The prosecutor passed by, tugging a wheeled brief-case behind him. He looked calm, which I thought was a good sign. It was the second day of the trial. Hopefully, his peaceful demeanor meant yesterday had gone well. Doors in the back of the courtroom opened and a different bailiff escorted John David into the room. I was surprised to find him clad in a gray suit and white shirt. I figured he would be wearing an orange jumpsuit like I had seen on TV court shows. Instead, his close-cropped beard and expensive blond coif reeked of money. A slight sneer radiated his disdain for the proceedings.

His gaze skirted over the onlookers as he took his seat at the defendant's table. I sank lower in the bench, hoping to hide behind five rows of people. There was no way he would have seen me, but my emotions weren't convinced by rational facts. Instead, my pulse pinged, playing catch up to my escalating breaths. I squeezed my hands into fists to still their trembling. *Lord, please help.*

A well-tailored man with perfectly styled hair and an air of authority paraded into the gallery. In his wake shuffled another well-dressed, but stooped, man with thinning hair, sallow skin, and a sad paunch.

Stunned, I realized it was Tommy Billings.

Bluster gone, Tommy seemed to have shrunk in size.

His shoulders slumped as if carrying an unseen weight, and I felt a curious surge of empathy for the man.

The attorney joined John David behind the table and conferred with his client. Tommy leaned across the railing to listen in to the conversation. I watched him nod and settle into his seat. A moment later another door in the back of the courtroom opened, and the judge sailed in, his black robe floating behind him.

"All rise," the bailiff commanded.

The entire audience stood.

"Hear ye. Hear ye. Court is now in session. The Honorable Judge Wayne Peterson presiding."

"You may sit," Judge Peterson said.

We did.

"Mr. Lee and Mr. Montrose, are we ready to proceed?"

A duet of, "Yes, Your Honor" echoed from the two tables.

"All right then. Mr. Lee, you may begin."

The prosecutor rose and called his first witness.

The courtroom doors opened again, and a petite blonde woman entered. I caught her gaze as she glanced around the room. Her jaw was set, but her chin and hands shook. She paused and squared her shoulders, then stalked down the aisle to the witness box. As she agreed to the oath, her voice rang clear and strong.

Mr. Lee rose from his seat and began his questions. Did she recognize the defendant? On what occasion had she seen him? What happened that night?

Mr. Montrose, John David's attorney, rose and objected. Argued, then questioned.

Pleas and denials were bandied about like a whiffle ball.

I could feel myself straining for any bit of oxygen I could inhale. I glanced around. No one was looking at me. All eyes were on the other victim sitting in the box, spilling her experience and tears.

Time passed. I had no idea how much. The witness—the victim—stepped down from the box. Eyes rimmed with red, cheeks damp and pale, gaze haunted. Mr. Montrose looked satisfied. John David smug. Mr. Lee called his next witness.

A police officer. He was sworn in. The questions began. Evidence was presented. Pictures stark and unflattering. Harsh light highlighted dark bruises. Torn clothing. Rape kit results.

I flinched as the words flew at me like bees, zoned in on their target, stinging, leaving welts as a departing gift. I prayed for lightning to strike. For a fire alarm. For anything that would put an end to the onslaught.

I was dying. But not. My heart could beat. My mind could think. Yet the rest of me was frozen in place.

*Please, Lord, let this end. Get me out of here.*

Mr. Montrose rose. He twisted words, questioned motives and intents, insinuating doubt in what appeared to be only truth.

I knew in that moment there was no way I could sit up there and share my shame. I couldn't, wouldn't do it. My chin dropped to my chest. A heavy fatigue soaked my limbs as despair settled over me. I hadn't healed. Instead, I had buried it. I'd chosen to move on, trusting everything that happened was God's plan.

But Georgia was right, the rest of me, of my life, stopped on the day I was raped.

The police officer rose. The bailiff called the gallery to rise. I ducked out and ran to my SUV.

୫ 

By the time I lunged into my seat, my whole body trembled. My teeth chattered. My skin crawled. Recalling the conversation with Janine, I forced myself to breathe. But the shaking continued.

A tap on my window made me jump. A dark-skinned man in a suit stood by my door. His eyes were kind and his smile comforting. His graying beard was closely cropped.

I knew him. Panic skirted through me. I was caught.

I rolled down the window and searched for an explanation for my presence. The scent of newly mown hay and jasmine wafted into the car. I took in a deep breath and absorbed the peace it offered. My eyes closed as the panic eased.

I realized he hadn't said anything. I opened my eyes. He was still there. Still calm. Still smiling. He nodded.

I blinked.

And he was gone.

The scent, his beard, his eyes all registered in my over-tasked mind. And I knew who—and maybe even what—he was. He had been there by the road, thirteen years ago, right after I'd read the results of the pregnancy test. His presence had calmed me then, allowing my thinking to override the emotions. And he had done so again.

I reached for my cell phone, but this time I dialed a different number. "Janine? You're probably not going to believe this, but ..." I filled her in on the events of the morning ending with the man who I was beginning to believe was an angel.

"Well, I can't say I'm surprised about your reaction," Janine said. "And about the man you saw. After all, angels are God's messengers, and He uses them to minister to His children in times of distress. Those two situations certainly qualify."

I nodded. It was comforting to know I wasn't going crazy—at least not about the man. But as for the rest? "Janine, what's happening to me? I thought I had moved on. I mean, I chose to accept everything that happened as God's plan. Why am I falling apart now?"

Sympathy wove its way through her professional tone. "I always thought you handled everything too well, Madeline. I didn't want to push because you had so much change to accept. You couldn't process what happened to you at the time. I think this is God's timing too. Whether you realize it or not, you're finally ready to work through the emotions and violation." She paused then said, "Do you trust me to help you?"

My chin trembled and my hands shook at her offer. But perhaps she was right. It made sense. Georgia's homework assignment. John David's trial. They'd created the perfect storm to shatter what I now knew was a façade. I closed my eyes and nodded. "You're the only person I would trust."

"Okay, then. We need to set up a time to talk in my office." I could hear her clicking on the computer. "My schedule is already booked Thursday, but I can move some things around tomorrow morning. Can you get here at ten?"

"I'll be there."

Feeling better, I pulled out of the parking spot and turned the SUV to head for the ranch. Despite the traumatic events, the morning had answered questions and opened doors. I heaved a sigh and decided to take it as a win. Now, I had to tell Georgia.

# CHAPTER SEVENTEEN

*Blue Springs, Texas*
*July, 1997*

D AD CLOSED THE CATTLE TRAILER DOORS WITH A
metallic *thunk*. Inside, the next round of steers shuffled and thumped as they adjusted to the tight quarters.
"I feel bad they're going to be in there so long," Madeline
murmured.

Dad pulled her into a quick reassuring hug.
"They'll be fine."

"But it's also an hour farther for you, which means
more gas. And there's no guarantee they'll sell as well."

"Pumpkin, the cost is one I'll happily pay to never set
foot in a Billings' auction house again." He released her
with a squeeze. "Sure you don't want to go with me?"

She shook her head and smoothed her t-shirt over her
growing bulge. "The morning sickness is a lot better, but
I don't think I could bear the looks and, even worse, the
questions. Church was bad enough."

Dad cupped her cheek with his heavily calloused hand.
His cheeks wrinkled into a sweet but sad smile. "I'll be
back by dinner time. Call me if you need me, Pumpkin."

Madeline nodded and gave him another hug.

He climbed in the truck and pulled out of the barn lot. She waved at him, smiling at his answering honk. Her cell phone rang a moment later. "Already worried, Dad?" Tugging it out of her back pocket she chuckled as she flipped it open.

A familiar, but very unexpected, voice greeted her.

"Girl, what the H-E-double hockey sticks? Preggers?"

A shudder whispered over Madeline. Maribeth. "Hey, uh, yeah about that—"

Maribeth continued as if she hadn't heard Madeline's half-hearted response. "Dad gave me what for when I got here to pick up my things—he's got this new job in Podunkville—and I'm all like, 'how is this my fault?' and then he tells me how. If I'm to blame you have got to give me the facts so I can back you up."

She wasn't mad? Relieved, Madeline still gulped as the full meaning of Maribeth's words registered. "You're here in Blue Springs?"

Madeline could almost hear Maribeth's eye roll. "Dad's moving to run the sheriff's department in some backwater town. Ugh. So I'm getting the last of my stuff from his house." She took in a breath and the indignation slipped from her voice, readily replaced by an eagerness for scoop. "But forget about me. Dish!"

"Well, it's a long story," Madeline said with a sigh. "Any chance you could come to the ranch?" She watched Dad pull out of the driveway with the trailer, grateful for the truthful excuse. "Dad's hauling cattle and has the truck."

"No prob, girl. I borrowed Mom's car. See you in a few."

About an hour later, Madeline opened the front door and smothered a gasp. Maribeth's previous auburn hair had morphed to an amethyst purple with undertones of ruby. The pixie cut was moussed into spikes and bright, thick makeup drowned her pretty features.

"Hey, look at you," Maribeth said as she pulled Madeline into a hug.

Madeline laughed as she released Maribeth. "And look at you. When did you dye your hair?"

Maribeth rolled her eyes. "Not long after your visit. Dad absolutely hates it. Which means I love it." She ran a hand through the spikey shoots and asked, "It's me, don't you think?"

Madeline wasn't so certain about that, but if Maribeth was happy, that was what mattered. "It definitely fits the Austin music scene."

"I know." Glee radiated from Maribeth's eyes. "It got me a job at the hottest music bar on the circuit—and not the one Mom works at, thank goodness."

Madeline led her back to the living room as her friend continued her update.

"It's only waitressing, but every open mic night the manager lets me do a set with the house band. He says I've got star quality. One of these days, I'm going to get my break, and then it'll be nothing but up."

Madeline's brows lifted. She'd heard Maribeth sing in church, and the girl definitely had potential. Maybe she'd make it big and Madeline could tell the baby their mama was once best friends with a rock star. Madeline flashed a supportive smile and gestured to the couch.

Maribeth snagged a seat and tucked her feet under her legs. "So tell me what happened,"

"You want something to drink?"

Maribeth shook her head. "Get down here and quit stalling. I want the deets. And don't leave anything out."

Madeline eased down beside her friend. The steady ache in her abdomen forced her to be careful as she sat. According to the books she read, the pain was her body adjusting to a growing baby, but that knowledge didn't ease its intensity.

Once settled, Madeline sighed. Despite Maribeth's plea, there were some details, or "deets," that would remain unsaid. "Well, first off, I want to apologize for making you my scapegoat."

Maribeth's eyes widened. "Are you kidding me? I love it. Really, I'm honored." An elated smile lit up her face. "It's too fun being part of a scandal. You should've seen my dad's face when he told me. Everybody has got to be talking about it."

Madeline blanched at the reminder, but Maribeth didn't seem to notice. "Now, you have to tell me all about it. I mean you were the last person on earth I thought would get preggers in high school." She scooted closer on the couch and leaned forward. "Tell me, some gorgeous guy just knocked you off your feet, right? I mean, I know you were dating Bobby, but he's pretty tame when you get right down to it."

Madeline winced. What could she say? It couldn't be the truth. And yet, could she lie again? It would be one more thing to keep straight even though Maribeth was unlikely to return to Blue Springs after this visit.

No. She couldn't lie. But she could manipulate the story she'd told Bobby. She took in a deep breath and thought fast. "It happened one weekend when Bobby was hunting with his dad. A guy he knows invited me to hang out with a group of their friends. He gave me a drink and one thing led to another ..." her voice trailed off, unable to find words to build the lie.

Maribeth's mouth dropped in amazement. "Who? You've got to tell me who it was. Oh, wait, let me guess." Her gaze grew distant as she wracked her brain to identify the boy. "I know. Was it Billy Daniels? Girl, I wouldn't blame you one bit. That boy is just fine. I had my eye on him before we left."

Madeline shook her head. "No. And I can't tell you who." She willed Maribeth to understand at least that much. "If it ever got out, it would cause all kinds of problems. And you have to promise not to tell anyone what I said."

Maribeth flashed a look of mock irritation. "Duh. I want to stay part of this story. It's too delicious." She leaned back into the couch and gave Madeline an appraising look. "But, girl, I've got to say, you've got the worst luck."

*You have no idea.* Madeline's heart clenched. Conviction sliced through her. Her gaze dropped to her lap. *I'm sorry, Lord. I know this is Your plan and garden variety luck had nothing to do with it.*

Silence permeated the air, widening the gap distance had already created between them. Madeline tried to think of some way to continue the conversation and finally landed on the main thing they had in common. "So have you and your mom found a church in Austin?"

Maribeth huffed. "Nah. Dad was the religious one. Mom prefers to sleep in on Sundays since she works late hours at the bar." Her cell phone dinged. She looked down and heaved an irritated sigh. "Sorry, it's the old man. He's ready to head out to Timbuktu and needs me to get back to the house to give the realtor my key." She offered a disappointed smile. "Sorry to have to cut and run."

She rose and extended her hand to Madeline. While she wasn't so far along she needed it, Madeline appreciated the gesture. As they walked to the front door, a familiar sadness welled up inside her. *Feels like we're saying goodbye for the last time.* Madeline gave Maribeth a long hug. They were complete opposites in every way, joined together by circumstance rather than commonalities. But still, they'd had good times and their friendship meant a lot to her.

As Maribeth pulled away, Madeline caught a glimpse of her former best friend under the outrageous hair and makeup.

"It's been good to see you, Madeline," Maribeth said with a sincere smile. A heartbeat later, a mischievous glint lit her eyes and her smile turned cheeky. "And the next time you get up to Austin, look me up. I can turn your lie into truth."

Madeline closed the door and leaned against it. "Lord, keep her safe."

Maybe this whole thing with Maribeth was a good thing. Madeline was transferring to Red Lick High for a new start anyway. Surely, she would make friends there.

There would be other girls in her situation. Wasn't motherhood a bond of its own?

She hugged herself and bowed her head. "Lord, please. Don't let me do this alone."

# CHAPTER EIGHTEEN

*Blue Springs, Texas*
*March, 2011*

G EORGIA POUNCED ON ME AS SOON AS I WALKED into the den. "How did it go? Is he going to get con-victed?" She tossed aside the book she had been reading and watched me with curious eyes.

I joined her on the couch. "I don't know."

Her face fell. I hated to disappoint her, to show how weak I was, but she needed to know the truth. "What I do know is I can't testify."

"Why not?"

"I don't know." Unable to watch her reaction, I closed my eyes and forced out my confession. "I-I just can't, Georgia. I know parents are supposed to be strong and able to handle everything without batting an eyelash. But between yesterday and my reaction today in the court-room, I've realized I'm still a wreck about it all."

I wrapped my arms around myself, and I turned my gaze to the window. "I watched one of the witnesses and what she endured. The grilling by John David's attorney.

I'm ashamed to admit it, but I wouldn't hold up under that same questioning. I'm not that brave."

Georgia gripped my elbow and tugged. My gaze flitted to hers. Pride and love radiated from her. "Mom, you're the bravest person I know. You can't see it, but you are."

I opened my mouth to argue, but she shook her head and spoke with conviction. "Mom, stop. You chose to protect me and Grandpa at your expense. You chose to keep me instead of aborting me or giving me up for adoption, raising me as a single mom while working and putting yourself through college. Then you moved us to Austin and started a brand new life with no family or friends around there to help. And you faced all the gossip and judgment this town threw your way. How can you not see yourself as brave?"

I couldn't believe her words. Her confidence and encouragement amazed me. *Lord, the heart You gave this child.* I blinked back tears and pulled her into a hug.

"I thought I heard you come in," Dad said as he joined us in the den and sized up the energy in the room. "Sugar pie, I think Buddy's missing you. Why don't you head out and play with him?"

Georgia looked at me and then back to Dad. I loved her for wanting to stay, to help ease my fears. But he was right, it was time for the grownups to talk. I shooed Georgia off and sank back into the couch. Dad eased into his leather chair and put his elbows on his knees as I filled him in on my reaction in the courthouse and calling Janine. Unsure how he might take it, I left out the angel. But I did tell him about my appointment the next day.

"I think that's a good thing to do, Pumpkin," he said

after a long, thoughtful pause. "And you need to find out more about the trial. I don't believe you can ignore this any longer. When I found you curled up on the floor the other day ..." He left the sentence unfinished, but his fear was plain.

"My reaction at the trial wasn't much better. I can't go through that again."

"Madeline, I didn't stand up for you in the past, but I'm going to now." His eyes narrowed as he considered his words. "You need to report what happened to you. Call the prosecutor and tell him."

I scooted to the other end of the couch, desperate to avoid his advice. Not wanting to disappoint him, I said, "I'm going to talk to Janine. Isn't that enough?"

He dipped his head. "Maybe, but getting justice could help you work through what happened. Bring some closure. Finally give that man what he's deserved all along."

"But what if it's been too long since my ... incident?"

He didn't look convinced. "You don't know if you don't ask. I'm sure attorney-client privilege would extend to you. But if it makes you feel better, confirm it before you tell him anything."

His voice was firm and his gaze steady. There was no way I was avoiding a call to the prosecutor. That much was clear.

"Madeline, I know you're scared. But I also know you can do this. You are stronger than you realize. Look at the life you've built in spite of all these challenges. Think of the life you can have when all of this has been dealt with. Don't you want that for yourself? I want it for you."

Closing my eyes, I buckled under his firm resolve. Then

I gave him a sad nod and reached for my phone. I found the number for the prosecutor's office and clicked on it. A moment later an older female voice answered.

"I have information regarding the John David Billings case."

There was a brief hold, then a male voice came on the line.

"Anthony Lee speaking. Brenda said you had information about a case?"

"Mr. Lee, what I have to tell you must be kept confidential. Can you do that?"

"Yes, of course."

"My name is Madeline Williams, and I think I was John David's first vic—um, I think I was his first."

A stunned silence filled the air. "Madeline Williams, you said?" he asked. "Madeline. I'm Anthony. We were in Mrs. Hastings's English class together. Junior year."

I fell back into the couch, stunned and incredibly grateful I confirmed confidentiality before I said anything. "Oh, Anthony. I-I didn't recognize you yesterday."

He chuckled. "Yeah, I grew out of the emo stuff."

I briefly told him the story about the rape and deciding to keep Georgia, leaving out the Hastings's offer of adoption.

"Madeline, I'm so sorry. I remember the last day of school and hearing the rumors." He paused. "Unfortunately, I can't add you to the case now. The statute of limitations for your experience passed two years ago."

Tension melted from my shoulders. I was home-free. Georgia could have her questions answered, and I wouldn't be forced to testify. "I'm actually relieved. I went to the trial yesterday morning. There's no way I could testify. The only reason I called is because of my dad and my daughter. Georgia feels a connection to the women and what they experienced."

"I can appreciate that." Empathy infused Anthony's words.

"She wants to know John David will be found guilty. Not only for the other women, but also for me, I think."

"Well, I believe our case is strong. The evidence is there and, so far, the expert witnesses are holding up. But his accusers are taking a beating on the stand from opposing counsel." Anthony let out a harsh bark of rueful laughter. "He's even had me questioning what I know to be fact."

I could believe it. Lisa Jean hadn't lied about the defense attorney's ability to tap dance in a courtroom. I had watched him twist words and lace doubt in the jury members' minds. "Good thing the judge decides sentencing," I said, basing my information on all the legal shows I'd seen in the past.

"Actually, the jury will decide his sentence. Not the judge."

My heart clenched at his frustrated tone.

"And unfortunately, there have been several cases where the sentence was much more lenient than what the victims hoped." He paused and his tone brightened. "One thing works in our favor, though. John David has said he doesn't want a deal. He believes he'll get off and fully exonerated—probably because of the recent cases in the state."

*How is that in your favor? What if he gets off? What will happen to those women?*

"Montrose is pushing every detail that could support his argument, that the women are lying and the experiences were consensual."

Consensual? If what happened to me was what they experienced, there was nothing consensual about it.

"If the jury blames the victim, then we are definitely up a creek. These days, a lot of juries have sided with the rapist, unwilling to tag them with that label for the rest of their lives."

The label of rape victim wasn't any better. Lives were ruined on both sides of the violation.

"As horrible as it is, the fact we have multiple victims with believable stories and evidence to back them up makes this case stronger than most. And John David's criminal past will help support jail time as opposed to probation. I won't say it's a slam dunk, but as it stands right now, I believe he'll get more than probation or time served. How much time? Well ... that's still up for grabs."

It sounded like Lisa Jean needed new sources for her gossip. *Thank God.* "Anthony, thank you so much for talking with me about the case." Relief fluttered through me. I ended the call with a smile and relayed Anthony's side of the conversation to Dad.

His fingers were steepled together, and he tapped the pads together as if counting out an unheard tune.

I waited for him to speak. My initial relief disappeared with each passing minute.

"Okay then. That's good to hear. But, Pumpkin, be ready for that to change."

# CHAPTER NINETEEN

*Red Lick, Texas*
*August, 1997*

M ADELINE PULLED INTO THE PARKING LOT OF
Red Lick High School. It was the first day of her se-
nior year and the first time she was the new kid in school.
Her nerves skittered, but she gave her head a forceful
shake. Now was not the time to fall apart.

She pushed open her car's door and a metallic screech
pierced the morning air. Janine hadn't lied. The car was
a banger. Though it was one of the first Honda Accords
with the new body style, it was four years old and already
had seventy thousand miles. The red paint was sunburnt
by the blazing Texas heat, and the tires were missing two
hubcaps. Clearly the soldier hadn't been much on maintenance before he'd shipped out, but at least his mom had
given Dad a good deal, trading the car for a steer.

In reality, though, Madeline didn't care. The car freed
her from the hostility at her old high school, offering her a
fresh start—or at least as fresh as she could find while carrying twenty extra pounds of baby weight. She grabbed her
backpack from the passenger seat and heaved her bulging

frame from the seat. The door's hinges protested again as she pushed it closed with her rear. She pulled her class schedule from her backpack and headed into the building. The school counselor had tucked a note in the welcome packet requesting she stop by the office on the first day.

Students milled at the entrance waiting for the homeroom bell. As Madeline neared the group she flashed a quick smile, intent on her destination.

"I wondered if I'd see you here," said a weary but wise voice.

The voice's owner looked familiar, but Madeline couldn't place her.

The girl's mouth curved in a knowing grin. "You may not remember me now that I'm fifty pounds lighter." Her gaze sharpened as she studied Madeline's confusion. "Dina McIntosh. We met by the water fountain that day you were sick?"

Madeline paled as recognition crashed through her. So much for a fresh start.

Dina gave Madeline a self-satisfied once over. "So, I was right after all. You are preggers." A light dawned in her eye as pieces seemed to fit together. "Wait, but isn't there more to it? Weren't you the one who cheated on her boyfriend and got knocked up?" She turned to her companions and began filling them in on the details. "I wasn't there, but my little sister told me all about what happened in the gym ..."

Madeline didn't wait to hear if Dina's retelling was accurate. She ducked between the group and tugged open the front door, shame burning her cheeks. With a quick glance, she found the office and was directed to the counselor.

Mrs. Massey greeted her with an easy smile, a soothing balm to the abrasive welcome of her new classmates. While escorting Madeline to her new homeroom, they stopped by the daycare, a large open space cordoned off with temporary dividers. Play zones and stations lined the perimeter of one side. Low bookshelves bracketed a couple of beanbags. A Barbie house, castle, and blocks entertained three toddlers. Cribs and play pens were squeezed into the opposite end of the room, each occupied with infants of various ages.

Madeline's chest tightened. She was more than halfway through the pregnancy. It wouldn't be long before she would be staring down at her own child in one of those cribs. Was she ready for this?

Mrs. Massey waved the teacher over to talk. The woman extracted herself from a pair of toddlers and made her way through the throng of toys. "Mrs. Gardener supervises the students and children. There are fifteen children of various ages already in the daycare, so you'll get plenty of experience to prepare for your little one."

Mrs. Gardener joined them looking harried but comfortable with her duties. As she was about to say something, one of the toddlers caught her eye. "Tyrone, you leave Emma alone." She sighed and shook her head. "That child. Always got to be in everybody else's business." She walked over and separated the two once again. "It's her time to play with that toy." She shot him a pointed look before turning back to Mrs. Massey. Tyrone promptly grabbed the toy from Emma again and ran to the beanbags.

Madeline stepped back toward the door. What had she done? There's no way she was ready for this.

Mrs. Massey flashed a sympathetic smile. "Well, plenty of time for this later. Let's get you to homeroom and start your day."

Thankful for the escape, Madeline followed the kind woman down the hall. Curious glances and feverish whispers seemed to dog her footsteps. Within minutes, curiosity turned to frosty judgment and knowing leers. She walked a little faster, hoping to beat the rumors to her classroom.

Her new homeroom teacher called the class to attention and proceeded to introduce her. Murmurs floated through the class from student to student. He called for quiet and they settled, but the damage was done. As soon as he finished her introduction, she slipped to an empty desk and prayed for the bell to ring.

※

Madeline returned to the daycare room for third period. Four other teenaged moms had joined Mrs. Gardener. Wails and screeches pierced the air as blocks tumbled and tears fell. Madeline sat in one of the beanbags next to a two-year-old boy named Nathan.

Moments earlier, Mrs. Gardener had said it was his turn in the reading station. She'd directed Madeline to help him pick out a book and read it with him. Unfortunately, Nathan had other ideas. As soon as Madeline had turned her back to look at the book options, Nathan ran back to the blocks and pushed over the tower two other children were building.

She'd already tried grabbing his hand and leading him

back to the books once and had a small bite mark in her arm as thanks. Now, she soothed the abrasion with a light caress and wondered if she should have reported the injury. But he hadn't broken skin, and he already had two marks by his name on the white board. A third would put him in time out. She wasn't ready to be the mean mommy of the group.

Was it too late to call the Hastings and tell them she'd changed her mind? *Lord, please help. I can't do this. I really can't do this.* Madeline felt a shadow cover her. Glancing up, she found Mrs. Gardener gazing down at her.

Compassion filled the teacher's eyes. She knelt down until she was eye-level with Madeline. "I know you're scared, Madeline. And it's all right to be scared. Motherhood is a daunting task—especially when you're a teenager. This is why you came here to Red Lick. We'll help you get ready. And it's okay if you mess up. No one is perfect."

Madeline nodded.

"It'll get better. You'll soon find your feet in all this." Mrs. Gardener squeezed Madeline's shoulder as she rose and turned back to the children.

Watching the kids around her, Madeline leaned back in the beanbag and counted the seconds until her next class.

§৯

Madeline pulled the banger into the garage and put her head on the steering wheel, grateful to finally be home. Her shoulders slowly un-bunched as she released the awfulness of the day. The other new or pending mothers had been polite, but distant. The rest of her classmates ignored her. Then there was her near meltdown in the daycare room. It was only for a year, but from the looks of it, it was going to be the longest of her life.

With a sigh, she pushed open the car door and grabbed her backpack. Dad waved to her from near the barn, encouraging her to join him.

He had banished her from the barn weeks ago out of concern for her safety. At six months pregnant, a definite waddle had crept into her walk and her ankles had begun to swell in the last few days. Neither change was helpful when it came to working with cattle, and she didn't want to risk getting kicked. She waved and headed that way.

"How was the first day?" he asked when she arrived.

Madeline shook her head. "Well ... that fresh start I hoped for isn't going to be there. Remember the girl I saw at the water fountain the day I took the test?"

Worry clouded his eyes.

"Well, she was already there when I arrived and she recognized me. Now, I'm Hester from the *Scarlet Letter.*"

He lifted an arm for her snuggle into his side. She did. "And, I know. It was my choice to tell it that way, but it doesn't make it hurt any less."

She felt his nod and heard the rumble in his chest as he said, "I can understand that." The soft thud of his heartbeat soothed her bruised emotions.

"What's that saying, you've got to sleep in the bed you make?" Madeline huffed and pulled back. She turned and surveyed the barn, feed lot, and the fields dotted with black cows. "I'm so sorry, Dad." Her voice trembled as the weight of failed responsibility clenched her heart. "I know you always dreamed of me taking over the ranch, raising kids and grandkids with a husband, continuing what your family started, but I can't stay here. Not now. Not with everyone knowing. I'm sorry, but I can't do that to my baby."

She swallowed hard, bracing herself to see disappointment in his eyes.

"No, Madeline, I'm the one who's sorry. This was my father's dream, my dream. I never meant it to be a millstone or an obligation to you. I never wanted you to feel trapped here. I'm sorry if you have." His damp eyes pleaded for forgiveness.

Unable to find words, she hugged him harder.

"I only want your happiness, and if you need to leave to find it, I'll do everything in my power to support you. But you know this will always be your home."

She pulled back and gazed up into his eyes. "Thanks, Dad."

He cleared the remaining tears from his throat and released her. "You think you can make it 'til graduation?"

"Oh, I'm definitely graduating. I'm not letting them run me out. I'm leaving on my terms. Only when I'm ready."

He shot her a sympathetic look, then sighed. "Well, your mama went to community college and got her nursing degree. Maybe you could do that."

Madeline grimaced. "I don't want to be a nurse."

He smiled and shook his head. "There are other things you could study. And getting a degree would give you more options."

She considered his idea. He was right. She couldn't do much with a high school degree—at least not enough to live on her own with a baby. But her time in the daycare affirmed what she already suspected. Motherhood was a full-time job in itself. How on earth could she do more school *and* raise a child?

Dad steered her toward the barn. "We'll make it work if it's something you want to do."

She leaned into his side grateful for his unwavering support.

"So how about some happy news, then?"

She heaved a sigh. "Please."

Amusement rippled through his voice. "When I went to the feed store, someone brought in a handful of chicks to sell."

Her eyes widened and she stopped in her tracks. "Tell me you brought them all home."

He nodded and kissed the top of her head. "I did. Three hens and a rooster. And they're ready for you to start naming them."

# CHAPTER TWENTY

*Blue Springs, Texas*
*March, 2011*

THE SHRILL RING OF MY CELL PHONE JERKED ME awake. I threw my arm over my face. There was only one reason for the call, and it wouldn't be good. "H'llo, this is Madeline Williams."

"Ms. Williams, this is Rita Ortega. I'm on duty tonight as the ER charge nurse." The nurse's familiar soft accent eased through the phone line, her tone professional but repentant. "I'm sorry to wake you, but there's been an incident here."

I nodded. Rita had been an ER charge nurse for the better part of ten years. During my tenure at the hospital, she had become a trusted coworker. If she called, then there was a definite HR issue. I switched on the lamp, and I rubbed my eyes. "No, you're fine. Thanks for calling, Rita. What happened?"

"We had an overdose victim come in at two-forty this morning. During our attempts to care for him, he punched one of my new LPNs. Broke her nose."

I closed my eyes. Working the ER night shift was not for

the faint of heart. Gut wrenching accidents and trauma were often par for the course. And unfortunately, it was often the new hires who received this baptism by fire. But a violent incident after admission was a rarity. "How is she?"

"Pretty shaken up. She's been treated, and I've started the incident paperwork, but you needed to know."

"Yes. Did a police officer come with the EMTs?"

There was a pause on the line. I could hear muffled questions. Rita must have tucked the phone to her chest while she checked for an answer. A moment later, her clear voice returned.

"Yes, he's waiting to take the patient into custody as soon as he's stable."

"Okay, good. Grab him if you would and ask the LPN if she wants to press assault charges. Tell her it's her choice, but I would highly encourage it. I'm about an hour out of town right now, but I'll get there as soon as I can."

Rita's soft accent warmed. "Thank you, Ms. Williams. I'll make the suggestion. She's a recent grad and has a tremendous heart. I hate for this to happen to anyone, but especially to her."

"I'll do everything I can to help. See you in a little while." Ending the call, I fell back in bed. The phone dropped from my hand onto the comforter. As terrible as the situation was, it was a welcome reprieve from my own emotional drama. I checked the time. Four in the morning. There was no way I could get back to Austin and have everything settled in time to meet Janine by ten, as agreed.

I felt horrible. She had already rearranged her schedule once for me, but there was no avoiding it. Given the early hour, I sent a text rather than call with the details. I apologized profusely, asked if it would be possible to re-schedule again, then tapped send. That done, I flung back the covers and went in search of appropriate work clothes.

☙

Thirty minutes later, I sneaked into the kitchen to leave a note explaining my absence. The scent of coffee greeted me. "Oh, Dad. You are the best man on earth."

Dad chuckled and handed me a travel mug already filled and doctored with cream and sugar. "When I heard your phone ring, I figured you'd be needing this. What happened?"

In between long sips, I filled him in.

He nodded. "I'll take Georgia with me on the tractor. She can help me finish up the fence work."

I smiled and reached for the coffee pot for a refill for the road. "She'll enjoy that." I glanced at the clock on the wall, then leaned over and kissed his cheek. "Hate to drink and run, but ..."

Pride lit his eyes. "Go, Pumpkin. Be the boss lady."

☙

My phone buzzed with a text as I pulled into SouthSide Hospital's parking lot about an hour later. I found my designated space and cut the engine. The phone buzzed again, and I tugged it out of my purse. One of these days I was going to get Georgia to turn off the double notifications.

I thumbed open the screen and was surprised to see Janine's name above the text.

She said she was sorry to hear about the trouble at the hospital and understood needing to cancel the appointment. She added that her twelve o'clock had to reschedule so that time was open. I could have passed on it and put off the session a little while longer, but something in my gut whispered to take the open time. I sighed and thumbed my acceptance.

When I reached the ER, I found Rita Ortega sitting in an open bay with the young LPN and the officer. The trio were putting the final details together for the assault charges. Bruises were beginning to darken the young nurse's bronze skin to a sickly grayish purple. It wouldn't be much longer before they turned into a full mask. A piece of white surgical tape gripped the bridge of her nose. I offered a compassionate smile as I joined them.

"That should be everything, ma'am," the officer said as he tucked a notepad into his chest pocket. "I'll be taking him into custody now that he's ready to be released. We'll be in contact." He dipped his chin at me and left the bay.

I moved to the side of the bed. The three of us sat without speaking. On the other side of the thin curtains, monitors beeped and voices called. The young LPN looked like she was still in high school, but based on hospital regulations, she had to at least be in her twenties. The name Celia Hernandez, LPN gleamed from the her SouthSide ID badge. I vaguely recognized her. Most of the hiring, especially for nursing positions, was conducted by the Director of Nursing, who was conspicuously absent. My brow furrowed.

Rita must have read my mind. "The DON was also out

of town. His father passed away unexpectedly on Sunday night. He's flying back in from El Paso later today."

I flashed a sympathetic smile. Dr. K must have handled the bereavement leave. "When it rains, it pours," I murmured. "Celia, I know this has been a horrible day, and I'm so sorry."

Celia sniffed as best she could through her swollen nose. "It's nothing like I expected when I went into nursing."

I winced. Getting punched by a patient was definitely a rude awakening, but thankfully it was an unusual event. "Let's look at getting your shifts covered for the next week to give you chance to heal up. How does that sound?"

Uncertainty filled her eyes. She looked from me to Rita. I made a slight incline of my head toward the door and Rita nodded.

"I'll go look at the schedule," she said with an understanding smile. "I'm sure we can work something out."

I patted Celia's hand and whispered, "Tell me, what's on your mind?"

Celia took in a long breath. She blinked rapidly and glanced away. "I-I'm not sure I'm cut out for this, Ms. Williams."

My heart broke for the young woman. "The ER or nursing altogether?" I asked, hoping it was only the former. Like most hospitals, there were open positions across all departments. And if Rita thought highly of the young LPN, then she was one we didn't want to lose.

"That could have been my older brother on the stretcher." Her stunned voice was a hair above a whisper. "He has been using drugs since high school and has been in rehab twice now after at least one overdose that the family knows of." She fell silent for a moment. I waited.

She shook her head and a tear slipped to her cheek. She wiped it away with a quick swipe of her hand. "If Daniel had done something like this and the person pressed charges, he would have been sent to jail too. That on top of the drugs would just kill my parents. My family is my life. I don't think I can be someone who can destroy someone else's family. And if that's what I have to look forward to as a nurse, I'm just not sure I can do it."

That was not the explanation I was expecting. But it was understandable. *Oh, Lord, how did this world get so broken?* "I won't begin to tell you I have any experience with drug use, but I do know what's it like to have your worst fears stare you right back in the face."

I blanched at my words. The confession was easier than I would have imagined after so many years of being buried. How had that happened? Had my innate protective nature somehow overridden the fears or had her situation simply dodged my landmines?

I cleared my throat and refocused on Celia. "How you choose to face those fears is up to you. But please know, what happened today is a rare occurrence in the ER. And everything I've heard about you, and seeing how you've handled today, tells me you have a bright future in the field. I would hate to see you throw that away."

Celia flashed a wan smile. "Thank you, Ms. Williams."

I squeezed her hand and said, "The hospital's insurance company offers a free counseling hotline. Take advantage of it, and talk this over with someone before you make any big decisions. Okay?"

Celia nodded. Rita stuck her head back in the ER bay. "Celia, I have all your shifts covered for the next five days. Go on home and get some rest."

"Do you need anyone to drive you?" I asked.

Celia shook her head. "No, I take the bus. The stop is two blocks from my house."

I nodded. "Okay, then. Please call me if you need anything. And remember what I said."

She nodded. "Yes, ma'am. I will."

I slipped out of the bay as Rita said, "Take as much time as you need in here until you're ready to leave. We've got plenty of open beds if any other emergencies come in."

Rita joined me a moment later at the nurses' station. "What's your read on her?"

"She's got a tender heart, that one." Rita glanced over her shoulder at the bay where Celia continued to sit. "I think she's more hurt that he was in so much pain than she is about actually getting hit. And then, there's her brother."

I nodded. "Keep me informed. We have other openings if she wants to change departments. Let's help her work through this."

Rita agreed. "You know, she might enjoy Peds or Labor and Delivery. I could see her being good with the little ones."

"Thanks, Rita. I'll keep that in mind." I gathered the incident report paperwork and headed to my office. It was almost eight o'clock, and the hospital was waking up. I pushed open the door to the HR department and smiled at my assistant's stunned face.

I handed Dacia the paperwork and filled her in on the goings on. "Since I'm here, I'm going to check my email and voicemail. But,"—I lowered my voice and looked around—"keep it on the down-low. I don't want a slew of people filling up the waiting area hoping to run something past me."

Dacia chuckled and nodded. "Mum's the word, Boss."

I shook my head at the title and shut my office door behind me. A quick tap to a power button was followed by a quiet hum, and I began to make good on my plan.

Two hours later, my stomach complained about its lack of food. Apparently it wanted something more tangible than coffee. I glanced at the clock, then my mostly empty email inbox. Not too shabby. It would make my return next week much easier. Deciding I had made the best dent possible, I powered down my computer and headed out.

"Is the coast clear?"

"Negative, Ghost Rider, the pattern is full," Dacia said in a hushed tone.

I just managed to keep my eye roll from showing. Dacia's penchant for quoting eighties movies was one of her few idiosyncrasies.

"Dr. Whitmer just called and wants two minutes."

I shook my head. "No, those two minutes will be an hour. At least. He's unhappy with Blue Cross's new guidelines on tele-practice, and is sure I have some power to change their minds."

"Yeah. That's what I thought." Dacia winced. "He's coming up anyway, but if you take the stairs I think you can avoid him."

I flashed Dacia a smile in thanks, grabbed my purse, and ducked out of the office making a beeline for the stairwell.

# CHAPTER TWENTY-ONE

*Blue Springs, Texas*
*November, 1997*

M ADELINE'S BULGING BELLY BUMPED AGAINST the kitchen counter as she and Dad assembled sandwiches for their Thanksgiving lunch. She had survived more than three months at Red Lick, and Mrs. Gardener had been right. The daycare class had gotten easier. She and the other moms had developed a sort of partnership. The kids now recognized her as an authority figure and responded to her quiet matter-of-factness. She supposed growing up on a ranch and dealing with recalcitrant calves and their mamas had given her a steadiness that could handle the kids' antics.

Unfortunately, that hadn't exactly translated into friendships. Each girl was too busy during the class period to chit chat, and Madeline's near-hour drive home didn't encourage lingering after the school day was over.

As the fall eased into winter and she moved into the final weeks of her pregnancy, she had become more cautious as she drove. School was out for Thanksgiving, and then there would only be three more weeks of commute before they were out for Christmas. At some point during the coming weeks, she would have a newborn.

"I can't believe how fast the months have gone," she said as she sliced a tomato.

"You think that's fast, wait 'til the little one is here." Dad chuckled as he sawed off a thick slab of smoked brisket and nibbled on the leavings. "I blinked and here you are, all grown up on me." He forked the brisket on the bread then watched as she added lettuce and tomato before closing the sandwich.

Madeline studied their plates, piled high with the brisket sandwiches and potato chips. They'd had brisket last Thanksgiving too. But it had been with Bobby's family. She had taken snap beans along with the meat to an already overloaded table. Uncle Richie, his wife, and all of Bobby's cousins had rounded out the loud afternoon filled with food, football, and funny stories. She and Lisa Jean had made tentative steps toward a friendship. By the end of the day, they'd even agreed to hang out and do girl things.

The day couldn't have been more perfect.

She shook her head. That was gone and she and Dad were making new memories. One of those was finishing up the nursery while she was out of school for the holiday. She smiled at the thought of their progress. The walls were now painted a soft lilac and her old baby cradle, a crisp white. The sonogram picture was framed and hung. The wood floor was cleaned and sealed. But she still needed to sort through a few boxes and put away the gifts.

"It was so sweet of the other moms to throw me a baby shower at school." There hadn't been games or cake, but Mrs. Gardener and the girls in her class had purchased thoughtful and necessary items. Diapers, a baby blanket, a package of burp cloths, and a huge stuffed teddy bear.

Dad agreed as he carried their plates to the table. He said a quick blessing, remembering her classmates' generosity in his thanks.

"That rocking chair you found at the church yard sale is going to be perfect in the room."

He nodded. "Just needs one more coat of lacquer, and it'll be all set."

She had so much to be thankful for, and the person at the top of her list sat right across from her. Without him and his unwavering support, there was no way she could have made it this far. She thought back to the night she'd woken up and heard him crying and praying. She'd never mentioned it and never would. But it seemed God answered Dad's prayer that night, providing him just the right wisdom and strength to help her.

Her gaze caught on the form letter stuck to the front of the refrigerator. She smiled and pinched herself under the table. UT-Austin's community college had accepted her even before she'd finished high school. She would start off the next summer with three general education classes and graduate two years later with a business degree. What she would do with it once she got it, she had no idea. But the realization she had a future for herself and a way to provide for her unborn child filled her with more hope than she could have imagined.

Sandwiches finished, Dad cleared the plates and stuck them in the dishwasher. He turned and raised his eyebrows at her. "Ready to get back to it?"

Madeline sensed he had more to say, but wasn't quite

sure of his words. She smiled and nodded. "I'll head to the room and start going through those boxes. Do you think the chair is ready for another coat of lacquer now?"

He nodded. "It was a bit tacky first thing this morning. That cold humid air isn't helping, but by now, it should be good."

"Okay then." Madeline accepted his offered hand and eased out of the chair. "Oh, I'll be glad when I can get up on my own again. And it'll be nice to tie my own shoelaces."

"Soon enough, Pumpkin," he said with an odd smile.

Her lips pursed at his cryptic look, but she decided not to press and instead headed back to the new nursery.

They had taken a kitchen chair into the room so she could sit and sort through her old baby items. She had already made it through half of the boxes that morning. Her old doll now sat tucked on a shelf next to a threadbare bunny rabbit she had gotten in an Easter basket. *The Fuzzy Duckling* book and a couple of others from that series lay on the top of the small dresser that would soon hold diapers, blankets, and changing items.

Madeline tugged the box of family history out from the closet and pulled her parents' baby photos from between the quilt folds, laying them on the dresser. She traced the baby faces and glanced to the wall where her sonogram print-out hung. She'd found her own baby picture and placed it in a matching frame, knowing one day she would add her baby's first photo to the wall arrangement. If only she could hang these alongside them. A collage of family baby snapshots would be perfect for the nursery.

But seeing Mom's photo would only hurt Dad. And she

couldn't do that to him. Madeline sighed. How different their lives might have been ...

"Pumpkin?" Dad peeked around the nursery door. "Got a surprise for you." He grinned and held out a wooden pole with hand carved stars and hearts, painted yellow and white, swaying from white twine. A handmade mobile.

She gasped and reached for the gift. "You did this?"

"While you were at school and when I was waiting for a cow to calve."

She shook her head, unable to believe the time and love that dangled before her. "It's perfect." Lifting it from his hands, she walked over to the cradle. "Can we add it now?"

When he didn't answer, she turned and found him staring at the top of the dresser. She swallowed a mild curse. Mom's baby picture lay in full view. "Dad?"

He turned and cleared his throat. With a few rapid blinks, he nodded. "Of course, Pumpkin. I'll go get my drill."

Madeline lay the mobile in the cradle and quickly tucked her parents' baby pictures back in the box. Dad returned a few minutes later and glanced over at the dresser. He made no comment about the missing photos, nor did she. Instead, she leaned into his side and whispered, "I love you."

# CHAPTER TWENTY-TWO

*Austin, Texas*
*March, 2011*

TAKING THE LAST BITE OF MY LUNCH BURRITO, I reached the turn off for Real Choices. I rarely made it to this end of town but, after twelve years of development, the area brimmed with new life. A strip mall, complete with a grocery store had replaced the old service station and used car lot. Real Choices itself boasted a fresh coat of paint and now offered benches for outside seating.

As I found a parking space, my phone rang.

"Hi, Madeline." Anthony's voice sounded distant and a bit more formal than his customary twang. "I just got out of court, and I wanted to update you."

I cut the engine and said, "Please do."

"Well, it's not a slam dunk. As I expected, Montrose moved for a dismissal."

My heart dropped to my stomach. "I didn't realize that could be a possibility."

"The judge denied it, thank God. But I watched the jury as they listened to the testimony." He paused and cleared his throat. "Madeline, the evidence is strong, and my witnesses have done well. But I'm not convinced the jurors will give him an appropriate sentence, nor that it'll even be unanimous."

I gripped the wheel. "What? Why not?"

"Well, for starters, most people don't like the idea of labeling someone a rapist. They hesitate to slap a man with a sexual offender designation for the rest of his life."

"Even if it's true?"

He sighed. "Yeah, even then."

"But you just said your case was strong, and the witnesses held up on the stand."

"I did, and they did. But even when juries have plenty of evidence to convict, they can still decide to weigh in favor of the defendant's good family name and character."

"John David isn't the most stand-up guy in the state. He's already served time for embezzling."

"And I emphasized that. But his name is also well-known. And that means something. Especially in these parts."

He paused, and for some reason I braced myself.

"You know I hate to ask, but I think it would be helpful if you testified."

My blood froze. My back stiffened. "You said the statute of limitations was up on my case."

Anthony's voice warmed. "I can get around that by calling you as a rebuttal witness. You wouldn't be filing charges." After a gap of silence, he said, "Madeline, I wouldn't be asking if I had much confidence in the jury's reactions."

Guilt whispered through me. I swallowed hard and said, "I-I can't do it, Anthony. I do feel for those women, and of course I want John David to get the time he deserves. But testify? Telling you my experience was one thing, but saying it in open court? Facing John David? I'm sorry. I just can't do it."

"I won't push you, but please at least think about it."

"Anthony, I've got to go now—I'm late for an appointment. But, yes, I promise I'll think about it."

"Unfortunately, we don't have much time, Madeline. I'll need to know something soon."

"I'll call you back," I said, ending the call as quickly as he could say goodbye. I leaned my head against the steering wheel. I couldn't stay much longer in the SUV without the AC running, and I needed to head into the building to meet with Janine. But I couldn't bring myself to move.

I hadn't looked John David in the eyes since that day. I could barely think about what happened without falling apart. I'd had a panic attack just from observing the trial.

Now, Anthony needed to me to testify.

My hands shook. My stomach turned over. The world swam around me, and I closed my eyes to gain some sort of emotional purchase. But the onslaught of memories continued. I tried to focus and remember what Janine had said on the phone the other day. And finally, the whirl began to slow.

Breathe. Slowly.

I forced my lungs to take deep, slow breaths, counting silently in my head until the wooziness passed.

Then in a heartbeat, a quiet calm fell over me. In the silence, a verse whispered in my mind: *For God does not give a spirit of fear. But of power, love, and a sound mind.*

"Lord?" I asked.

*God does not give a spirit of fear.* The voice came again. So clear.

*God does not give fear.* The whisper settled inside my heart.

The words were somewhere in one of the letters to Timothy. And if they were in God's Word, then they had to be true even if they ran counter to every emotion I felt. "If You didn't give me this fear, Lord, then who did?" The question was elementary. Every VBS kid could answer it correctly.

But what could I do to fight it? How could I believe the Word when every emotion inside of me was screaming otherwise?

Who did I believe? My emotions or my God?

My phone buzzed. An appointment reminder flashed across the screen. Praying Janine would have some insight, I forced myself to step out of the SUV.

The receptionist gave my professional clothing and flat stomach a curious look, but she smiled as I said, "I have a twelve o'clock with Janine."

Before she could answer, the hall door opened, and Janine stepped through. Instead of the scrubs I remembered, she wore a pair of linen pants and a pale blue jacket. Her brown hair was still long, but it was loose at her shoulders rather than pulled up in a ponytail. A few lines bracketed her lips and eyes, but the kindness that radiated from them remained the same. She opened her arms and I rushed into them like a child returning to her mother. "It's so good to see you, Madeline." She pulled back and gripped my elbows. "You look wonderful. And I am so proud of the woman you have become."

I eased back until our hands interlocked and gave them a tight squeeze, communicating the words my lips couldn't form. She nodded and pulled me into the hallway that I remembered led to the offices and treatment rooms.

With a generous smile, she waved me to one end of the love seat while she took the other. "You've already had the quite the morning, haven't you?"

I pushed out a huff. "You don't know the half of it. The prosecutor called me while I was parking."

Concern flickered in Janine's gaze.

"He's still worried John David may not do enough—or even any—jail time." I half turned on the cushion and grabbed a throw pillow that was scrunched against my back. Hugging it to my chest, I leaned my chin on the cord-trimmed edge and played with one of the tassels. "He wants me to testify."

Janine's eyes widened. "I can see how that would throw you for a loop."

"I don't know what to do, Janine. Everything in me is screaming in terror. Thirteen years ago, I lied to protect my family from John David. How can I possibly bring myself to tell the truth right in front of him?"

I paused and once again the verse played in my mind. With a shake of my head, I told Janine about hearing it. "I know it's truth, and I accept it ... at least in my head ... but my heart, my emotions, are telling me it can't be true. Because this fear I have is real, no matter who sent it. I can't bury it again, and I can't just dismiss it and go on."

"Yes, that is true," she said. "You have experienced a trauma your brain doesn't understand. And because of that, your emotions and your fear are running rampant.

So yes, absolutely cling to God's Word and the truth of it. However, also recognize there are psychological things that need to be healed in order for you to fully embrace and walk in that truth."

That made sense. I told her Dad's opinion about the trial. "Am I letting the fear win by not testifying?"

"I wouldn't say that. Instead, I would encourage you to appreciate the steps you are taking. You pushed what happened into a section of your mind and closed the door on it. These last few days you've opened that door just enough to realize there are things, scary things, still behind it. The fact you've opened the door at all is huge."

I winced, even as I saw her point. I had buried that day rather than working through it. But was I ready to take another even scarier step and testify to the truth?

Janine patted my hand. "There's no reason to inflict more trauma on yourself by testifying when you're not emotionally ready." She paused and watched her words sink in.

I felt a bit of relief at the possibility of skirting the issue once more. But with her next words, she ruffled my uneasy calm.

"That being said, I do agree with your dad. Facing your fear and working with the district attorney could help you heal. And if he believes your testimony could be pivotal in sentencing, then it's worth considering. Not just for you, but for the other women too. But it is your choice. Don't let anyone push you into doing something you don't want to do. That's already happened once."

I shivered at the memory. Maybe that was why I had reacted so badly to Georgia's questions. When she'd pressed,

I pushed back to stop her onslaught. Was it possible that my response was a sign I was more capable than I believed? Could I face my fears just as I'd encouraged Celia to do when she'd been assaulted in the ER?

"What are you thinking?" Janine asked. Her voice was low and soothing.

I shrugged and released a long sigh. "I don't know. I was young. Just trying to make the best of a bad situation. And then I fell in love with my baby, there was no longer any question about what I would do. We just lived the lives we were given." I fell silent and thought about Georgia's words. "Georgia says she thinks I'm brave."

"How does that make you feel?"

"Like an imposter." A bark of wry laughter floated from my lips.

"What makes you think that?"

I shot her an incredulous look. "Weren't you the one talking me off the floor in Dad's kitchen?"

"Yes, you've had some really scary reactions to triggering situations, but you've handled them with incredible bravery. You've reached out and accepted help to learn how to deal with them. You've pushed yourself to face circumstances that are terrifying even though you haven't wanted to. In short, you are facing your fears. Fears you've been avoiding since childhood."

I huffed. "You know, I told one of my employees something similar after the incident this morning. She'd been attacked by a dangerous patient, and the situation had opened up some of her own personal fears. I suggested that how she decided to face those fears was her choice, but that I hated to see other people's actions derail a promising career."

Janine smiled. "Sounds like pretty good advice."

I fell silent and considered my words. Just this week, Georgia had told me I was the bravest person she knew. Janine said she was proud of the woman I had become. And Dad was stepping up to encourage me to do what would help me heal, even if that meant revealing our family's deepest secret.

If the three people I held most dear in the world believed in me, how could I not believe in myself? How could I not trust, yet again, that this was God's plan? Panic welled in me at the thought of testifying. But now another emotion wove its way between the fear-driven sensations.

It was hope.

I took in a deep breath and released a watery sigh. A new, firmer resolve squared my shoulders. With a nod, I took the next big step toward healing. "All right. I'll testify."

# CHAPTER TWENTY-THREE

*Blue Springs, Texas*
*December, 1997*

M ADELINE LAY IN BED AND GAZED OUT THE window. Dad had gone up to the barn to check on a sick cow after breakfast while she, feeling a little off, returned to bed. Thick fog had rolled in overnight, blanketing her usual view of the front metal gates almost a mile away. The weather fit with her mood. Somber, quiet, waiting. She was nearing her due date and the impending title, mother. Over the last few months, the weight of the baby had become more emotional than physical.

She soothed her swollen belly and dreamed, picturing her child as they grew, praying there would be little similarity to their father. She would never be able to put the past behind her completely, but seeing his eyes peering at her every day would be more than she thought she could bear—despite Janine's assurances.

But what was the old saying? *God won't give you more than you can bear?* She chuffed and shook her head. "You must think I can handle a lot, Lord." Something inside her shifted. She thought it was God's reassurance. And perhaps it was, but the sharp heavy cramp that followed on its heels made her wonder.

The pain eased to a dull ache. Madeline rolled to one side in bed and tugged her pillow behind her shoulders. Feeling settled for the moment, her hands returned to her belly and began the circular movements she'd learned in her prenatal classes.

She smiled. "Little one, despite how you got here, I'm looking forward to meeting you. I'm glad I didn't find out if you're a boy or a girl. I'll love you no matter which you turn out to be."

A sweet sense settled over her. She had names chosen for both genders. If a boy, he would be Charles James after both of his grandfathers. If a girl, Georgia May, after her mom and maternal grandmother. Her salt of the earth, faith-filled ancestors would be honored. And the child would start their life with a good legacy.

As for herself, she wondered what those same ancestors—especially Mom—would think of her. Janine was proud of her, but as great as she was, Janine was not Mom. Would she be pleased? Was she looking down on everything that happened and saying to everyone, "That's my daughter. Look at the woman she is becoming." Madeline truly hoped so.

Another sharp pain jarred her from her musings. Her due date was two weeks away—she had begun to think of the baby as her Christmas present. Brow furrowed, she shifted in bed again. A gush of wetness soaked her sheets. Her lungs stilled and her mind reeled.

*Did I just wet the ... oh ...*

She sucked in a quick breath and reached for her cell phone.

Two rings.

Dad answered.

"I think I'm in labor."

§

Two days later, Madeline lay in her bed on the hospital's labor and delivery floor. Dad's soft snores whispered from the armchair in the corner. Sweet coos reverberated at her breast. She stared down at the newborn in awe. Georgia May Williams had entered the world eighteen hours after Madeline's water broke. Six pounds, eleven ounces, twenty inches long. A tiny hand now wrapped around her index finger as she snuggled the baby closer. Leaning in to kiss the little girl's forehead, she breathed in the sweet baby scent. Georgia fussed a bit. Madeline hummed a soft melody from her childhood, marveling how quickly the baby was soothed and returned to suckling.

Madeline absorbed every detail. Downy fine hair. Shell-like ears. Pale blue eyes. Pink rosebud mouth. Love, pure and heady, washed over her. Tears of joy dripped down her cheeks.

This was her child. It no longer mattered how she came to be.

"Welcome to the world, Georgia May."

Georgia pulled away and yawned. Madeline smiled at the sight. "You are just too cute, little one." She chuckled then sobered as she traced the line of Georgia's brow. "This world you entered is a tough one, sweetie. But I promise I will give my life to protect you. And I will do everything in my power to give you a life filled with love."

Dad blinked awake. After a huge yawn and long stretch, he unfolded himself from the chair and eased over to the bed. He placed a soft hand against the baby's head and leaned in to kiss Madeline's temple. "My girls." His cheeks crinkled around his smile. "Your mama would be so proud of you. And so pleased to have her grandchild named after her."

Madeline blushed. "She looks just like Mom's baby picture, doesn't she?"

"She sure does," he said with a nod. He cleared his throat and blinked away sudden tears. "I'm glad you found those old photos. I'm sorry I haven't been able to talk about her—"

A knock interrupted them and a nurse stuck her head around the door. "You about ready to get some rest? I'll take Georgia back to the nursery."

"Can she stay a bit longer?" Madeline asked. "She just fell asleep."

The nurse slipped into the room and said, "You need to take advantage of the time to rest."

With reluctance, Madeline eased Georgia into the nurse's waiting arms before the woman settled the baby back into the portable cradle.

Another knock to the door was followed by another hospital worker. The nurse offered a reassuring smile and nodded to the new addition. "Why don't we complete her birth certificate paperwork while she's sleeping?"

Madeline glanced at Dad who nodded. She took in a

deep breath and said, "Okay." She gave the clerk Georgia's complete name as well as her own.

"And the father?"

Madeline bit her lip. "Leave that blank, please. There is no father."

The clerk's brow lifted. She made no comment, but exchanged a quick glance with the nurse. She added a few more details to the papers then said, "All right. We'll get this submitted for you, and you can request the formal certificate within a week or so."

The nurse smiled and checked on Georgia. "I'll be back in a few minutes for her."

Madeline nodded then waited for the women to leave. She turned on her side and reached into the cradle to stroke Georgia's back. "I know what I told them, sweetie, but you do have a Father. He loves you deeper than the ocean and wider than the sky. And His name is God."

# CHAPTER TWENTY-FOUR

*Blue Springs, Texas*
*March, 2011*

I FOUND DAD AND GEORGIA ON THE FRONT PORCH indulging in servings of the apple pie I had bought at Whitlock's. Climbing out of the X3, I settled against the porch railing and smiled at their combined delight. Whitlock's always did have the best baker in these parts. Georgia handed me her half-full plate and fork.

"Here, Mom. I got a piece big enough for both of us."

I wrinkled my nose in thanks and took a bite. Tart and sweet, the Granny Smith apples bit the back of my mouth, but the sugary glaze soon softened the blow. I licked my lips and somehow kept myself from licking the plate as well. Setting it on the railing, I glanced around the porch. Sometime in the last few years, Dad had replaced the cherry-red bench cushions with emerald green and my geraniums were traded out with a pot of low maintenance ivy. But the porch remained a welcome place to sit and ponder.

With a sigh, I turned my gaze to Dad and Georgia, filling them in on Anthony's concerns about the trial.

"He won't serve time? That's not fair!" Georgia sat up in the bench, jostling Dad with her elbow.

He placed a calming hand on her shoulder.

"He's asked me to testify. Even though the statute of limitations is up on my case, he can still call me as a witness."

Georgia's face brightened. "Are you going to do it?"

"I had decided to, but then on the drive back, I realized I'm not the only person who has to agree."

Her eyes narrowed, and, frowning, glanced to Dad. "Who else do you have to ask?"

"The two most important people, you and Grandpa."

She leaned back in her seat, her agreement evident. Dad was another story.

Consideration darkened his eyes. "Have you talked with Anthony yet?"

"No." I shook my head. "I didn't want to get his hopes up. Because if either of you says no, then I won't do it."

Georgia's brow wrinkled and her gaze turned curious. "Why would we say no, Mom?"

"Well," I sighed. "I might be the one testifying, but you two will still experience the results. Think about what might happen when you go back to school and everyone knows about it."

Georgia shook her head. "I don't care—I want to help. Besides, I'm better than a person's word. I'm hard evidence. I can take a DNA test to prove your story."

I reached forward and cupped her cheek. "Sweetie, are you really sure this is something you want to do? Once we do this, we can never go back."

Georgia nodded. Her gaze sharpened as an idea

occurred to her. "Mom, you remember that story in the Bible about Esther? The beautiful Jewish queen who kept her identity a secret until that guy decided he wanted to kill all the Jews?"

I closed my eyes in resignation. I knew where she was going with this, and I could tell Dad did too. It was her favorite story from the Bible, and Heaven help me I wished I had never introduced her to it.

"What if that's me now? What if this is my time? What if what her uncle—what was his name? Morrison?"

"Mordecai," I said with a small smile.

"Yeah, Mordecai. Well, what if what he said to Esther is the same for me? What if I was born for this time? To be the ultimate proof that puts John David away?"

*Oh, Lord. How can I argue with the truth of Your Word and her application of it?* Of course, my wonderful, idealistic, selfless child would think nothing of herself in the face of the greater good. I caught a glimpse of Georgia as an adult. Beautiful, poised, and a champion for others. "I can assure you, sweetie, this is not your sole purpose here on earth. But I will agree it may be a big one."

Dad cleared his throat. "Sugar pie, I think I hear Buddy playing with his food dish. Why don't you go feed him?"

Georgia flashed Dad a disbelieving look. Buddy ate up in the barn office and bedded down in one of the stalls at night. I, too, doubted his hearing, but I was grateful for his redirection. I nodded to Georgia but she planted her hands on her hips.

"I'm not a little girl, Mom. I want to stay. I'm part of this too."

Sighing, I nodded. "As much as I hate to admit it, you

aren't little anymore. You are growing up." I cupped her cheeks and stared into her determined eyes. Though I appreciated her logic, I still couldn't relinquish the entirety of her innocence.

"But that doesn't mean you're a grownup. And you've had to learn a lot more at twelve than I ever wanted you to know. So please, do as Grandpa asked. He and I need to talk, and, don't worry. I'll let you know what we decide."

Georgia frowned and turned pleading eyes to Dad.

"Go on, sugar pie. And make sure he eats every bite," Dad said with an encouraging push toward the steps. "He's not crazy about the food the vet wants him to eat. But he needs all the energy he can get for the work he does around here."

"Yes, sir," she said. Though disappointed she would miss out on the grownups' conversation, it didn't take long before she was skipping up the drive. She'd been asking for a dog for the last year, and I foisted her on Buddy every chance I got. Good thing he appreciated the extra attention.

Dad grabbed the plates and forks and headed into the kitchen. Setting my purse on the table, I took over dish duty, rinsing and arranging the plates in the dishwasher. "Dad, what am I supposed to do? The fallout could be horrendous."

"That's an answer I don't have, Pumpkin. Have you asked God for His take on the situation? You've trusted His plan, well, at least for the most part. Don't you think you can trust Him to guide you with the right answer?" He paused and flashed a wry smile. "Only this time, why don't you let Him control the outcome?"

Dad was right. That was exactly what I had done. I trusted Georgia was God's plan, but I didn't have faith in Him for the outcome. I chose to step into His shoes and tell Bobby the lie that changed all our lives even more. Could our lives have been different if I had told the truth back then and relied on Him to handle the fallout?

I couldn't go back and change the past, but I could choose differently this time. I headed back to my room. As I settled on the bed and let my head fall against the headboard, I released everything to the only One who had all the answers.

"Lord, You have been faithful. Between school and job opportunities, You have provided abundantly for me and Georgia. I never dreamed I would be doing what I do and loving it as much as I do. Georgia is the absolute best gift You could ever give me as Your child. I can't imagine life without her. I know You know what's going to happen. And even though going forward scares the life out of me, I will choose to trust You'll keep us safe. I'm sorry I didn't choose that path sooner. Please forgive me."

I pulled my phone out of my purse and found Anthony's number in my call log. One press and it was ringing. It rang only once.

"Madeline, it's good to hear from you."

"I talked it over with my family. And even though I'm still not sure how well I'll do on the stand, I'm willing to do it. If you still think you need my testimony ..." I silently hoped the answer would be no, but the peace I felt as the offer left my lips told me it was the right decision.

Anthony breathed a relieved sigh. "Thank you, God."

I couldn't help but smile at his thanksgiving. "And Georgia wants to take a DNA test to prove paternity."

"Absolutely. Would it be possible for y'all to meet me in Austin at the crime lab? That way the tech can take her swab and start processing it immediately."

My shoulders sagged. I had just gotten back to the ranch not thirty minutes prior. With the early start and work drama, all I wanted was a warm bath and a mug of hot chocolate. But I appreciated time was of the essence. "Yes. We can leave in the next thirty minutes."

My phone buzzed with an incoming text.

"I just sent you the address."

I glanced quickly at the screen and said, "Got it." I paused as a thought niggled at me. "Anthony, the other day, when I was unpacking in my room here at the ranch, I found something. I don't know if it will help or ..."

I was babbling, but I couldn't bring myself to say the words. I took in a fortifying breath and said, "I found the clothes I wore that day at the auction. I don't remember doing it, but I obviously stuffed them in this bag after the attack when I got home."

"You still have your clothes?" I could hear the incredulity in his voice.

"Uh, yes. Is that awful?"

Awe filled his words. "No, it's amazing. We can test them as well. The judge may deny it because there's no police chain of custody, but I can use it as anecdotal evidence if nothing else. Please, bring them too."

I closed my eyes and tried to muster the confidence to reach back under my bed and remove them once again. *Remember why you're doing this. For healing. Closure.*

*To protect the next woman he tries to hurt.* "Okay." I was pleased my voice held no sign of the trembling that coursed through my body. "We'll see you soon."

❦

As we turned off the highway, Dad glanced over at me and flashed an encouraging smile. Georgia sat in the back seat of his truck, happy as a lark to be playing her part. I couldn't help but want to weep at the reality.

We reached the Texas Department of Safety in a little over an hour. The parking lot was still filled with cars and Anthony stood by the entrance, briefcase in hand. Dad pulled to a stop in front of the building. "Y'all go ahead and get out. I'll hunt up a parking place."

I nodded and we joined Anthony on the sidewalk. The plastic trash bag dangled from my hand. He made no move to take it when I offered. Instead, he said, "Let's wait until we get inside where there will be a witness when you hand it over."

That made a sort of sense, but my tired mind couldn't grasp exactly why it did. I shook my head trying to clear it. "Any chance there's some coffee around here somewhere? It's been a long day."

Anthony nodded as he held open the glass doors for us to enter. "Sure. We'll need to talk after the crime tech is done with his portion. Prep you for your testimony."

*Talk? Prep?* Yeah, that made sense too. Unfortunately, I wasn't certain how much information my brain would hold.

"What about me? Can I testify?" Georgia asked as we made our way to the glass-encased counter.

Anthony shook his head as he let his briefcase drop to the floor. "No, a witness can only testify to what she directly saw or experienced. Sorry, Georgia, but if you testify about what your mother told you, then it would be called hearsay and that's not admissible."

Georgia looked disappointed, but brightened under Anthony's reassuring smile. "But you taking a DNA test is perfect. That's evidence to support what your mom tells on the witness stand. And it might be the deciding factor in the case."

Proud to have her role confirmed in the proceedings, Georgia grinned with satisfaction. "Hi," Anthony greeted the woman behind the counter. "Ricky Clark is expecting us."

"Yes. He gave me a heads up. I'll just buzz him." She tapped an extension on her phone and relayed our presence. Her thick Texas twang raced the information together with a brisk efficiency. When she hung up, she asked, "He mentioned you had other evidence to log?"

Anthony gestured for me to bring the bag. "Yes. This is Madeline Williams. These are her clothes. There was no police report filed, but we want them logged for DNA testing for a rape thirteen years ago."

The woman shot me a sympathetic look, but her mouth pursed as she flicked her eyes to Anthony.

Anthony nodded. "We know it's a long shot, but I want to try anyway."

"Anthony," called a deep melodic voice. Ricky Clark looked more like a former tight end for the Cowboys than a crime lab tech. He held a small box in one giant hand and a clear plastic bag in the other.

"Ricky, thanks so much for putting a rush on this."

"Anytime, Anthony. You know that." He turned his pale green gaze toward me. "So. Let's start with getting the clothes bagged."

I blanched. I hadn't thought this part through. I flicked a hesitant glance toward Georgia then back to Ricky. Sighing, I untied the bag. "These were the clothes I wore when John David raped me. They've been under my bed ever since."

Ricky nodded and opened the clear, plastic evidence bag. I closed my eyes and pulled each piece out one at a time, cringing as my underwear slipped inside to join the t-shirt and shorts. But as I released my grip on each item, I also released my grip on the outcome.

*God, I'll trust you fully for whatever happens.*

Ricky sealed the evidence bag and wrote something on the outside. Anthony added his own notation, and then they handed it to the receptionist.

She gave me an encouraging nod as she began typing on her terminal. I reached out a hand toward Georgia and she moved closer.

"My turn now?" she asked, her eyes dancing with hope.

Ricky greeted her with a smile. "Yes ma'am. Here's what we're going to do. I'm gonna take this gigantic Q-tip and rub it inside your cheek, and then stick it in this tube of testing solution."

"Cool. Will you test Mom too? I mean, I know she's my mom, but is it important to confirm that as well?"

Ricky glanced at Anthony, who nodded.

"Sure, Georgia, we'll take her sample as well. You can't have too much confirmation these days."

Ricky swabbed both of our cheeks then snapped the plastic tubes closed. "I'll run the cheek swabs through the rapid DNA testing. You'll have those results this evening." He paused and glanced at the evidence bag. "The clothes might take the usual twenty-four to forty-eight hours, though, given how long it's been."

"Thanks, man," Anthony said. "I owe you one."

"No, you don't, and you never will," Ricky said over his shoulder as he pushed through the door heading back to the lab.

I shot Anthony a curious glance and he explained. "I helped Ricky's little brother get into rehab after a DUI charge when he was a teen. He's now playing football at UT with a shot at the pros."

"So the size must be a family trait."

He chuckled, and I was grateful for the levity. "Yeah, Ricky was more interested in developing his brains than his brawn." He said with a wry smile, "Although it looks like he couldn't outthink his genetics."

Dad tugged open the entry door as Anthony gestured us toward a consulting room just off the main waiting area. Georgia waved him over then wrapped an arm around his waist as they walked together, following us down the hall.

Anthony held open the door and gestured for us to sit. "I don't think I've told you this, Madeline, but I want you to know what you're doing is incredibly brave."

A dry bark of laughter slipped between my lips. Even though everyone kept saying that, I still didn't feel particularly brave.

Anthony opened his briefcase and tugged out a legal pad and a pen. He flipped about halfway through until he found a blank page and then scrawled my name and the date across the top. Tapping the pen against the pad, he read back through his notes. "Montrose has built his case around the premise that John David has never engaged in nonconsensual behavior."

I shot a quick glance down the table to where Georgia sat absently spinning her chair. I wasn't comfortable with her hearing the specifics of my rape and testimony. Growing up visiting the ranch, she'd learned about the birds and bees early. But having them presented as anything other than in a mutually respectful and loving situation made me cringe.

Before Anthony went much further, I caught Dad's eye. "Dad, do you think you and Georgia can find me a cup of coffee somewhere? I'm going to need some caffeine."

Dad gave an understanding nod and placed a staying hand on Georgia's chair. "Come on, sugar pie, let's go round up some coffee for your mom and maybe a candy bar for us."

"Really, Mom? A candy bar?" Georgia asked with a delighted smile.

"Yes, okay. But make sure you split it with your grandpa. You've already had apple pie. I don't want you bouncing off the walls tonight on a sugar high."

Comprehension lit Anthony's eyes. "There's a concession area down the hall on the left. But you may have to ask the receptionist if she can get the coffee."

Dad smiled. "That'll be okay. We'll be back in a little while."

As the door closed behind them, I fell back in my chair and closed my eyes. "I'm sorry. I just couldn't ... not in front of her ..."

"Say no more," Anthony said in his soft twang. Concern radiated from him. "Do you want to wait for that coffee or are you ready to get started?"

I opened my eyes and shook my head. "No time like the present."

# CHAPTER TWENTY-FIVE

*Blue Springs, Texas*
*August, 1998*

**"T**HERE'S A GOOD GIRL," MADELINE SAID, rubbing Georgia's back one last time before handing her over to Mrs. Johnson. Cheeks the color of ripe strawberries and eyes brimming with tears, Georgia released a screech like a barn owl. Madeline's stomach turned over. She could do this, right? "I know, sweetie, but you can't come to school with me anymore."

Mrs. Johnson blew raspberries into Georgia's cheeks, turning the girl's wails into hiccuping laughter. The widow lived down the road from the ranch and had jumped at Madeline's timid request to watch Georgia while she commuted to Austin. "We'll do just fine, Madeline. Don't you worry one bit. You concentrate on your schoolwork and bring back that fancy degree."

Madeline bit her lip, but nodded. "I'll check in between my classes. And I'll be back by four today." Georgia grabbed a long tendril of Madeline's hair and yanked. Madeline blinked away her tears, certain the hard tug wasn't the only reason for them.

Mrs. Johnson uncurled Georgia's death grip and bounced the baby in her arms until she settled again. "I'll be near the phone, but I can't tell you how much I've been looking forward to this, what with my babies grown and their babies hours away."

Madeline caressed one of Georgia's chubby legs. "Let me know if she gets to be too much—"

"You go on, now," Mrs. Johnson said with a chastising huff and a delighted grin. "You're gonna be late if you dawdle here much longer."

Madeline nodded and kissed Georgia's forehead. Georgia cooed and smiled and Madeline heaved a somber sigh. Over the past eight months, Georgia had gone with her everywhere, becoming both driving and school buddy. Although she'd left her in the school's daycare during class, she'd never been more than a few yards and minutes away. Today, the distance would be several miles and more than an hour. What if something were to happen?

"Girl, your daddy's just down the road," Mrs. Johnson said, as if reading Madeline's worries. "I've got his cell number right under yours on my phone list. And you and I both know he'll drop everything in a hot minute if this young 'un even scrapes her knee."

Madeline smiled. Mrs. Johnson was right. She could do this. "He'll be by sometime today with your eggs and meat to pay you for babysitting."

"I'll be here and ready. You go on now. Get yourself to Austin and study hard. Make this little one proud."

With one last kiss to Georgia's cheek, Madeline nodded and climbed into her car. She waved at the pair until they disappeared in her rearview mirror. Pulling out her handwritten directions to campus, she settled in for the drive.

A little over an hour later, she reached the city limits and found her exit to UT's community college campus in downtown Austin. She and Dad had passed it every time they'd driven to Real Choices during her pregnancy. Madeline had paid little attention to the billboard signs advertising their degree programs, never dreaming the campus would someday be her destination. She glanced ahead to the exit she knew by heart and lifted a quick prayer of thanks and blessings for Janine. She never would have made it without her mentoring during the pregnancy. Maybe one day, she could stop over and say hello.

Madeline pulled into the designated student parking lot, grabbed her backpack, and made her way to class. Students of all ages sauntered in casual clusters or lounged on benches that lined the walkway.

Further off, they lay sprawled across towels on an open lawn, books and laptops open, tall cups and sunglasses at the ready to beat back the hot August sun. If that was the same lawn on her map, then the English building had to be just up ahead. She wiped her brow, readjusted her backpack, and continued her hike. Tomorrow she would make sure to bring a water bottle.

She reached her first classroom building and spied a group of students milling around the entrance. Memories of her first day at Red Lick flickered. *You can do this. This is your fresh start.* Grabbing the door's handle, she tugged it open and took her first step into her future.

སྙ

Several hours later, Madeline closed her state government textbook with a satisfied smile and slipped out of her final class of the day. The teachers were interesting and insightful and encouraged every student to voice their thoughts on the day's topics. Though their excitement might not last the duration of the semester, the discussions pricked her curiosity, prompting a surprising desire to build on what she'd learned.

Dad was right. College was a good choice. Yet another blessing from Georgia's presence in her life.

Madeline glanced at her watch as the dismissal bell reverberated through the hall. Three o'clock already? She'd checked in on Mrs. Johnson and Georgia at lunch and learned all was well. Georgia had eaten a little bit earlier and was down for her afternoon nap. The widow spoke nothing but praise for the baby's good behavior, calming Madeline's nerves and concerns.

"Hey, Madeline!" a voice called from behind her. She turned and saw a boy about her age waving. Dark hair worn long and free flopped over his eyes with an easy charm turning more than one female head as he slipped between the throng of students.

Madeline paused allowing him to catch up. "Hi, um, Jorge, right?" He sat behind her in this morning's English 101 class and a few rows over in Government.

His grin widened with appreciation. "Right. How was your first day?"

"It was good. Great even."

"Oh, cool." He glanced around as if suddenly nervous. "Hey, so I was wondering—a bunch of us are forming a study group for the semester. Care to join in?"

Madeline hesitated. He seemed sweet and a study group would be helpful as the semester progressed. But the drive was already over an hour home, and Georgia was waiting. She ducked her head and said, "Sorry, I can't."

Jorge's grin gained wattage and urgency. "Aw, come on, it'll be fun. It's a bunch of us from my high school and everyone's cool."

She shook her head and glanced at her watch again hoping he'd take the hint. "Thanks for the offer, but I've got to get home."

Jorge ignored her excuse and pressed. "Where do you live? We could all meet up near there. I'm sure there's a coffee shop or a book store around there somewhere."

"Oh, no." Madeline shook her head and took a step back. She looked up the hall and blushed as their conversation gained attention. "I'm way out of town. A little over an hour south of here."

Jorge let out a long, low whistle. "Yikes. You gonna drive that every day?

Madeline nodded, but said nothing.

He pursed his lips then shrugged. "Well, okay then. But hey, if you change your mind, here's my number. Call anytime. About anything." He thrust a piece of paper with a series of numbers slashed across it.

She read the number then glanced up. Hope lit his dark eyes. This was about more than a simple study group. How had she missed that? She bit her lips, trying to smother her embarrassment and squelch the pang that clenched her heart.

At Red Lick, she'd been marked with a scarlet A and avoided by all the male students. But even then, Bobby still lurked in the corners of her heart. Jorge, however, didn't know either of those details. To him, she was just another cute girl in his class.

What would he say if he knew she was a single mom? Would he ask about Georgia's father? Dread sank thick and sticky into her limbs. "I'm, um, I'm sorry. But I can't. You—I—"

Jorge eased back, his smile faded. Rejection shaded his eyes as he gazed up the hallway. "Hey, no prob. I get it."

*Oh, no. It's not that. Never that.* Desperate to remedy her misstep, Madeline reached out, squeezed his arm, and bulldozed through her fear. "No, you don't understand. I'm ... my daughter is waiting for me. I have to pick her up from the sitter."

Confusion wrinkled his brow as her explanation worked its way through his mind. He studied her as if reassessing his previous views. Judgment flickered in his gaze. "Wow. Okay then. Well, drive safe. See you tomorrow."

Sticking his phone number in her pocket, she watched him walk away, leaving him to whatever conclusion he'd made from her explanation. Relief mingled with disappointment. Since becoming a mother, she'd never given dating any thought, but she was only eighteen. Would that always be the case? Time was supposed to heal heartache. And if it did, what about Georgia? She had vowed to keep the truth of Georgia's conception secret until she was an adult. But how could she do that and be truthful in a relationship?

Madeline stood straight, resolute. Georgia was a responsibility she wouldn't shirk, even if it meant more sacrifice on her part. Jorge's judgment flashed through her memory. *Lord, help me find better words next time.*

# CHAPTER TWENTY-SIX

*Blue Springs, Texas*
*March, 2011*

"**M**OM, ARE YOU SCARED?"
Georgia's quiet question pulled my attention from the mirror as I put on the last touches of my blush. Though I had learned to love dressing up, I still wasn't much into makeup beyond the basics. But I wasn't about to go into court without some war paint. I nodded as I set the brush down and turned to face her. "Yes. Life will be different not living with the lie any longer."

Georgia leaned against the door, eyes narrowed. "Is that bad?"

I shrugged. "I don't know. But I do know it's time to let it go." I turned her toward the hall, flicking off the light. "Sweetie, will you do something for me?"

"Sure, Mom. Anything."

"When I get on the stand, will you put your earbuds in and listen to your music?"

Georgia sighed, but nodded. "Okay. But Mom, I told you. I'm not a little girl anymore."

My heart cringed. I ran my hand through her hair

tucking it behind her ear. "Don't I know it. I just—I just want don't want you to hear all the details. You don't need to know them now." I settled my hands on her shoulders and gave them a light squeeze. "I want to hold on to your innocence for as long as I can. The world will open your eyes to all of its evils soon enough."

"Ready to go?" Dad asked as we reached the kitchen.

I nodded. My phone buzzed with an incoming text. I grabbed it off the counter and read the message. "Janine is going to come too. She canceled her schedule today and will meet us at the courthouse."

Georgia wrapped her arms around my waist and leaned into me offering her silent support. I squeezed her, but there was something more I needed.

"Dad?" My voice trembled. "Before we leave, will you pray for me?"

Surprise lifted his brow. His cheeks warmed, but he seemed honored by my request. He cleared his throat and nodded. "Of course."

We grabbed hands, Dad, Georgia, and me, and bowed our heads. Dad's easy baritone broke the silence with a solid strength. I could hear the faith of his fathers in the soft timber. "Lord God, we come to You as a family to ask for Your wisdom and peace as Madeline goes to testify today. We trust You have planned this day, and take comfort You'll be with her. We give You praise and all the glory for whatever the result. Thank You for being our God and our Father. We ask this all in Jesus' name."

Our chorus of amens were soaked with tears, but finally I felt ready to face John David.

Dad drove us to the courthouse, and I was grateful for his chauffeuring once again. Even though yesterday had started out sleep-deprived, I tossed and turned as visions of today played out in my dreams. The town was even more packed than when I had been at the courthouse on Tuesday. But it was closing argument day—at least as far as any of these people knew.

Dad led the way as we pushed through the throng and found the seats Anthony had saved for us in the second row. I gulped as I looked around the courtroom. I had mentally prepared myself, but reality was a rude awakening. All of these people would hear my secret the moment the truth left my lips, and within an hour, thousands more would know.

I should have called Dr. K and let him know, to prepare him for the potential calls from the press. As the HR Director, the hospital should have been utmost in my mind. I closed my eyes and prayed he would forgive my lapse once he heard the news. A soft hand squeezed my shoulder. I glanced up and into the warm comfort of Janine's gaze.

I stood and embraced her. "Thank you for coming. You don't know how much this means to me."

"I wouldn't be anywhere else." She pulled back, and I stepped out into the aisle. "You must be Georgia," Janine said and held out her hand. "I am so pleased to meet you."

"You're Janine?"

She nodded and shook Georgia's hand.

And suddenly, my extroverted, never-met-a-stranger

daughter seemed unsure of what to say. Georgia mutely watched Janine settle on the bench as an obvious awe stole over her. I shook my head at the change. But then I remembered Janine had talked me down from a terrifying panic attack—probably within Georgia's hearing.

"Hi, Jim. It's good to see you again," Janine said with a smile.

Dad dipped his head in welcome. If my eyes weren't deceiving me, I registered a distinct pinking of Janine's cheeks. Before I could say anything, I heard Anthony's voice behind me.

"Madeline."

I turned and nodded. His suit was neatly pressed and his eyes beamed with confidence. The sight settled my nerves. "Morning, Anthony."

He flashed a reassuring smile. "You ready?"

I looked at my family and thought about Dad's prayer, Georgia's praise of my bravery, and Janine's pride in my choices. But mostly, I remembered my commitment to trust God's timing and His plan. I nodded. "Yeah, I think I am."

"Okay, great." He lowered his voice, despite the cacophony of conversation that surrounded us, and leaned a bit closer. "Just hang tight. I'm going to ask for a continuance first to give us time to get the results of the testing from your clothes. But I'm not holding my breath the judge will allow it this late in the case."

He glanced down at his briefcase and offered a reassuring smile. "Ricky faxed me the results of Georgia's DNA test last night." He paused as sympathy flooded his eyes. "They show what we expected."

Even though there would be no other answer, my heart still sank. I closed my eyes and nodded. My child was now forever and inextricably tied to her paternity. She would make her own choices for how to live with that, but part of me still wished she didn't have to. That she might have lived forever with a mystery instead of a horror.

I shook off the feeling and forced myself to focus on the present. Out of the corner of my eye, I caught a movement in the aisle. Montrose split the crowd like Moses at the Red Sea. But instead of a staff, the attorney used his ego and a smug grin. Tommy, looking lost and defeated, trailed behind him. I held my breath as we locked eyes. Would he recognize me? Would he wonder why I was there?

A vague recognition passed over his features, but then, as if he realized where he was and why he was there, he ducked his head and found his seat. I couldn't help but have some compassion on him.

"You okay?" Anthony asked.

I took in a quick breath and nodded.

"It'll be over soon." Anthony slipped through the gate and laid his briefcase on the table, ready to begin.

I eased back into my seat. Sandwiched between the end cap and Janine's shoulder, I felt secured rather than suffocated. The door in the back of the courtroom opened and a bailiff escorted John David to his seat. My stomach clenched. In a few minutes, I would have to look him in the eye and recount what he had done to me.

Had I really said I was ready?

No, I had lied.

Yet again.

A warm hand settled over my clenched fingers and

Janine's soft, soothing voice whispered in my ear. "Just breathe. Slow and easy. You can do this, Madeline. I know you can."

With a single nod, I sat up straight and tamped down the fear.

The bailiff called the gallery to order as Judge Wayne Peterson settled behind his desk. He glanced at both attorneys. "Counselors, are we ready for closing statements?"

Mr. Montrose shuffled his notes and said, "Yes, Your Honor."

Anthony rose. "Your Honor, if I may?"

"Yes, Mr. Lee?"

"I'd like to ask for a one-day continuance."

Montrose turned in his seat and cast an askance look toward Anthony. "Your Honor, in asking for a continuance at this late hour, the prosecution must know their case is weak and they're only trying to delay the inevitable."

Judge Peterson leaned his elbows on the desk and glared down at Anthony. I was glad I wasn't on the receiving end of that stare. But in the next moment, I realized my turn was forthcoming.

"I'm not inclined to belabor this trial any longer. Request denied, counselor."

"Then, Your Honor, I would like to call a rebuttal witness."

Judge Peterson looked even more irritated. "This is highly unusual, counselor."

"I understand that, Your Honor, but this witness only came forward and agreed to testify last night. She is critical in rebutting Mr. Montrose's argument that all of Mr. Billings's contact with women has been consensual."

Mr. Montrose gestured widely. "Your Honor, please. Counsel is now sounding desperate."

The judge looked from Anthony to Montrose. John David's arrogant regard hadn't faded. The judge pursed his lips and looked over at the jury. They waited quietly in various states of interest. After a moment, he nodded. "All right. I'll allow it, but, Mr. Lee, understand you are walking a very thin line right now."

"Yes, Your Honor, and thank you. The prosecution calls Madeline Williams."

As I stood, I caught Tommy's surprised inhale and watched as recognition dawned in his eyes. I looked back to Georgia and nodded. She unraveled the cords to her earbuds and fit them in her ears. I waited until I saw her thumb push play. Dad placed an arm around her shoulders, and Janine nodded her reassurance.

I turned to begin my walk to the witness stand. My mind returned to my first visit to the courtroom and watching the other victim enter the gallery. I could feel the tremble in my shoulders and the skittering along my nerves. Was I shaking any more than she?

As I approached the witness stand, I surveyed the jury. Some fidgeted, others sat still, but every eye watched me. Their expressions ranged from curiosity to irritation. The bailiff rushed the oath, repetition salting his words with a pat boredom.

And then it happened.

For the first time in thirteen years, I looked John David Billings in the eyes.

In one glimpse, all thirteen of those years disappeared, and I was once more standing before him in that horse stall. His eyes gleamed with that same self-satisfied smugness, the entitlement of privilege and money.

But in the next moment, I remembered. I was no longer that same innocent seventeen-year-old girl. My shoulders squared, my resolve firmed. I would not give him the satisfaction of seeing me cower.

"Please state your name for the record," Anthony said.

I tore my gaze from John David and leaned toward the microphone. "Madeline Williams." My voice was strong with only the slightest hint of a tremble.

"Ms. Williams, how do you know the defendant, John David Billings?"

"I knew John David from attending the Billings Cattle Auctions throughout my childhood." Anthony had prepared me for his line of questioning. He said he would begin with general information to lay the groundwork and lead up to the revelation of the rape and Georgia's paternity. I sat in the witness stand and answered his questions with a calm distance that belied my shaking hands.

No, we didn't socialize.

When I was seventeen I was dating a boy, and we were discussing marriage.

No, we were not sexually active. We were waiting. It was my choice, and he respected it.

No, I would never have consented to a sexual encounter with John David.

Yes, John David sexually assaulted me.

No, I did not report it.

I was scared I wouldn't be believed and there would be repercussions from his family.

Yes, I have a daughter. She's twelve years old.

I discovered I was pregnant two months after the rape.

Yes, John David Billings is her father.

Mr. Montrose erupted from his seated shouting his objections. The jury and gallery buzzed with discussion. John David's smugness evaporated. A stunned panic fell in its place. Tommy's mouth hung agape. His shoulders slumped. And Lisa Jean ...

*Oh, God* ... Lisa Jean.

Bobby's sister sat in the courtroom audience next to a blond woman about my age.

Lisa Jean stared at me. Her mouth dropped open. A hand covered it. Tears formed in her eyes. They fell to her cheeks. She heard, and she knew.

Reality dropped over me like a heavy, wet blanket. It was closing statement day. Of course, they would be there.

I closed my eyes.

*Bobby, I'm so sorry. You should have heard it from me.*

*Bang.*

*Bang.*

*Bang.*

Heart pounding, breath hiccuping, I flinched and looked for the source of the raps—the judge banging his gavel, calling for order. Shuddering, I searched for my family. Dad's cheeks were pale, and his lips bunched in a concerned frown. Janine fixed me with a steady look, nodding her reassurance. Georgia gazed at her iPod fulfilling my request to the letter.

The judge's irate tone pierced the din of the crowd. "Mr. Lee, I hope you have evidence to back up this testimony."

Anthony held a piece of paper aloft. "Your Honor, I'd like to admit these DNA test results of Georgia May

Williams as defense exhibit forty. They were taken last night at the Texas DPS by Richard Clark, a long-standing crime tech, and logged into evidence. Her DNA was tested using the rapid DNA testing protocol and compared to the DNA sample that is on file from Mr. Billings's previous felony conviction. And they prove Ms. Williams's statement." He turned and pointed to Georgia.

Dad tapped her on the shoulder, and she looked up. Anthony motioned for her to stand, and she did.

"Twelve-year-old Georgia May Williams is John David Billings's biological daughter."

Georgia stood tall and proud and gazed around the courtroom. Tears pricked my eyes. Queen Esther couldn't have stood before the king with more grace or aplomb.

"And she is the proof that Mr. Billings has indeed perpetrated a nonconsensual sexual act against Ms. Williams."

The gallery erupted again. The bailiff handed the results to the jury foreperson, who watched me, brows lifting as a considering gleam lit her eyes. Each member took time to thoroughly read the report as it passed from hand to hand. A few glanced from the paper to Georgia and then to John David. She had little resemblance to him in my opinion. But then, the eyes of a stranger would look at her without the love I held and might see something different.

John David leaned over and whispered furiously at his attorney. Montrose nodded and held up a hand, quieting John David's words.

"Cross examination, Mr. Montrose?" the judge asked.

The defense attorney nodded and rose. A cool, sanctimonious smile slipped over his lips. "Ms. Williams. You were seventeen you said when this happened? And Mr.

Billings here is a handsome man. Wealthy too. Do you really expect this jury to believe you weren't a willing participant? I understand the setting wasn't quite romantic enough for a young girl, but hormones are hormones, and they get the best of all of us. Are you sure your situation wasn't more along those lines?"

"Mr. Montrose, I am completely certain my experience with John David Billings was not consensual. It was rape. I never agreed to his actions, and I told him so repeatedly."

"So why come forward now? Is it a lust for vengeance? Opportunity to join in some sort of civil suit that will take the Billings family to the cleaners?"

"No, none of those things. For one, I wanted to help these women and make sure he doesn't hurt anyone else. But also ... I'm tired. I'm tired of living with the lies I told to keep my daughter safe. The lies that upended the life I always planned to have. Lies I chose to tell because of what John David did to me and the resulting pregnancy."

"So you admit you have a habit of lying?"

"Only when it came to protecting the nature of my daughter's conception." I scanned the jury panel, looking each in the eye searching for empathy, for understanding. "Which of you wouldn't do whatever it took to make sure your child grew up knowing only love instead of judgment and fear?"

"But we only have your word that what happened between you and John David Billings was rape."

"No, I told my pregnancy counselor and my father once I found out I was pregnant. I know they'll testify to that if necessary."

"Oh, so you cried rape after you discovered the

pregnancy. Seems awfully convenient to me, Ms. Williams."

"Objection! Argumentative."

"Sustained."

"Do you think anything about my life since John David raped me has been convenient, Mr. Montrose? Really? I broke up with the boy I loved, the boy who wanted to marry me. I left my home and moved to Austin holding down a job, raising a child, and going to school as a single mom. I worked my tail off to protect her and provide her a good life. What about any of that would you consider convenient? Why would I have kept this secret when I could have gone to the Billings, told them about the pregnancy, and demanded they pay me?"

Montrose's cheeks paled as shame stole across them. His mouth opened, then closed, unable to find accusations to counter my truths. Without another word, he sat back down. The audience erupted around us. The judge pounded his gavel against the wooden block, calling for order in the chaos, but the noise only grew.

Somehow the judge's voice cut through the din. "We will recess for lunch. Counselors, we will proceed with closing arguments in an hour." He turned to me. "You're dismissed from the stand, Ms. Williams."

I sat staring at the pandemonium my words, my truth, caused. My mind separated from my body just as it did the day of the rape. John David and Tommy argued as the reality of John David's impending future washed over them. Mr. Montrose sat stunned as he realized his fancy footwork couldn't dance around the blatant truth. Georgia stood and absorbed the scene.

I had spoken up. I had released the lie that held me captive to a singular event. My goal was done.

And I had no idea what would follow.

Would the truth set me free? Or would it unravel the life I created?

"Ms. Williams."

I heard the judge's voice, registered his patient urge. But still, I couldn't move.

My eyes found Dad and Janine.

And behind them, my angel.

I blinked.

He stood with a smile and extended his hand.

And finally, my body moved. I rose, and he disappeared. Just as I knew he would. *Thank You, Lord.*

I joined Anthony at the prosecutor's table. He waved over a bailiff and asked him for an escort out of the courtroom. Questions flew left and right from the reporters, but I focused on only one person.

Lisa Jean once again shoved her way toward me elbowing through the crowd with dogged intent. But instead of hatred and anger, her eyes were filled with shock and sorrow. She reached for me and wrapped me in a fierce hug. Her tears drenched my shoulder as years of hatred and animosity were wept away. "I'm so sorry, Madeline. All those things I've said—I don't know that I could have done what you did. I'm so sorry for everything. Can you ever forgive me?"

Tears flooded my eyes as I returned her grip. A heady blend of relief, joy, and surprise tumbled through me. I leaned into her, and we held each other upright under the deluge of released pain and regret. I smiled and whispered, "I already have."

# CHAPTER TWENTY-SEVEN

*Austin, Texas*
*May, 2000*

MADELINE UNWRAPPED THE FINAL PLATE, ADDED it to the stack, and shut the kitchen cabinet door. The dishes, compliments of a thrift store shopping spree, were chipped in various places and missing a plate and a couple of bowls from a full set. Water glasses from that same excursion and sippy cups from the ranch collection lined the next shelf, a comforting blend of ranch and city, mother and daughter.

Her new home, an apartment complex near downtown Austin, had seen better days. The roofs were a mishmash of varying shingle colors, and the shutters and stairwells could use a fresh coat of paint. But it was in a safe area, the landscaping was neatly trimmed, and the neighbors she'd met seemed welcoming and nice. Thrill pinged against her senses. She had done it. A new life for herself and Georgia had arrived.

"Where do you want this bag of clothes?" Dad asked as he held up a black trash bag by its red drawstrings.

Madeline glanced around the tiny living room already

packed with boxes and toddler toys. "Um, I guess just drop them in bathroom for now since we still have to put the bed frame together."

Dad returned a moment later scooting boxes and bags to make a wider path to the bedroom. "You ready to start on the furniture?"

Madeline nodded grateful for the hundredth time she'd decided to leave Georgia with Mrs. Johnson while she and Dad set up the apartment. Two-year-olds had the attention span of a gnat and the curiosity of a cat, a potentially lethal combination during a move.

Dad looped an arm around her shoulders and led her out to the rental van. "I know you wanted a second-floor apartment, Pumpkin, but you'll be glad for the first floor once we're done."

"I don't know what I would do without you, Dad." She said it in jest, but as he paused and looked down at her the truth and finality of the words sank deep into the memories of the past three years. The silence stretched, encompassing the future that lay before her like the unmapped landscape of a new world. She started work on Monday with a temp agency. Georgia would go to daycare. But the reality was she was twenty-years-old and on her own with a two-year-old child.

Dad squeezed her into his side. "You're gonna do just fine, Pumpkin. And I'm only an hour away for anything you need. Day or night."

Madeline tucked her head against his chambray shirt. All of a sudden, her new life felt more like saying goodbye to her old one. What was wrong with her? This was what she'd worked so hard to achieve. She had a degree and could provide for both of them. Georgia could safely grow up knowing only love and acceptance from those around her. Blue Springs was a chapter that was now closed.

"You know the ranch will always be your home, right, Pumpkin? The door's always open. No need to even call ahead."

Madeline snuggled deep into his arms and offered a silent prayer of thanks to God for all of His provision in her life, starting with the man she called Dad.

# CHAPTER TWENTY-EIGHT

*Red Lick, Texas*
*March, 2011*

"SO WE'LL TALK SOON, RIGHT?" LISA JEAN ASKED as she released my hands to wipe her tear dampened cheeks. Her earnest plea melted what little hurt remained between us after our earlier group cry.

"Here. Wait a minute." I tugged a tissue packet out of my purse and offered her something other than her sleeve.

She grinned then rolled her eyes. "Yeah, that's probably a better idea. Mascara's a pain to get out of clothing."

I chuckled and grabbed her free hand as she dabbed her face. "And yes, I'd like that. I'd like that a lot. Talking, that is." I savored the rush of peace that replaced all of the years of animosity. "I'm sorry—" I began as she pulled me into another hug.

"No, don't ever be sorry, Madeline. Let's just start over, okay?"

I closed my eyes, nodded against her shoulder, and gave her a tight squeeze. She returned it then released me and left with a final smile and a quick wave. As the door thumped closed behind her, the courtroom's regal serenity seemed to heave a relieved sigh. Now quiet and calm, it was hard to believe the chaos I caused within its walls.

My secret was out. The truth was spoken. The world hadn't crashed around me, though I also hadn't yet ventured out into it. But I had decided to trust God for the outcome. And I would hold to my decision. No matter what happened.

I turned and found Dad and Janine still sitting in our row talking quietly. Georgia leaned against another row tapping through her playlist trying to downplay her rampant curiosity over Dad and Janine's conversation. She tucked her iPod in a pocket, tugged out her earbuds, then slipped to my side.

I pulled her into my arms and drew slow circles across her back. "I can't tell you how proud I am of you, sweetie."

Georgia leaned into me. "Back at ya', Mom."

"You ready, Pumpkin?" Dad stood and, with a glance to Janine, gestured to the door. "I think we could all use some lunch right now."

I gave Georgia another squeeze, then pulled open the courtroom door. Blinding camera flashes welcomed us at the courtroom steps where the bailiffs had cordoned the press off at the main entrance. I glanced to Dad. "Think there's another way out?"

He looked around and found the sheriff's department door still open. "Let's go ask." He held out a hand to Georgia as his eyes focused on something behind me.

"Madeline."

That voice. Gone was the bluster and ego, but the billowing twang remained. Tommy. I cast a grateful look to Dad for his thoughtful intervention and nodded to Janine's questioning gaze. She followed them leaving the pair of us alone in the hall.

I turned and winced as his raw pain hit me. Compassion flooded me unchecked. We stood in silence, broken only by the call of a reporter or the flash of a camera.

Tommy spread his hands wide as remorse stooped his shoulders. "I never knew—never had any idea." He fell silent.

I had no words to give him. He had done nothing wrong to me, but I could not offer the forgiveness he sought.

"He's my son. And I should have done better by him. Should have held him accountable for so many things." Tommy's eyes fell to the floor. Shame blanched his cheeks. "I indulged him to offset my own failings, never understanding my son was not who I thought he was. I gave and he took, growing how he wanted, reckless, mean-spirited, entitled."

He looked up. A plea for understanding, for mercy.

My heart broke for the man, the father.

"I kept hoping he would change. And I thought he had when he married Maria. But I know now that was an act. What he did to you and the others was heinous. I know it is horribly inadequate and he may never say it, so let me say it for him." Tommy paused, and took in a fortifying breath. "I am so sorry."

I nodded. "Thank you." I couldn't hold Tommy responsible for John David's actions. It wasn't right or fair. Like my own dad, I had to believe Tommy had done the best he was able to do. But I sensed the conversation was about more than acknowledging a wrong.

Tommy glanced over his shoulder and lowered his

voice. "Looks like you've raised an amazing young woman, Madeline."

My hands clenched, fingernails digging into my palms. Yes, Georgia was amazing. And she was also his granddaughter.

Years dropped away as my initial fears of the Billings family lurched to the forefront of my mind. Would he fight me for her, pushing for custody and removing her from my life? Would he force her to visit John David in prison?

I took in a deep trembling breath. No. I trusted God enough to confess my secret. I would have faith in Him even now with my most valuable gift. He had come through for Abraham with Isaac centuries ago. Surely, He would do the same for me.

Tommy cleared his throat. "I won't force this in court. No one would win. And I'll make sure John David releases any parental rights to her." He paused as if at a loss for words. Or perhaps maybe daring to hope for the impossible.

"But if you would allow it ... I would like to know my granddaughter." He swallowed and glanced away, preparing himself for my response.

Air left my lungs. My clenched hands eased opened. *Thank You, Lord.* He had left the door open. Though the DNA results would forever link us, I could still walk away. I could say no. But as the idea worked through my mind, I caught sight of Georgia further up the hallway, and I realized it wasn't really my decision. She had a right to know her grandfather. My gaze returned to Tommy. The barest hope lit his eyes. He had lost so much in all of this too. "I think Georgia should be the one to decide."

His hazel eyes brightened to a light green, and a tentative smile lifted his cheeks.

"She's still very much a child, and I want her to stay that way for as long as possible. But I believe it should be her choice." My voice firmed, and my shoulders squared. "And if she says no, you have to respect that."

Tommy nodded. His chin trembled. "Of course. Of course. We'll take this as slow as we need to. Goodness knows you've been forced to do enough that you didn't want to do."

"Madeline?" Dad joined us, concern and curiosity warring in his eyes. "I've found a back door."

Tommy's cheeks reddened under my father's gaze. "I'm sorry, Jim. I-I don't know what else to say."

Dad nodded, but said nothing more.

Offering a weak smile, I gave Tommy what grace I could. "I'll talk with Georgia today."

He pulled a business card from his wallet. "All my contact information is listed here. However she feels most comfortable reaching out is fine with me."

I took the card and tucked it in my purse. "We'll be in touch."

His relief and hope radiated, lifting his stooped shoulders and brightening his eyes. "Thank you."

❧

A deputy sheriff had driven Dad's truck up to the back entrance and, with a recommendation for an out-of-the-way Mexican restaurant, we sped away from the courthouse. I texted Janine the location and, within thirty minutes, we were seated.

Food and drinks ordered, Georgia turned her curious gaze toward me. "What were you and that man talking about outside the courtroom?"

"Well, you." I smiled and her curiosity turned to confusion. "That man is John David's father, Tommy Billings."

Georgia's brow furrowed. "So that makes him my grandfather."

She fell silent, and I watched her contemplate the new branch on her family tree.

"What did he want?" She bit her lip and cringed. "Is he going to take me away from you?"

I reached an arm around her in the booth and hugged her to my side. "No, sweetie. In fact, he assured me he would never do that." My eyes flicked to Dad and Janine, and I read their mutual relief. I swallowed hard and nodded.

Georgia tucked her head in the crook of my shoulder and played with her napkin. Her voice thinned with concern. "What does he want?"

"You're his only grandchild. He wants to get to know you."

Her sky blue eyes filled with disbelief. "Really?"

"Really." I nodded.

Dad and Janine watched the conversation in silence. Knowing Dad would have his own opinions, and, of course, Janine would have a professional viewpoint, I appreciated their reticence. I had promised to let Georgia decide, and I would hold to my word. "What do you think?"

She wrinkled her brow. "I don't know. Do I have to answer right now?"

"No. Take all the time you want. And don't feel like you have to say yes. It's okay if you don't." Part of me desperately hoped she wouldn't open that door, but I pushed my own fears aside, overruling my protective instincts. *Not my will, Lord. Yours.*

The waitress delivered our drinks and said our food would be up in a few minutes. I released a relieved breath, thankful for the change in conversation. I glanced at Janine who smiled and said, "So Madeline, catch me up on everything. How do you like living in Austin?"

By the time we finished eating, court was back in session. Dad shot me a curious glance as he looked at his watch. I shook my head.

Anthony had said there was no need for us to stay beyond my testimony, and for that I was grateful. The emotional roller coaster and carb-laden meal had lulled my senses. I was past ready to head home. Dad paid for the meal and met us in the parking lot. I gave Janine a long hug and promised to let her know the results as soon as Anthony called.

"And let's keep talking, Madeline," she said. "The trial may be almost over, but you're just at the beginning of working through everything."

"I'll call when we get back to Austin to set up a regular time," I said, noticing her pink tinged his cheeks as she smiled at Dad. *Lord? They would be good for each other. Will You watch over this and help it develop?* A calm peace settled over my heart.

"Mom, is something going on between them?"

"I don't know." I smiled. "We'll just have to wait and see."

*♄*

We arrived back at the ranch about an hour later. Dad went up to see to the cattle, and Georgia grabbed a book and headed to her room. I crashed on the couch, magazine in my lap, and listened to the ticking of the clock, waiting for my phone to ring. I tried not to think about my part in it all. Tried not to think about the impact of my testimony, for good or ill. I tried, but I failed.

A little while later, Georgia and I made dinner while Dad washed up from the barn. He joined us as we set the table. Food was served and the blessing said. I picked up my fork just as my phone rang.

Dad looked up from his plate, and Georgia put down her glass. I read the name on the caller ID and nodded. A quiver shook my hand as I answered the call. "Hello?"

"The jury came back from deliberations with a unanimous vote. Guilty on all charges." Jubilation rang in Anthony's words. "Sentenced to fifteen years, and he'll serve at least ten even with good behavior. We did it, Madeline."

Tears streamed down my cheeks as I looked toward Heaven. "Yes, we did."

# CHAPTER TWENTY-NINE

*Blue Springs, Texas*
*March, 2011*

D AD'S LANDLINE RANG FOR THE TWENTIETH TIME since word of the sentencing broke and the fifth time since dawn. He took a last draw on his coffee and rose. I thought he might answer it that time, but instead, he pulled the phone off the wall and yanked out the cord. "That's enough of that." He laid the phone on the counter and proceeded to do the same with the other extensions.

Georgia grinned, and I couldn't help my giggle. It had probably rung more in the last two hours than it had all last week. But it did remind me of a call I needed to make. I grabbed my phone and left my half-finished breakfast on the table.

"Samuel Kitteridge."

"Good morning, Dr. K."

"Madeline, what is going on?" His usual easy tone was strained with worry. "I'm fielding calls from the press left, right, and sideways about a court case you were involved in. They said you were raped?"

I flinched at his words, but the concern that undercut

his tone made me smile. "Yes, the reports are correct. I'm sorry I've been focused more on holding myself together and didn't consider what the hospital would experience. I should have warned you."

"Don't worry about that. I'm just so sorry to hear of your experience." He paused and I could feel his concern. "You never mentioned Georgia's father, but I figured it was due to a bad break up or a death. I never thought it could be from a violation."

"No, I didn't tell anyone. It wasn't something I wanted Georgia growing up knowing."

"Well," he said, "I always knew you were a wonderful coworker and employee, but you are also an amazing woman."

My cheeks heated at his praise. "Oh, no, I'm not amazing at all. Just trying to figure out my life. Like every other woman, I'm sure."

Dr. K ignored my deferral and marveled yet again at my wherewithal and bravery. "I don't know many women who could have made such a difficult decision, let alone any teenagers. You are truly remarkable. I hope you realize that."

Embarrassed by his words, I thanked him and tried to shift the conversation back to damage control. "I hadn't planned to be back in the office until Monday, but I can put together a statement for the hospital and email it to you if you want."

"No, no." Professionalism returned, but the caring undertone remained. "I can handle that. You spend the time with your family. The chaos can wait."

I chuckled. "Unfortunately, the chaos found my dad's

phone. I fully expect camera crews to camp out at the ranch's entrance as soon as they can find it."

Dr. K laughed, then his voice grew serious. "Let me know if you need anything, Madeline. Anything at all. The entire hospital is behind you."

I thanked him again and ended the call. He hadn't condemned me as a victim. Instead, he'd praised me and acknowledged the difficulty of my choices. On top of that, he'd said the whole hospital, all my coworkers, supported me.

I closed my eyes as the knowledge seeped into my heart, washing over all my fears and doubts. Was it possible that, in addition to telling a lie, I had also believed one? Would his reaction be isolated or shared? I looked at Dad and found his proud smile beaming at me.

The phone buzzed with an incoming text, and I had to laugh.

"What is it?" Georgia asked as she picked up her dishes and took them to the sink.

I sank down in my chair, stunned at the texter's identity. "It's Lisa Jean. She wants to meet for lunch before we go back to Austin."

"Are you going to do it?"

"Yeah, I'm looking forward to it." I tapped my acceptance and we set a time for Saturday.

Dad cleared the rest of the dishes and refilled our coffee mugs. He pulled a ranching magazine out of the mail stack and began to leaf through the pages while I continued my text conversation with Lisa Jean, awed by the turn of events.

"Mom?" Georgia sat with a bare foot tucked beneath her and stared at me.

"Hmm?"

"Do you think you'll ever talk to Bobby again?"

My breath caught. *I really need to better prepare myself for her questions.* "I don't know," I managed through my tightened chest. "A lot has happened over the years, and we're much different people than we were in high school."

I paused. Though I didn't want to burst her optimism completely, she needed to hear a bit of realism. "I don't know that he'll ever forgive me for what I did. Even if he knows the truth. He's paid a big price for my lies."

Georgia's lips turned down as the hearts, flowers, and possibilities faded from her eyes. We each took a magazine from the mail stack and began to pass a few hours learning about the latest in farming and ranching.

⁂

Later that morning, I wondered if Georgia had an inside source. The call came from a number I didn't recognize. Usually, I sent those to voicemail, if I didn't ignore them altogether. But in that moment, something encouraged me to answer.

"Um, hi, Madeline."

A low warm drawl filled my ear. I sat up in the chair and gripped the table. My heart stuttered. "Bobby?"

Georgia's eyes widened and a delighted smile wreathed her face.

I turned away, unwilling to leap to any of her conclusions.

"Yeah," Bobby said. "Um, I heard about what happened yesterday. I ... we have a lot to talk about."

A weak chuckle slipped between my lips. "Yeah, you could say that."

"Will you meet me today? There's a coffee shop downtown on the square."

I savored the voice I thought I'd never hear again and whispered, "I'd like that."

"Is one o'clock okay?"

"I'll see you then."

I ended the call and waited for Georgia's response.

A gleam lit her eyes. "So what are you going to wear?"

❦

The Friday lunch hour had the town square hopping with people. I ended up squeezing my X3 into a narrow slot between a dually pickup and a Ford Excursion. Climbing out of the SUV, I nervously smoothed invisible wrinkles from my blue sundress. Georgia was disappointed by my limited outfit options, but she was pleased I had at least thought to bring the dress. I stepped onto the sidewalk and tried to distract my anxious thoughts with some window shopping.

A couple with three kids walked purposefully toward the shoe store. Well, the couple did at least. Their blond pre-teen son paused to look in all of the store windows while the two younger, dark-haired girls dragged on their parents' hands, more interested in the playground than in their actual destination. The girls looked to be twins and each clutched a stuffed animal. One dropped her bear and let out a wail. The mother paused and scooped her up while the son ran to grab the toy and offered it to her.

"Matthew, thank you so much," the mother said. "You are the best big brother."

The woman's slow Alabama drawl caught my ears. I paused mid-stride. "Mrs. Hastings?"

She looked up from her children and flashed a wide smile. "Madeline Williams?" She adjusted the little girl on her hip and ran a hand over her son's head. "Matthew, go run on with your daddy and Maya. I'll follow in just a bit." The boy did as she asked, but turned and pointed to us when he reached his father and sister.

The man had a full head of salt and pepper hair, but when he looked back I knew he was Pastor Mike.

"Oh, my goodness. How are you?" Mrs. Hastings asked as she drew closer. "We heard about everything. Are you okay?"

As I met her gaze, I found only concern and care in its depths. "Yes, I'm actually really good."

Remembrance reflected in her eyes, and a blush stole over her cheeks. "And your daughter?"

"Georgia is wonderful." The little girl shoved her bear toward my head and giggled. I smiled and stroked her pudgy arm. "And look at your beautiful family."

Mrs. Hastings grinned. "It's amazing how things work out, isn't it? We got a call out of the blue from a crisis pregnancy counselor in Austin saying she had heard we were looking to adopt." She paused and shook her head. "I don't know how she knew, but we are so grateful to God for how He arranged everything." She nodded toward the boy and her smile turned misty. "We couldn't have asked for a better answer to our prayers. Matthew is an absolute gift."

The little girl shifted in her arms, and Mrs. Hastings bounced her on one hip. She ran a hand across her back as she clung to her like a koala bear to a tree. "And then we met Maya and Fatima on a mission trip to a Guatemalan orphanage. We knew within days they belonged in our family too."

Matthew ran back and tugged on his mom's elbow. "Mom, they've got the shoes I want. The green and blue Nikes. Come see."

Mrs. Hastings flashed an apologetic smile. "We are so thrilled, but it is definitely a much busier life." She glanced down and said, "Matthew, this is Ms. Williams. She was one of my students a few years ago. Say hello."

"Hello," came the dutiful response. "Mom? Will you come?" Hope and urgency lit his eyes.

"It's great to see you," I said with an amused smile.

She nodded then sobered. "Madeline, I don't mean to sound patronizing, but the choices you made had to be the most difficult—I am so proud of you for making them."

"Thank you." I nodded and watched them go, praising God for His provision and mercy. When I turned back, I prayed again, but this time it was for wisdom and healing.

※

The whirr of the espresso machine didn't make a dint in the conversations that flowed as fast as the coffee. I looked around the crowded room, but found no one who resembled Bobby, even in passing. With a start, I realized I might not recognize him at all.

A breath later, the air thickened and my senses focused. I turned and found Bobby standing in the entrance holding the door wide and staring at the customers. He was leaner, his face harder and his frame chiseled.

Gone was the boyish charm, and, in its place, was an edge of awareness, an anticipation of danger. Poised to strike at the first sign of trouble. His eyes found mine, and a shiver whispered over my skin. Despite my concern, I was drawn to him like a magnet. I reached his side and murmured, "Hey."

He nodded. "Sorry, I didn't realize how crowded it would be when Lisa Jean suggested it."

"No, it's okay with me." I glanced around to search for an empty table, but found none. A barista yelled out a name and a drink order and Bobby's shoulders stiffened. "If you want, we can sit out in the park instead. I'm not that thirsty."

Relief flashed through his eyes. He gave a quick shake of his head. "Crowds aren't my thing. Sorry."

I offered a sympathetic smile. Lisa Jean hadn't lied about the PTSD. Crowds had never bothered him before, though he always had preferred the woods and a tree stand.

We crossed the street and entered the park. In a couple of hours, the place would be crawling with kids, but for now, the playground was quiet. We settled on the swings just as we had on our last official date. I darted a quick glance over to him and saw the soft surprise of a familiar memory pass over his features.

A glint lit his eyes as he pushed back in his swing, but he said, "I can't remember the last time I actually swung in one of these things."

My heart fell. He hadn't remembered. Was that part of the PTSD as well? Had he lost time too? I glanced at him again and read the reticence in his shoulders. He shot a quick look my way, and I caught the reluctance in his eyes. Surprise washed over me. He was feeling his way in this. Trying not to push, only to offer an opening and allow my reaction. Trying to read me as I tried to read him.

Feeling my confidence returning, I said, "Well, I don't know about you, but the last time I sat on a swing was here with you." I watched as my admission registered.

A small smile danced around his lips then disappeared. "Yeah, that's right."

We fell silent again. I swiveled in my seat watching him, but not too closely. War had changed him—as it probably would every person who experienced it.

And yet, in some ways, he was still so familiar. The golden hazel of his eyes, the soft curl of his hair as it grew back in from the military's razor. I ached for the boy I remembered, even as my heart broke for the man sitting next to me.

Who would he have been if not for my lie? Who would we be? Two semi-strangers seated in a park surrounded by memories? Or two partners in a marriage watching our children play in the sand? I would never know. A sad sigh eased between my lips. So much was lost.

"Hey, don't do that." His soft voice whispered over me. Contrition and longing wrapped around the words.

"I'm so sorry, Bobby. For lying to you. For how you

found out. I never wanted to hurt you." I stumbled over my words. Inadequate, but no less heartfelt.

"I know. And I'm sorry too. For so many things." He ducked his head. "But mostly for leaving you."

I glanced up, stunned. "I didn't give you much of a choice."

He shook his head. "No, I should have known there was more going on, Mads. The words you said, how you said it happened, those actions weren't ones the girl I loved would have taken. And even if you had made that one mistake, it shouldn't have been enough to make me walk away. I should have stuck by you. I'm the one who is sorry, Mads. I'm sorry for leaving you to handle it all on your own."

Tears filled my eyes at the torment I caused, and yet, my heart lurched. He still thought of me as Mads.

Bobby cleared his throat. "I was too young. Immature. And I was so hurt. The life I thought we'd live together vanished in a second, and I just couldn't wrap my brain around what you'd said. All I wanted to do was get as far away from here as possible."

He paused his swing. I felt more than saw his movement through my sudden tears. I glanced up and found his eyes, sincere and bright, staring at me.

He reached over to grab my hand but stopped the impulse. He gave his head a tiny shake as if reminding himself he had no right to touch me now. "I've looked back on that day more than you'll ever know." He glanced away and lowered his voice. "Lisa Jean said she told you about the PTSD."

"That's my fault, Bobby. You wouldn't have gone if I'd told the truth."

His eyes found mine again, and he shook his head. "No, Mads. That's not your responsibility at all. Even though your words might have pushed me further toward the Army, I made my own choices about enlisting." He smashed his lips together as pain filled his gaze. "And things I didn't choose happened to me. But absolutely none of them are your fault."

I wiped my cheeks with the back of my hand. It would be a good while before I could accept his reprieve.

He flashed a quick, but genuine smile. My breath caught. It was the faintest glimpse, but there he was, my Bobby.

"There were good things that happened there too. I made some great friends, brothers in combat, and local kids. I have good memories to go along with the bad. There was this one." He fell silent and blinked hard.

I placed a hand on his arm. The wiry muscle under his tanned skin flexed then settled. "Bobby, if it's too painful, you don't have to tell me."

He shook his head. "No, my counselor says it's good to talk about it. To share the experience. It helps release the memories and their power over me—psychobabble, I know. But it does seem to work."

I nodded. I knew.

"So this kid, Jamaal. He was about twelve and loved to hunt and track. He was the son of one of our interpreters. Great kid." Bobby chuckled at the memory. "I actually convinced him there were snipe over there."

Unable to help myself, I laughed then rolled my eyes. "You didn't."

"Yep. Told him they had stowed away on the American airplanes, and they all rushed out after dark. But I knew how to trap them."

I watched his eyes flood with unshed tears, and I shook my head. I desperately didn't want to know, but he needed to tell me.

"Well, this one morning, the unit was out on reconnaissance searching for landmines to clear. I didn't know it, but Jamaal tagged along. I had convinced him the previous night we, the unit I mean, were going snipe hunting. I don't know why."

He spread his hands wide and shook his head. "I guess I just wanted him to have some innocent fun instead of more atrocity. He called to me from out in one of the fields saying he had found the tracks. I was terrified. He was standing in the middle of a field that Intelligence reported had been recently mined." His voice trembled and I watched the memory play out over his face.

*Lord, please no.*

"I told him to stand perfectly still, but he was too excited. He took a wrong step, and in a flash ..."

His words trailed off, but I could finish the story without them. "Bobby, I'm so sorry. That's horrible."

"Yeah. The crazy thing is, he had a smile on his face. He'd been so happy to find a darn snipe." Bobby ran his hand over his face. "I'm sorry. I didn't mean to scare you with one of my horror stories. That's not why I wanted to talk. I just wanted you to know I understand why you did it. Why you chose to lie." He let out a long slow breath.

"And I don't blame you one bit." He shook his head. "Don't get me wrong, I was angry for the longest. But the further I got into my training, and when we were deployed, my unit became my family. And I understood your instincts to protect family at all costs."

He looked out over the square, but his eyes were seeing something much further away.

"Over there, they were all I had. You lost your mom and all your grandparents. We had only been dating for a little while. Your dad and that baby—Georgia—they were really all you had."

He looked me in the eye, and I read the sincerity in his gaze.

"I'm sorry it's taken me so long to tell you."

Something in me shattered. It was as if a shell lay broken in a million pieces. And my heart began to truly feel again. I reached over and slipped my hand into his. We sat in silence bumping into each other as the swings swayed. I closed my eyes, savoring the sensation of sitting next to him once more.

"I've missed you. So much." The words were out before I could stop them, but their truth couldn't be denied.

Bobby linked his calloused fingers with mine. His thumb swept over my index finger, then lingered over the soft skin at the base of my thumb. "You know I wanted to marry you, right? I even had the ring picked out. Just a matter of saving up for it."

I swallowed hard. I had thrown away so much out my own desperation. "I didn't know about the ring, but about wanting to marry me? Yeah, I had a good idea. You weren't exactly subtle."

He chuckled. "Yeah, guess I wasn't."

"We were so young. And I was scared. But I should have trusted you. Trusted God."

He squeezed my hand. "I understand."

My feet dug into the sand stopping the sway. "You know, I haven't dated, not once, since we broke up. Coworkers have tried to set me up. I always told them I was too busy raising Georgia. But that wasn't true." I turned, clasped both of his hands, and took a deep breath. "It's because I've never stopped loving you."

I watched the words register in his golden eyes, but instead of joy, I found sorrow. Taking a quick breath, I said, "I know a lot has happened. We're both very different people with very deep wounds that need to heal. But I would like to get to know you again. Would that be possible?"

Bobby shook his head. "Don't, Mads. Don't offer if it's out of any guilt or grief. I couldn't take that."

"No, it's not out of guilt. Or grief. But for the most important reason. What we had back then was real. It was something lives are built on. I'd like to see if it's still there." I glanced away. "That is, if you want to."

Bobby gave a slow nod, and then I saw it. That look he would give me. Only me. He slid his hand over my cheek, and he rubbed his thumb across the smooth skin. My heart pummeled my ribs as breath caught in my lungs.

I closed my eyes and felt his warm sigh. Then a moment later, his kiss. As our lips melded together, the years and traumas disappeared. We were simply Bobby and Madeline, high school sweethearts sitting on the swings in our favorite part of the park.

When he pulled away, he leaned his forehead against mine. His low voice rumbled, "Well, now what?"

I blinked and pulled back still clutching one of his hands. "I don't know. I have a life in Austin. And now, things I need to heal from."

"Yeah. And I need a job that gives me the time to continue to heal."

We fell silent, allowing the moment, the responsibilities, and the needs to simply hang between us. Not separating, but bonding us on our new journey together.

After a few minutes, Bobby cleared his throat. His gaze flicked to mine, and his lips lifted in a tiny smile. "So tell me about her."

My heart clenched at the flash of pain his eyes. I hated that Georgia remained a sore subject for him, but maybe with time he would come to love her, too. "She's wonderful. And I can't imagine my life without her."

Bobby surprised me with his next words. "I'd, uh, I'd like to meet her."

Relief eased through me like a sigh. I turned in my swing to look him full in the eyes. "I'd like that, too." Heat rose to my cheeks as I remembered her earlier enthusiasm. "And I know she would love to meet you."

Surprise lit his eyes.

"She asked Dad to tell her our story a few days ago once she learned the truth. The girl's a budding romantic, and I'll have you know your call only made her heart-and-flower dreams bigger."

"Ah." He smiled and hopped off his swing.

I shot him a curious glance then felt him move behind me and grab the chains on my swing. He pulled me back to his chest and held me there for a long moment. Sandalwood and clove permeated the air. I inhaled and choked back a sob at the aching familiarity of his cologne. A moment later, he released me, and I began to swing.

We had so much more to discuss. So much ground to cover, memories to share and healing to achieve, but as he pushed and I soared, it was enough. We were enough.

# CHAPTER THIRTY

*Blue Springs, Texas*
*March, 2011*

A SLEEPY "G'MORNIN'" TURNED MY HEAD. I couldn't help my fond smile at Georgia's rumpled hair and wrinkled sleep shirt. She joined me on the couch, and I laid my Bible aside.

"Morning, sweetie," I said. "You want some breakfast?"

She shook her head. "Not—not right now," she said around a yawn.

I lifted an arm, and she snuggled into my side.

"I've been giving it a lot of thought, Mom."

"What's that?" I ran my fingers through her hair, trying the tame the bedhead.

"Mr. Billings's request. To get to know me."

My fingers paused, then continued their run through the honey-colored length.

"And I think I want that. I mean, we're family. He's part of me, and I'm a part of him. I think I'd like to get to know him." She turned and craned her neck toward me.

I pulled my fingers from her hair and leaned back. She

had given the matter serious consideration, but it seemed she was still open to input.

"I mean, it wasn't his fault what happened, was it? I don't see how it could be. So I can't hold that against him, right?"

This child, no, this young woman, astounded me. "No, you really can't. John David made his own choices."

"So will you ask Mr. Billings to come over?"

"Sure. When do you want to meet?"

"What about this afternoon? Do you think that's too soon for his schedule?"

"Sweetie, I think Mr. Billings would move his entire world to spend even a minute with you."

⁂

"Talk about going home," I murmured as I pulled open the door to Uncle Richie's pizza parlor. Lisa Jean waved at me from a booth. I smiled and moved to join her. The parlor was starting to pack in with families and road crew workers. Demolition was underway on the north end of the expansion that would take out the old Billings Cattle Auction building.

"Hey, Madeline," Richie called from behind the counter. His coal-black hair still shined like it was coated with shoe polish, and his smile was wide and welcoming. "You want to pick up a few shifts?"

I laughed. "Not right now, but maybe one day."

He grinned and gestured toward the booth. "I've already got your order in. I think I remember what you used to get on your lunch break."

"Stromboli with extra marinara," we chorused.

"And they say the mind is the first thing to go," he chortled. "Go sit down. Lisa Jean's waiting for you." His smile softened as he said, "And hey, it's good to see you again. Don't be a stranger."

As soon as I settled into the booth and greetings were said, Lisa Jean leaned across the table. "So I'm dying to know. Bobby said y'all talked yesterday."

Same old Lisa Jean, looking for tidbits and gossip, but I didn't mind.

Her eyes glowed, and her smile invited confession. "When I saw him last night after work, he looked better than he had in months. I'm guessing y'all's conversation went well?"

I nodded. "Yeah. It went really well. There's a long way to go, but I'm hopeful."

Lisa Jean glanced at my bare and misshapen fingernails and grinned. "Let me know if you want to go with me to get our nails done some time."

I couldn't help my blush and rueful chuckle. She must have known all along how much I had hated our nail dates. "Sure." I nodded. "But it's my treat."

My phone buzzed inside the pocket of my purse. Wincing, I glanced from Lisa Jean to the noise maker. "I'm sorry, I have to get this. It could be Georgia or the hospital."

"No, go ahead. It'll be fun to watch you in boss lady mode."

I snorted then pulled out the phone and read the text. "Oh, um. It's not work or Georgia. It's um ... it's Bobby."

Heat seared my neck and cheeks as Lisa Jean's grin widened bigger than the Cheshire cat's.

I thumbed open the text and read his sweet request asking me to dinner the next evening. Biting my lip, I texted back my agreement slipped my phone back in its pocket.

"Well?" Lisa Jean leaned across the table once again, but this time her conspiratorial air was softened with hints of remorse.

Awe and bemusement swirled through me. "We're going out to dinner tomorrow night before Georgia and I head back to Austin."

"That's great." Lisa Jean nodded and played with her napkin, suddenly nervous. "You know, back in high school, I couldn't tell you ... couldn't show how much I wanted to like you. You were so different from me, from Mama, and I was so afraid that if you and Bobby dated, he would leave or forget about me. It's crazy, I know—and he did end up leaving anyway." She fell silent. "But I wanted to say I'm sorry about how I treated you back then."

Stunned, I nodded. I was loved and missed by more people than I'd ever realized. Bobby, Uncle Richie, and now Lisa Jean. I never recognized all her animosity and vitriol had hidden a hurting heart.

Holding her gaze, I allowed the moment time to linger giving us each the opportunity to heal just a bit more. "I can understand that. And I always wondered if I missed out on something being an only child."

Lisa Jean's eyes gleamed and a teasing smile so reminiscent of her brother's stole over her lips. "Well, if you and Bobby get married, we can be sisters."

My heart fluttered at the thought. *Can you really restore*

*the years the locusts ate, Lord?* Everything thus far was looking promising. Warmed by her words, I nodded. "I'd like that."

"Okay, girls," Richie said as he laid two dishes overloaded with saucy Stromboli on the table. "Dig in. And I want empty plates coming back to the kitchen, you hear?"

Lisa Jean bowed her head and began the blessing. I closed my eyes as her words of thanksgiving flowed between us, and I lifted my own silent, simple prayer. *Thank You, Lord.*

꿈

The doorbell rang just as the clock turned over to three. I had been home maybe an hour from my lunch with Lisa Jean, and my amazement at the experience still hadn't worn off. I opened the door and found Tommy clutching a photo album. He tugged off his Stetson as he followed me through the door.

"Pictures?" I asked glancing at the album.

Tommy blushed. "Yes, unless you think it's too soon."

I shook my head. "No, it's actually perfect, but I'll let her explain."

Relief washed over Tommy's face. "I'm glad. I-I wasn't sure, but it felt right, you know?"

We walked into the kitchen where Dad and Georgia were already settled. "Would you like some tea?"

"Tea would be nice, thank you." He glanced over at Dad and dipped his head. "Jim. Good to see you."

Dad nodded then turned to Georgia. "Sugar pie, this is Tommy Billings, your other grandfather. Tommy, if you don't mind, I've got some calves to attend to. I'm sure you understand."

Tommy nodded. Hurt flashed in his eyes, but I figured he had to appreciate Dad's discomfort. Dad and I had planned for him to introduce the two, and then he could stay or go, whichever he felt most comfortable doing. I was disappointed he opted to leave, but I didn't say anything. Dad would make peace with this in his own way and in his own time.

I was surprised when he turned as he opened the back door. "Stop by the barn before you leave, if you would. I'd like to hear your view on the new bull I just added to the herd."

Tommy brightened at the invitation. "I'd be glad to, Jim."

Dad nodded and with his customary, "Call me if you need me." He pulled the door shut and headed to the barn.

Tommy grinned and held out his hand for Georgia to shake. "Georgia, I'm so proud to meet you."

Georgia took his hand, gave it a few shakes, and tossed a quick glance my direction. I nodded my encouragement, and she offered him the chair next to her.

Tommy's cheeks glowed as he sat and laid the album on the table. He patted its cover. "I figured you might have a few questions, so I brought some pictures."

Georgia grinned and reached for the album, flipping open the cover. The first photo filled the page. A much younger and thinner Tommy and a beautiful blonde woman stared out from the paper. Joy radiated from the pair. He sported a tan western suit, and she wore a long white dress complete with a white cowboy hat and boots.

Tommy cleared his throat and blinked hard. Curious, I

caught his eye. He glanced away and ran a stubby finger over the woman in the picture. "Georgia, this is Winnie Billings, your grandmother."

My jaw dropped. No one had ever spoken of John David's mother, except for rumor and innuendo. It was almost as if John David had been dropped off on Tommy's doorstep by the stork.

"She's beautiful, Mr. Billings," Georgia breathed.

Tommy blushed then flicked a worried glance toward me. "Please call me, um, Tommy?"

I smiled and gave him a reassuring nod. She had to call him something and *Grandpa* was a little too personal—at least at this point.

Tommy grinned and leaned back in his chair, settling in for the visit. "Yes, she is. I fell for her at first sight. She was a rodeo queen. Won every roping competition she entered and nearly half the hearts she met."

Georgia looked at Tommy's hand and asked, "But you're not married anymore?"

Tommy grimaced. "Well, here's the second skeleton for your closet, darlin'. Winnie, much as I loved her, loved my bank account more. She was sure I'd finance her run on the rodeo circuit for as long as she batted those gorgeous blue eyes at me. It wasn't long after we were married that she turned up pregnant with John David."

Georgia's face fell. "I guess she wasn't happy about that."

"No, darlin', she wasn't. I was overjoyed, though. When she gave me a son, I thought our family was complete." He wiped his brow and lifted one side of his mouth in a half-smile. "And for a little while it was."

He cast a pain-filled glance my way. Sympathy settled

over my heart, and I realized why he had always commented about my mom and dad. He'd been jealous, not of Dad winning Mom, but of their happy marriage.

Pain flared in his eyes, but he smothered it. "I didn't intend for this to be a sad affair. I've got something else I want to show you." He flipped a few pages over. Unfamiliar faces peered out from photos of varying sizes, but Tommy seemed focused on finding one in particular. He flipped another page, then tapped a small photo of a boy in a cowboy outfit riding a stick pony. "There it is."

Georgia stared at the photo then shot Tommy a curious glance. "Is that you?" she asked with a small smile.

Tommy nodded. "Yep, when I was about your age. That pony there was the finest steed in all of east Texas."

I couldn't help the grin that formed as I heard his old bluster return. Perhaps this day was about more than introductions. Perhaps there was healing to be found for someone other than me.

Tommy regaled Georgia with stories of his childhood and listened intently to her talk about her school project. "I'd like to help with that," he said. "That is, if it's okay with you, Madeline."

I glanced at Georgia. Her heart was in her eyes and hope brightened her cheeks. "Sure, Tommy, I think that'd be really nice."

Tommy blushed then flipped the pages in the album. He tugged out a photo of himself standing in front of a caramel-colored calf and then one of Winnie atop a loud-colored paint horse. "I'd like you to have these, Georgia. If you want them."

Tears filled Georgia's eyes. "I'd love them. I'll make copies for my project and then get them back to you."

"No, darlin'. They're yours. You do with them what you want."

Georgia flung her arms around Tommy's neck. "Thank you. I'll put them in frames and hang them in my room."

They talked for a little while longer, then Tommy's phone buzzed. He looked embarrassed. "Sorry, I thought I'd turned that off."

I glanced at the clock. It was just after five. "You know, Dad wanted to show you that bull. He should be about ready to come back down. You want to go check it out?"

Tommy nodded. "Yes, yes. I'd like that a lot. Would you do me the favor of walking up with me, Madeline?"

I could tell by the question lurking in his eyes there was more to his request. I nodded. "Georgia, sweetie, why don't you go get cleaned up and start pulling things out for dinner. I'll be back in a little bit."

Georgia nodded. As she rose and gathered up her new pictures, she said, "I'd like to see you again sometime, Tommy. If you'd like to."

Pride and joy radiated from his eyes. "I'd like that more than anything, Georgia."

Georgia's answering smile warmed my heart. I was incredibly glad for her. Despite the skeletons he brought, I could tell she thought answers were much better than mystery.

※

Tommy and I walked in a companionable silence toward

the barn. I watched as he looked around at the cattle and the land. After a while, he said, "She's amazing. Just amazing."

I smiled. "Yeah, sometimes I can't believe she's my daughter." He shot me a concerned glance, and I said, "I take you at your word about only wanting to be a part of her life."

He nodded. "There's something I think you should know. Something that Georgia doesn't need to know."

I looked at him and waited.

"After the sentencing and before John David was taken to the jail, I asked him why. Why you, why them. Why do this?"

I flinched, uncertain I wanted this type of closure.

"He looked me in the eye and said, 'Why not?'" Tears filled Tommy's eyes.

I shook my head unable to make any sort of sense out of the explanation. But I prayed God would comfort Tommy in the coming days and months.

We neared the barn, and Tommy touched my arm, pausing our walk. "Madeline, I never thought the boy I loved and raised could become so unfeeling, so wrapped up in himself. I have no idea what I did that made him that way, but I'll do whatever it takes to make up for his actions."

"Tommy, none of this is your fault. John David's actions were his alone."

Tommy winced and glanced around the barn lot. "I know that, but I can't help thinking that I could have done something to stop it. If his mama hadn't left when he was just a boy. If I'd taught him how to treat women instead of letting him figure it out on his own—"

I placed a hand on his shoulder and looked him in the eyes. "Don't go down that road. The 'what-ifs' will send you spinning. Trust me, I've been there."

Tommy nodded.

The door to the barn office opened, and Dad stuck out his head. Casting a concerned glance my way, he asked, "Everything go okay?"

I smiled and stepped back. "Couldn't have gone better. But I need to get back and help Georgia with dinner. We'll see you again sometime, Tommy."

"Thank you again, Madeline. Anything you need, I'll be there."

With a new appreciation for the doors God was opening, I left the two men in Georgia's life to work out their own peace and future.

꧁

After dinner, Georgia sat at the kitchen table with an assortment of photos spread out across the surface. A poster board lay on the far end. She had filled the white space with a tree and drawn two large branches and two smaller branches leading off each side.

She'd scanned the pictures of Tommy and Winnie using Dad's old printer and taped the copies to two branches on one side of the tree. Her neat printing listed their names, dates of birth, occupations, and relation to her under the pictures. She was currently sorting through photos of me and Dad trying to choose the ones she liked best.

"What about this one?" I pointed to a photo of me at college graduation.

She shook her head. "Nah, that funny hat covers most of your head. It's hard to tell who you are."

I chuckled. That cap was in a box somewhere back at the house, a treasured memory and keepsake. But I agreed it probably wasn't my best photo.

"I like this one of Grandpa." She picked up one of him standing next to the livestock trailer, straw hat in hand and sheepish grin on his face. I had snapped it for a college project.

"Yeah, I like that one too."

"I've got another picture for you to add." Dad's voice was husky as he reached for his wallet and pulled out a small rectangle. The edges were bent and rubbed, and it looked like it was folded at one corner. He joined us at the table and laid the small photo on the tree.

I swallowed hard. "Mom." Clad in her white nurse's uniform and white hat, it was her class photo.

"Georgia, this is your Grandma Georgia. I know your mom has told you what she remembers of her. But one of these days, I'd like to tell you both what I remember too."

I leaned in close. "Thank you, Dad."

"It's time, Pumpkin."

Georgia taped Mom's photo alongside Dad's and wrote the same information under their photos, checking with him for birthdates. She pulled another picture out from under the poster board.

John David stared out from its depths. It was the same photo I had seen in the newspaper on Sunday. "Where did you get that?"

Georgia shot me an uncertain glance as she taped the photo on one of the thicker tree branches. "It didn't feel right asking Tommy for a picture of John David. So I cut it out of the paper. Do you think that's okay?"

"I think that was very thoughtful of you, Georgia." I felt Dad's squeeze and asked the question we both wondered. "What are you going to say about John David in class?"

She picked up a yellow marker and drew a large cross between John David and herself. My vision blurred, but my ears heard her simple explanation.

"I'm going to tell them what you've always told me. God is my Father. It's the truth. John David Billings was just how He chose to get me here." Georgia smiled and looked up, a question in her eyes. "Mom, is it okay if I pray for him?"

I had no doubt who she meant. I nodded and placed my hands on her shoulders.

Georgia laid her hand on John David's photo, then closed her eyes and bowed her head. "Lord God, thank You for creating me and giving me to Mom and Grandpa. Please be with John David. Prison is going to be scary, even though it's what he deserves. Please help him to learn from it. Amen."

# CHAPTER THIRTY-ONE

*Blue Springs, Texas*
*March, 2011*

THE HUM OF THE REFRIGERATOR. THE TICK OF the clock. The muted calls of bird songs. The stillness was calming, comforting. I stared out at the field from the kitchen window as the sun set low on the horizon. A handful of cows grazed, their calves tucked in the rushes and tall grasses eager for a night's rest.

Had it really been only a week since Georgia climbed into my car in tears?

The secret was dead. Georgia would be fine. My relationships with Bobby and Lisa Jean were being restored. And new ones between Dad and Janine and Georgia and Tommy were beginning.

But there was still one last thing to be done. Georgia had asked if I hated John David and I had told her the truth. I didn't. And yet, I still hadn't forgiven him. It was the last nail that held me tethered to the past. And the hardest one to remove.

Because even though I didn't hate him, there was still a part of me that hated his deed. For taking something from me that wasn't his to take. Until I released myself from that hurt, the rest of the healing and the new relationships would never be complete.

And I wanted nothing short of everything that God was beginning and restoring.

It didn't matter that John David might never show remorse. It didn't matter that he would never hear my words. What mattered was that they needed to be said.

And so I did.

"I forgive you, John David. For taking my innocence and hurting me out of your own hurt. I forgive you for making me fear you and choosing to react out of that fear instead of trusting God. I forgive you, John David."

An overwhelming flood of love washed over me. I had never felt such purity, such depth. Not even when I held Georgia for the first time.

Headlights flashed up at the gate as a truck bounced over the cattle guard. Bobby.

When I told Dad and Georgia about Bobby's text, Georgia had danced around the den then promptly asked Dad out for their own date. They'd left an hour ago intent on dinner and a movie downtown. Bobby and I would head in the opposite direction, driving and talking, keeping our options open and continuing to feel out this new relationship together.

I locked the front door behind me and leaned against the porch railing, absorbing the reality of his return into my life. Climbing out of the truck, he tugged a camo ball cap embroidered with the US Army logo low over his forehead and flashed my favorite grin.

"Hi, ya', Mads. I've missed you," he whispered as he leaned down and brushed his lips against mine.

Leaning back, I cupped his cheek and his smooth, newly shaved skin warmed under my hand. Joy, pure and heady, bubbled inside me.

"You ready?" His golden eyes gleamed with hope, the shadows of the past at bay.

I nodded. "I sure am."

# ACKNOWLEDGMENTS

Writing may look like me sitting behind my laptop for hours on end, pounding the keyboard, creating, rewriting, and moving chunks of story around like giant puzzle pieces. But in my head, heart, and history are a group of pivotal people who sat beside me, knowingly and unknowingly, for all of those hours and more. I would not be where I am today without you. And I am tremendously grateful.

To Patsy Jones, my fifth-grade teacher, may you be singing with the angels. You tolerated the many handwritten Sweet Valley High stories passed like notes between myself and my first writing partner, Amy Croslin Wright. I don't know when it happened, but I can pinpoint that year as the moment I knew I wanted to be a writer. Thank you both for lighting the spark and allowing it the opportunity to burn.

To Tracy Inman, my high school Creative Writing and AP English teacher, who fostered my love of writing. Your kindness and insight nurtured my dream of one day being a wordsmith.

To Sarah Brown, my cohort in my early days of fanfiction writing. Oh, the fun we had swapping ideas and co-authoring stories, even co-managing a fanfiction website while we both dreamed of writing our own characters and telling their stories.

To Eva Marie Everson and the Christian writers' critique group, Word Weavers International, and especially the Destin chapter. You honed my skills, encouraging me to grow in the craft, lent me your experiences when I had none, and cheered me on through the long silences of the wait.

To Carol Ogle McCracken, Alice Murray, and Mike Logan. I couldn't ask for better or more inspiring company on this road. Y'all are unparalleled.

To Ginny Cruz, abundant, never-ending thanks for encouraging me to sign up for Victoria Duerstock's Building Platform 101 class, which God used to open the door to traditional publishing through End Game Press. Wow. Just wow.

To Connie Stevens, a gifted storyteller, who patiently listened as I talked through Madeline's story, offering her wisdom and insights to help me tie up loose story threads and deepen my point of view. You are a gem, dear lady!

To Julie Cantrell, best-selling author and developmental editor extraordinaire, whose eagle eye and caring heart took this book from a deluge of tears to a beautiful unfolding of restoration and purpose. Thank you for "getting" me and my stories.

To Victoria Duerstock and the End Game Press team, I pray a thousand-fold blessing on each of you.

And of course, I wouldn't be here at all if it weren't for Mom and Dad, Janice and Wade Ferguson. Thank you for, well, everything. Much love to you both on earth and in heaven.

Each of you watered the seeds, provided the sunlight, or fertilized the ground from which my love of writing and this book grew.

Thank you. Thank you. Thank you.

# ABOUT THE AUTHOR

Felicia Ferguson is an award-winning freelance writer who holds master's degrees in healthcare administration and speech-language pathology. A features writer for the national luxury lifestyle magazine, VIE, she was also the assistant publisher and lead writer for three N2 Publishing magazine products. She spent her childhood on a horse and cattle farm. In high school, she had classmates who became teenage mothers. Her school was the first in the county to install a daycare for teen mothers to allow them the opportunity to continue their education and graduate.

She is a member of the Daughters of the American Revolution, American Speech-Language Hearing Association, and Word Weavers International, serving as the Destin Word Weavers chapter president for a two-year term beginning January, 2021.